REBEL HEIR

REBEL HEIR

THE ROYALE VAMPIRE HEIRS, BOOK FOUR

by

GINNA MORAN

ISBN 978-1-951314-25-5 (soft cover)

This is a work of fiction. All of the characters, organizations, and events portrayed in this novel are either products of the author's imagination or are used fictitiously.

Cover design by Silver Starlight Designs
Cover images copyright Depositphotos

For Inquiries Contact:
Sunny Palms Press
9663 Santa Monica Blvd Suite 1158
Beverly Hills, CA 90210, USA
www.sunnypalmspress.com
www.GinnaMoran.com

To Bronx's babes, Everett's dolls, Mikkalo's wild ones, and Jameson's girls—this is for you.

1

INSATIABLE

"FIVE MORE MINUTES," I MURMUR, lifting my foot from the bubble bath to stare at my toes. "I'm not ready to get out."

Everett crosses his arms over his chest, giving me a longing look. "Okay, but only five. I want to get in some exercise before we head out. It's important for you."

I groan and sink underwater. The last three and a half weeks have been so strange. Ever since Bronx agreed to fight for a seat on the board, we haven't had a single encounter with the Baron Coven. And while it's been almost normal, I realize normalcy freaks me the hell out. It feels like Freeport is biding his time, waiting for the opportunity to steal me away.

Fingers grip under my arms, tugging me from the tub. I gasp a breath of air and automatically wrap my naked body around Everett. He greets me with a smile, not caring that I'm soaking his clothes with bathwater. I purposefully press my boobs into his chest, wiggling my body a little to dry them off. Goosebumps prickle over my skin, Everett's body seemingly cooler because of the heat of mine.

"Time's up. I can't stand watching you mope." He swipes my wet hair from my face and brushes his lips to mine.

"I'm not moping," I argue, pursing my lips. "I'm just bored out of my mind. The four of you are way too overprotective. You want me to exercise, yet you won't let me practice my combat skills. Or wrestle with you all. How am I supposed to prepare Bronx if he's too afraid to even hug me tightly?"

Everett sighs against my mouth. "It's a good thing it's my night."

I laugh. "You're as bad as Jamie."

Narrowing his eyes, he fake-glares at me. "I highly doubt it. Jameson doesn't even let you walk ten feet because he's afraid you'll trip and fall. I, on the other hand, plan to give you the best workout of your life tonight. Obstetrician's orders."

Everett sets me on my feet and grabs a towel from the warming tray. He drapes it around my shoulders and gently starts to dry me off. I stand utterly still, letting him rub the fluffy towel down my arms and to my sides. His eyes follow the rivulets of water that trickle down my breasts. Everett kneels in front of me, taking his time to dry off every inch of me. Wrapping the towel around me, he pulls me close and kisses my stomach.

I comb my fingers through his hair. "That's not the place I like getting kissed best." My teasing words get Everett to tip his head back to look at me.

His eyes flash silver. "Careful, Gwen. You know we have things to do."

"And that doesn't include each other?"

Mikkalo groans, his voice humming through the door to his room. I smirk and stop Everett from starting something by clutching his head. He stretches his arms out and catches me by the hips, pulling my body to his face. I laugh and squeal, trying to turn away. He manages to kiss my ass cheek. I drop my towel on his head and run for the door.

Swinging it open, I run right into Mikkalo's arms. He scoops me up and dodges out of Everett's way. The world blurs as Mikkalo crosses his suite to lay me on the bed far more gently than he used to. No one throws me on the bed anymore—not since we confirmed that I am in fact pregnant.

I still can't believe it sometimes. I don't feel much different apart from occasionally getting sick, not wanting to eat human food some days while gorging on it other days. Oh, and also how my guys treat me like I'm the most fragile being in the universe. And to think I thought they were bad before...

Mikkalo props himself over me and kisses me softly. I hum under my breath, stretching my arms down his back to link my fingers to the hem of his shirt. His muscles flex under my touch as he deepens our kiss. I attempt to pull his shirt off of him, but he breaks from my mouth and scoots lower, brushing his lips to my clavicle. He teases me with his tongue but prevents me from reaching down between us.

"Are you denying yourself of my affection?" I ask, arching my hips up to rub against him. Because he's obviously not denying me.

"You spent too much time in the tub," he says, working his way down my chest. His hand gently squeezes my side, trying to stop me from grinding my body to his. "No time to get carried away. It's easier to resist you like this. If I let you have your way..." Mikkalo stops short of kissing my breasts and eases off me. Tugging me by my ankles, he drags me to the end of the bed. "We have to get up."

Everett slips a pair of sheer panties onto me, kissing my ankle up to my knee in the process. Who knew getting dressed could feel so sexy and hot. "I warned you about the time."

Mikkalo wraps a bra around my chest and fastens it into place. He grins as he adjusts my boobs to enhance my cleavage. "Your needs are going to have to wait until later."

"Which kills me, if I might add." Tugging me to my feet, Everett links his fingers through mine to pull my arms over my head. He steps closer and trails his hand down the length of my back to squeeze my ass cheek to pull my hips into his. "The act of covering your body is not on the list of things I want to do with you."

I bounce on my feet, rubbing my pelvis up and down the length of his erection through his pants. Everett has the least amount of restraint when it comes to sex. He groans in his throat, his eyes sparking with silver desire. If Mikkalo wasn't pulling my dress over my head, I'm sure Everett would spin me around to bend me over the bed. Or lift me up to prop me on the dresser. Maybe the couch. It wouldn't be the first time tonight...

"Gwen," Mikkalo whispers, sandwiching me to Everett. I savor the sensation of being trapped in the middle of all sorts of hard muscle. "Please drink. Your eyes are flashing like crazy, and you have to walk through the lobby. It's busy tonight. A few covens have come to show Bronx their support."

"Maybe a few extra minutes here won't hurt," Everett says, kissing my throat.

Mikkalo slides his hand to my hip. "Better to be late than unleash my favorite side of her," he says to his brother.

I shiver under the softness of Mikkalo's breath tickling the crook of my neck as the delectable scent of his blood teases my senses. He extends his arm around me, so I don't have to move from my spot.

Locking my hand around Mikkalo's wrist, I bring his arm to my mouth and glide my tongue over the puncture wounds. Tingles explode over my tongue, and I lean my head on his chest. Everett's blue eyes lock onto me, and we stare at each other while Mikkalo gives me what my body needs. There's something incredibly sexy about Everett's anticipation and raw desire he shares with me while watching me drink from Mikkalo. It fills me with hot lust and need, making it hard to think of anything else besides being with the both of them.

"If you need more, let me take over," Everett says after another minute. He touches his fingers to my cheek. His lips curl up in the corner with his teasing smirk. But I can't get myself to ease away from Mikkalo just yet. I love the way he moans at the sensation of my mouth too much. My blood lust has been out of control lately. It's difficult not to just let my dhampir side free.

Mikkalo feels the same need I do and slides his free hand from my hip and down my stomach, holding me a bit tighter. "I'm good, brother. She can have more."

I moan under my breath, my whole body buzzing like crazy at his permission for me to continue. Mikkalo's blood tastes so good that the last thing I want to do now is stop.

He fills me up with everything I need. Everything I want in this moment.

Closing my eyes, I suck harder, trying to get his bite mark to give me more blood. I can't stop my teeth from sinking into his skin to bite him myself. I get more blood this way, and Mikkalo never complains. He loves it. He probably only bit himself because I'm testing his restraint. I've been giving him more and more pleasure bites lately because I can't sustain him with my blood like I want. I never want any of my guys to feel like that's all they are—a blood source.

"Fuck," Mikkalo whispers under his breath. "I might need your help after all, Ev." Mikkalo adjusts me in his arms, testing to see if I'll let him go.

I don't.

My body wants none of that, and I surprise myself by releasing the scariest growl from my throat. It's like my body is possessed by a wild beast hell-bent on drinking every last drop from Mikkalo. He doesn't stiffen or anything at my reaction. Instead, he moans deeply, his body arousing against mine. I knew I was a little ridiculous before, but it's usually only my guys who act in such a manner if I'm not ready to release them and someone else tries. Even so, it's been a while since Mikkalo's done such a thing. And never to this extent. It's usually Bronx who reacts this way toward my unintentional possessiveness. Not Mikkalo. But now? I never want to let him go.

Everett bites his arm to entice me to switch to him, but Mikkalo and I both growl this time. And then he backs up, pulling me away. His heartbeat thrums against my back, his breathing quickening.

I bite him again.

What. The. Actual. Fuck.

I can't control myself. It's like my body and mind separate. Nothing works together to get my savagery under control. Tingles rush through me, and I link my hand through Mikkalo's, guiding him to hold me tighter.

Everett raises his hands up in surrender. "Gwen, you have to stop. Mikkalo won't make you. You're taking too much."

I flare my nostrils, trying to slow my racing heart. Still, I don't want to stop. It's like a deep-seated hunger consumes me, and I'm afraid I won't ever get blood again.

"She's fine," Mikkalo snaps. "If she needs me, then she needs me. The baby takes its toll on her. You know this."

"Get it together, brother. I don't want to fight you. Gwen could get hurt. She could hurt us." Everett pulls out his com device and taps the screen a few times. "You know she wouldn't want that."

Mikkalo growls again, tugging me back with him more. "Then don't fight. Leave us alone."

Stepping closer, Everett risks his hand by grabbing my wrist. "I can't do tha—"

The door flies open at the same time Mikkalo falls back

with me still latched to his arm. I land on top of him, the force of our fall enough to make me gasp. The second I release his arm, Everett snatches me up and pins my arms to my sides, holding me away from him. Jameson materializes in front of me and frowns, his green eyes roving over my face.

I snap my teeth and thrash, anger rushing through me. I know I'm being unreasonable. I know I should chill out. But something is wrong. "Let me go! I wasn't done!" Did I really just say that?

Jameson shifts on his feet and waves his arm toward Mikkalo sprawled across the floor. My heart screams in fear, but my eyes can't help from drinking in the drops of blood seeping onto the floor. "Are you sure you want to finish him off, Gigi? I know how much you love his full-body massages and freaky pleasure bites."

"He's also your backup cook, dandelion." Bronx's voice draws my attention to him as he brings in a giant pitcher of blood. I don't have to ask to know it's gen. pop. blood. The scent permeates through the air, causing me to crinkle my nose. My sense of smell is out of control the last two weeks. "Or have you forgotten when I tried?"

I cover my mouth, my stomach twisting at the thought. While his version of pasta never touched my tongue, it was so burnt that I could practically taste it.

"Here, Gwen. If Jameson can't entice you to drink, let me try." Everett offers his arm to me again.

The rivulets of ruby liquid catch my attention, and I tense in anticipation. Everett brings his arm directly to my mouth and lets the blood dribble on my bottom lip to run down my chin. It's enough to drag my attention away from Mikkalo and his wasted blood completely as he finally manages to prop himself up to gulp the gen. pop. blood. Our gazes meet, and his eyes flash silver at me, but he manages to keep himself under control instead of endangering himself to give in to my intense craving for him. It's the strangest thing.

Jameson kneels on the ground and hooks his fingers to my hips, resting his forehead to my belly. "You make your mommy insatiable, mini-beast," he whispers. "Maybe try to get her to eat the human food. I put a lot of effort into it. You'll like it too. Promise."

My heart slows at his voice, my body managing to chill the hell out. If I could melt in a puddle, I would.

I comb my fingers through his soft hair. "Listen to Jamie, okay? I know they taste so delicious, but I love them and so will you. We want them around forever."

Flicking my gaze to Bronx's, I give him The Look. It's the same one I've given him every day since he announced he was challenging Freeport for the board seat. Just the thought of something happening leaves me on the verge of a breakdown. He's afraid that without the region, we won't be able to handle what is ahead of us, but I know we can handle anything...except I don't want the unnecessary danger of him fighting a vampire older than the Vampire Uprising. We're a team. We're supposed to fight together. But this? He has to do it alone. I hate it.

"Damn straight," Jameson says, kissing my stomach. "Which means it's time to let go of Everett and let me feed you."

Sliding his hand between my legs, Jameson glides his fingers over the soft fabric of my panties. Tingles explode through me, and I gasp and release Everett's arm. I hadn't even realized I had pulled it to my mouth again.

"Shit," I say, spinning to face Everett. He sucks in his bottom lip between his teeth, his eyes searching mine. "What the hell is wrong with me? Why didn't you stop me?"

Everett's fangs peek from beneath his lip, and he offers me a brilliant smile. "Nothing is wrong with you, and I didn't stop you because you weren't even drinking. Just giving me one helluva hickey. I love your mouth on me."

"Damn. Me next." Jameson hops up and drags his collar down to show off his neck.

Bronx materializes behind Jameson and grabs the back of his shirt, yanking him away. The two of them growl at each other but manage to keep it together under the weight of my stare. Jameson straightens his shirt and adjusts his tie. He sucks his bottom lip between his teeth and smiles.

"You know the rules, Jameson," Bronx says. "Only two of us at a time unless Gwen asks otherwise. We need to stay as strong as possible, especially because the two of us need to make a round tonight to our potential future allies. The Mercy Coven has come with Rio. They're looking to advance to a city head position when I win the board seat."

The fact that he says it like it's a sure thing helps my crazy nerves.

"Don't forget the Alonzos are here as well. Vienna is someone I'd like for Gwen to meet." Mikkalo closes the space to us and touches my cheek. "I'd like your opinion of her coven. They're a bit unconventional, but from what I know, they're extremely human-friendly."

I blow out a breath through my nose. "Are you sure that's a good idea? What if I get all flashy-eyed? Hungry? What if they say something that sets me off? I'm a mess these days."

Everett tugs out a small glass box from his jacket pocket. Popping the lid, he reveals a clear liquid to me. "I've got your eyes covered. Have you ever heard of contacts? Humans used to wear them in the back-world before the medical advancement in ophthalmology." Because vampires can't have humans with vision problems. I knew this. They can't manipulate a person's mind if the human can't properly see. Only the humans who age out of gen. pop donations are left alone and given glasses. But these contacts? What the hell?

Everett disappears into the bathroom for a moment and returns holding out his index finger to me. I catch sight of a clear, tiny, circular disk on his fingertip. I've never seen anything like it and can't stop myself from trying to whack his hand before he gets it near my eyeball.

"Gwen, you'll only feel them for a second. I promise. I've spent all my free time recreating these from some back-world technology I acquired. You'll still be able to see clearly and everything. It'll just mute your irises." Everett holds the contact out to me, showing me again. "If it bothers you too much, then I won't make you wear them. But please try for me."

Jameson cracks his knuckles. "I can pin her down for you. She loves when I do that."

I narrow my eyes at Everett and bob my head, ignoring Jameson's comment. "Fine. For you." I stick out my tongue at Jameson, who play-growls.

Everett tries again, and I swing my arm, nearly whacking his hand. He's too quick for me, and Bronx hooks his arms around my chest and waist, pinning me to him. His hulking muscular body rests flush against mine, his scent relaxing my nerves.

"Be good for your health keeper, dandelion. Don't you want to leave this suite?" Bronx kisses the crook of my neck. "I've been looking forward to showing you off. It's one of the few things I look forward to at these kinds of gatherings."

"Hell yeah. We all want to." Mikkalo smiles and wags his brows at me. "Our future coven mate."

I glance in his direction. "I love the sound of—"

Something blurs in front of my eyes, cutting off my comment. I blink a dozen times as they water. I wiggle in Bronx's arms, arching my back to grind my ass against him until he loosens his hold enough for me to break free.

Everett snatches my hands and yanks me to him, lifting me off my feet. "Give it a minute before you rub your eyes."

I groan and blink some more. "You guys are in so much trouble. I see what you all did, distracting me."

"Teamwork, Gigi. Get used to it." Jameson kisses me from over Everett's shoulder.

"If you weren't such a pain in my balls, we wouldn't have to." Bronx sandwiches me against Everett. "But I love it. And you."

"Now, try not to rip any hearts out while we make our way to the gym." Mikkalo straps a thigh holster to my leg and slips a dagger into it. In normal circumstances, they think I'm enough of a weapon, but now I can't even walk down the hall without being armed or surrounded by their muscular bodies that lock me in the best cage. I'm going to have to work on them. If they're this protective with me, our baby might never see the outside world.

"No promises," I tease, squirming enough to get Everett to set me on my feet. "So be prepared. You put me in a mood."

"Maybe we should stay here." Mikkalo adjusts the bodice of my dress for no other reason than he wants to. "I have nothing to do. You're my sole mission tonight."

Jameson groans. "Fuck, I nominate you to be the head of communications instead. I'll be defense. I almost beat you for the spot anyway."

"Brothers, quit it. We're all going. United." Bronx turns his attention on me, cocking his brow while pausing to see if I start arguing. I don't. I like it when he gets all gushy about standing together. "And Gwen, if you can resist causing a scene and make it through the lobby unnoticed by most, I'll give you whatever you want on my night." Bronx steps closer and drapes a jacket over my bare shoulders to reduce the amount of my showing skin. From the subtle pursing of his lips, I can tell he hates to do it, but he's not willing to risk me attracting more attention than I already do. At least the whole pregnancy thing stops most vampires from testing me, considering I'm completely off-limits under the Donor Life Corp law.

"I mean anything. Hell, I'll even let you drive around the block," he adds. "Though Mik will have to clear the area before you can do so."

Mikkalo chuckles. "Shit, brother. Give her better ideas."

"That's nice and all, but I need to know what happens if I don't." I place my hands on my hips, loving to test Bronx. He enjoys it as much as I do. "Because if it's like being your angel for a week or something...not happening."

"I prefer you a bit naughty, which means if you fail, I get whatever I want." Bronx's eyes flash silver. "I have a list."

"Unfortunately, you can't bite me. Health keeper's orders." I snap my teeth, teasingly. "I doubt you have it in you to spank me either."

He flicks my ass. "That's not what I want."

I smirk. "You want to lick every inch of me?"

Jameson sneaks behind me and shifts my hair. He draws his tongue up the side of my neck, making me laugh. "That's me, Gigi."

I twist my lips to the side, keeping my gaze on Bronx. "You want my mouth all over you? Because that's not much of a punishment."

He shakes his head.

"I'll take that," Everett says, his eyes drinking me in.

Tapping my finger to my chin, I run a million ideas of what he could possibly want through my head. "A new, crazy-ass position?"

"That sounds fun." Mikkalo wags his eyebrows.

Bronx moves closer and links his fingers around my wrist. Guiding my hand down my stomach, he stops my hand on my pelvis. "I want something a bit more personal from you."

I fake-glare at Bronx, puckering my brows. "Seriously? Out of all the things, you want that?"

"Damn, now I do too," Jameson quips. He nudges his hand against Bronx's shoulder. "Can I watch with you?"

"That would work for me." Mikkalo grins, his smile

lighting up his handsome face.

Everett chuckles. "That sounds more like punishment to us."

I poke his shoulder. "No one get their hopes up. I'm not losing this game. But I want to up the stakes. It's unfair if you guys all get rewarded. If I make it through the lobby like a good little dhampir—"

"A good dhampir? Does such a thing exist?" Mikkalo bumps Jameson with a laugh.

I hold my finger up, getting him to hide his smile with his hand. "If I make it through the lobby...without incident," I repeat. "You all have to let me have my way. I have my own list too."

"Damn, why do I suddenly want her to win?" Jameson whispers.

Everett presses his lips together and leans in closer to his brother. "Because she can't come up with anything that'll be a punishment. Win-win for us."

"Now it's on. I'm winning, and you're going to regret it." I stand on my tiptoes and wiggle my nose against Everett's.

Bronx tips his head back and laughs. "We'll see, dandelion."

I twist and grab Bronx's tie, pulling him from his brothers before the four of them start high-fiving or some shit. "You just wait. If you guys want to play this game, you will all do what I want. And now I want the same as you. All of you giving me the best show of my life. One fucking awesome bonding experience."

Jameson groans. "Shit. Now you've done it."

I tilt my head and smile. "Is it a deal?"

"Hell yeah. I have faith that you'll always be my wild one, Gwen. It's a deal I'll risk taking," Mikkalo says, striding toward the door. He opens it and checks to make sure the hallway is clear. "Now let's go."

I extend my arms to Everett to pick me up, but he takes my hand instead and tugs me along to the door. Jameson remains ultra-close to my other side, his movements mirroring mine like it's torture to see me out of one of their arms. If Everett didn't pull me into his side and wrap his arm around my waist, I wouldn't put it past Jameson to try to pick me up to carry me. He takes protecting me far too seriously when the floor now becomes one of his enemies.

"We're going to take the stairs, if that's okay," Everett says, peeking at me in his peripheral vision. He glances to Jameson next, expecting him to argue. "At least until you get tired. I wasn't joking about giving you the best workout of your life. You need to stay active."

I raise an eyebrow at him. "I thought that was code for something else." Because Everett still loves to sneak around all the time.

He chuckles, ruffling his hand through his hair. Licking his lips, he turns to meet my gaze completely looking so sexy with the desire sharpening his features. There is just something about Everett that always gets to me in the best way. "Don't worry. I plan to work it in. Later. After you torture my brothers and make them regret this little bet since it's my time after all. The wait will be worth it."

I swing our hands back and forth, excitement fluttering in my stomach. When he puts it like that... "I'm not sure I can wait. You tease me too much. It's almost like you want me to go wild."

He grins without comment.

"Damn straight. So get that hot ass of yours moving, Gigi." Jameson swats my ass, getting me to pick up my pace with a laugh. I tug Everett with me, slipping in in front of him to use him as a shield from behind.

The five of us head to the stairs, where Mikkalo checks the security feeds to make sure they're free from any possible threats. After four flights of stairs, I plop down on the landing to rest for a bit. Who knew I hated stairs so much. This isn't the kind of exercise I enjoy.

Bronx must sense it because he sits next to me and whispers, "We'll work the mats later, dandelion. I've come up with a more suitable routine just for you."

Everett hands me a flask of water, and I force myself to drink it, though my body would much prefer something else. My needs are all out of whack, and it makes me wonder about our future. If this could be a sign of something even more life changing than I imagined. None of us has a lot of experience with children. Not knowing what to expect terrifies me. No one has mentioned it, but I know my guys worry about that as well.

"Back on your feet, dandelion," Bronx says, standing tall over me.

"Just a second more. I'm enjoying the view." I flick my gaze from his dark eyes and down the rest of his body, stopping at his pants. If I show enough attention to him, even without touching, I can give him a boner. It'll serve him and his brothers right.

He turns his back on me, letting me appreciate every inch of him in that sexy suit of his. "Time's up," he adds from over his shoulder. "Jameson looks ready to pick you up, and that'll ruin our fun."

I bat Jameson away as he teasingly lifts me up to set me on my feet. Everett spins me away toward Mikkalo. He jumps down the next flight of stairs, sending my stomach into my throat. I screech and laugh, the world blurring. Bronx tries to intercept Jameson, but he dodges out of the way and snags the back of my dress. Mikkalo moves with us and uses me to pin Jameson to the wall. By the hardness of their cocks, I can really feel how much they enjoy this.

A door slams shut, and a figure stumbles onto the next landing. If only we could enjoy our games a bit longer.

"Shit, Macon. Get in here." The guy rolls to his side and looks at the stairwell exit.

I stare in shock at the sight of Ashton dripping blood on the shiny concrete. He can't see me from my spot, but he definitely sees my guys. Except they don't react how I expect. They don't speak or move.

"Ohmyfuck," I say, rushing down the stairs before they can catch me.

My brother presses his hands into the floor to prop up and turns to look at me. "Gwen? Is that you?"

My eyes widen. It's not Ashton. It's Declan.

And he's been bitten.

The stairwell door flies open, and I gawk at a short vampire with blood dripping down his chin. I can't recall ever seeing such a sight on a vampire who wasn't an outcast. Blinking his eyes, he gets them to stop flashing and straightens his jacket.

"Excuse me. This is my blood source," the man says, flashing his fangs. "We were in the middle of a competition."

His blood source? A competition? Ah, hell.

No one has a chance to stop me as I launch at the man.

It's me who bites first.

2

UNEXPECTED REUNION

"WHOA, SHIT. GWEN! GWEN, STOP!" Declan pushes to his feet and stumbles toward me at the same time Everett locks his fingers under my arms and drags me away.

Bronx, Mikkalo, and Jameson materialize between me and the vampire, all drawing their weapons. I heave a few deep breaths, staring at Declan from the small space between Mikkalo and Jameson. Declan's brows knit together, his familiarity bringing tears to my eyes. I blink a few times to suppress them. The last thing I need to do right now is cry.

The vampire manages to peer at me from next to Declan. Tugging a handkerchief from his pocket, he dangles it out. "Misters Royale, please forgive me. I didn't mean to startle Ms. Royale, though her reaction was quite entertaining. Is she practicing for her Blood Vow?"

"You could say that, Mr. Bowman," Bronx says, his hulking form remaining rigid despite the lightness of the man's voice. "Luckily for you, she wasn't in the nut-kicking mood."

The vampire laughs. "I'd have accepted the pain to experience such a thing. And please, no need for formality. I've come with my coven to formally announce our support to the Royale Region."

"That is appreciated, Macon." Bronx accepts the handkerchief and swivels on his feet and gives it to Everett. "Perhaps we can all sit down over dinner. Gwen is late for her appointment."

Macon's eyes turn to me in Everett's arms. He gives me a once-over, flitting his gaze down to my stomach. Word travels fast among regions, according to Jameson, and I'm sure everyone knows about me and my circumstances.

Everett carefully wipes my mouth off without a word and hugs me tighter. "We don't want to keep Rio Mercy waiting."

"Appointment? For what?" Declan's soft voice draws everyone's attention to him. He's been utterly quiet since

Everett pulled me away before I could devour Macon completely. "Are you sick, Gweny?"

"You know her, Dec?" Macon asks Declan.

He nods. "She's my sister."

Macon cocks his head to the side in curiosity. "I suppose you did mention you had one. And so you don't worry, Ms. Royale is in good health and only with child. The Royales permitted her request for an heir before her Blood Vow to join their coven. It seems the Gallaghers impress many." He grins at Declan. "Like you've impressed me."

"Fuck," Declan whispers under his breath, ignoring Macon's comment.

A dozen thoughts swirl through my mind. I have so much to tell Declan, but with Macon here, there is no way. We can't afford to slip up. Our excuse for my pregnancy is flimsy at best. Only Viorica, the head of Donor Life Corp's board, knows that it was a shock and surprise. As far as she is aware, the father is a donor from the Royale staff. It's a thought I hate, but it is what it is. No one can ever know.

"Don't be so down. It's an amazing thing. Not many covens allow such a request." Macon pulls Declan to his feet and straightens his suit jacket. It's now that I realize he's dressed as impeccably as the vampire. Both of them have various bloodstains, but they're still handsome.

Declan keeps his gaze locked on mine, choosing to talk to me directly. "Gwen, really? But..." He lets his voice trail off.

"Come along, Declan. It's best to process your feelings in private. We still have a bit of time to enjoy the city tonight. During these uncertain times, it might be easier to find you a female who will transfer into our household. Wouldn't you like that? I know you get bored." Macon glances to Bronx. "Do you think such a thing would be possible? I heard the board temporarily lifted the quarantine."

Bronx gives a sharp nod. "Let's discuss it at dinner."

Macon bows deeply. "Until then."

I don't get a chance to even breathe a plea before Macon disappears with my brother. My head spins, confusion twisting my thoughts. I knew Declan was sold into a vampire household in another region, but after Corona's shady-ass stunt, I thought it would be a while until I could find him. It's like fate brought him to me only to tease me. My heart hurts so much worse than it did now that I saw him, his absence weighing heavy on me in this moment.

Without a word, Everett relocates me, blurring the world. The five of us stop in the lobby, where Bronx takes over and holds my hand. He squeezes my fingers, showing me he's here for me without making a huge deal. It's better to ignore my rising emotions than to point them out. I just wish I could hug all my guys in front of everyone. While our Blood Vow is based on loyalty, we still must maintain appearances. Vampires are not known for sharing, and the last thing we need is for more people to test Bronx in regards to me. As coven leader, he chose me. I can't afford to show loyalty to anyone else. It must be strictly to him in public. Such a crock.

"We'll make this quick, since you lost our game already," Bronx murmurs under his breath. "Since I know you want more time with your brother, I'll invite our possible allies to dinner. Is that okay?"

I swivel my head and narrow my eyes at him. "What do you mean *I* lost our game?" I shake his hand, trying to get him to break his tense stance. "You said the lobby. We were in the stairwell."

He chuckles and reels me in, locking my hand to his chest so I feel the thrums of his heartbeat. "Out of everything I said, that's the thing you choose to focus on?"

Jameson bumps my shoulder from my other side. "Damn straight it is. Our girl is fiercely competitive."

"And I didn't lose," I argue.

"Sorry, Gwen. You did." Mikkalo rests his hands on my hips, closing the space behind me. "You had to make it from our suite and through the lobby. You lost when you bit a chunk from Macon's neck. But hey, at least he took it well."

"Just think of it as a win." Everett smiles at me. "You get to torture my brothers, and we get what I'm sure will be the hottest show."

Fuck. Me.

I don't get a chance to argue more when Rio Mercy strides in our direction. The handsome vampire runs the

Human Health Center in Shadow Hill Pointe, which used to be a part of another region. Now that I know his coven wants a city head position, I wonder why. Maybe Rio pushed for it. Maybe he sees the strong and powerful future I dream of.

Rio bows before me and greets each of my guys with a handshake. His smile lights up his face, his facial hair neatly trimmed compared to last week when I saw him. Because of the uncertainty of my situation, he monitors my health with Everett every week, but this will be the first time I've ever met his coven. None of them knows about my dhampir mutation, and they never will unless we tell them. Rio's the only vampire outside of my guys that I believe doesn't have some twisted ulterior motive for helping me. His compassion for humans speaks volumes.

"Misters Royale, it is a pleasure to see you again." Rio shifts on his feet, and three guys appear behind him. "You remember my brothers?"

Bronx extends his hand out to the tallest of the three. "Paris, it's been a while." Turning to me, he adds, "This is Gwen. Gwen, I'd like to introduce you to Paris, the head of the Mercy Coven, and his brothers Dallas and Angelo. They run the security division in their city for Brea Armstrong."

No one has to say anything for me to know that the Mercy Coven is using Brea's betrayal of aligning with the Barons to their advantage. I can't blame the Mercys for wanting to take over the city if Bronx wins the fight. Because as of right now, the current Royale Region city heads made it clear that they are on Freeport Baron's side, considering he stopped the board from executing them for treason. If Bronx wins, they're all out. Probably cast out or the board will proceed with their death sentences.

I give a small bow. "It's nice to meet you, Misters Mercy." Usually, I wouldn't give any of them my attention, but I know with my supposed Blood Vow, it's important to assert myself among vampires more, though Jameson warned me some will treat me as if I'm beneath them until I grow fangs. Something that we're all aware will never happen. I can't transform. I don't even know how we'll manage after the baby's born.

"And I'm enchanted, darlin'." The blond vampire with long hair and a slight accent steps forward and bows. "Bronx was lucky to find you. I always thought it'd be Everett to propose a Blood Vow."

"Don't think I didn't want to, Dallas," Everett says, grabbing my hand. He kisses the back. "I'm lucky it's a vow of loyalty."

"You're also lucky he's not the jealous type." Rio smacks Everett on the back, and the two of them laugh like it's the funniest thing in the world. It's strange that Rio knows about my relationship with each of them, and he's less weirded out than I expected him to be.

"I think we're all lucky," I say. "Because I wouldn't have it any other way. I can't wait to be a true Royale."

Rio's brothers all look at me with curiosity, but none of them ask any more questions or make comments. If a female vampire didn't stroll across the room with a human man clinging to her arm, they might've. She offers my guys a bow and the human follows her lead. Another vampire materializes at her side with a female human companion.

"Misters Royale, Ms. Royale. I wanted to personally extend my coven's support to you. It's a shame the board agreed to such an arrangement. Our previous board would have never allowed such a travesty to occur, allowing an outcast coven to try to take charge." The woman's bold presence gets the Mercy Coven to excuse themselves apart from Rio. She turns her attention to me but doesn't say anything. She draws her gaze to my stomach. I don't look pregnant yet, but it's like vampires can't help themselves.

"The board knows of my capabilities, Vienna," Bronx says, straightening his back. "I just consider this a small test to prove my worth."

"And you'll get what rightfully belongs to you. I'm sure it helps having this gorgeous woman here to cheer you on," the man says. "I know my Noelle makes me stronger than ever."

"As does my Henrique," Vienna adds.

It's now that I realize both humans wear matching vow necklaces with an owl decorated with black stones and diamond eyes. Attached to its talons is a teardrop vial of blood. I can't stop my rebel hand from reaching out and gently fingering the necklace on Henrique. Bronx grabs my wrist, trying to pull my hand back, but Vienna stops him.

"It's lovely, isn't it, Ms. Royale? My Henrique has been wearing it for four years now." Vienna smiles at the man and touches his cheek. "He's so kindly agreed to expand my coven's bloodline with my brother's intended."

I jerk my attention to the woman, my gaze darting to her stomach. She slowly unbuttons her jacket and reveals her pregnant belly, surprising the hell out of me. I don't even know how to respond or act. While rare, it's not un-heard of for humans to procreate before a Blood Vow. It's how we got away with the story Viorica made up for us. But this is strange.

"I suppose congratulations are in order," Rio says, speaking up. "Is this heir number three?"

"Four," Vienna and her brother say at the same time. "We've discovered one purely wasn't enough. This one is female, and the Hakkasan Coven looks forward to a future permanent alliance with us with her as their future coven head."

And I thought me getting impregnated by one of my guys was crazy.

I open my mouth to ask them to explain what the hell they're talking about, but Rio clears his throat and pulls out his com device. He glances over the screen and hands it to Everett. The two of them share a silent look.

It's Bronx who says, "We'd love for your coven to join

us for dinner if you plan to remain in the city. I can have our staff arrange a few rooms for you."

"That would be lovely. I'm sure Ms. Royale would love to dine with my Noelle. Perhaps she can help her prepare for such an occasion." The man turns to me. "How would you feel about that?"

I shrug. I don't know. "I guess that would be nice."

"Perfect." The man bows. "Now, please excuse us. We have a meeting with the Bowmans."

"And Ms. Royale has an appointment to get to," Everett says, touching my stomach.

The vampires and their mates congratulate me and disappear, leaving us standing in the lobby. A few other vampires converse quietly, but no one else approaches us. Taking my hand, Bronx guides me along with him, and we follow Everett and Rio toward the double doors of the Human Health Center. The place is empty this time of night. Any human who was here for the Blood Match Program would have already left.

Rio opens the door to my usual exam room with a king-sized bed, projection screen, a small kitchen, bathroom, and various medical machines and workout equipment. If I didn't know any better, I'd think someone lived here and it wasn't used to monitor my progress, but everyone wanted to make this whole experience the best one possible, and a place in neutral territory among my guys so they can all be a part of it without possessiveness sneaking up.

"I've looked over Everett's weekly progress notes, and so far, the only difference seems to be that your dhampir nature seems to be taking over more often. Your last round of bloodwork is also rather intriguing. If I didn't know any better, I'd think you had transitioned completely into a vampire." Rio pulls up a chair to sit beside me.

Holding out his com device, he lets me look at it first. I appreciate how much effort he puts into making sure I don't feel like I'm left out. Most vampires probably only talk to a human's mister or miss in this type of situation.

I hand Everett the com device next, and he shows his brothers, pointing out a few things on the screen. Jameson plops on the bed beside me and glides his finger over my lips, trying to check out my teeth. I snap my jaws and catch his finger faster than he can react. I don't bite him, though, even if the taste of his skin sets my stomach growling.

"Do you have any concerns?" Rio asks, pulling a rolling tray closer. Slung over the side is the huge belt that will allow him a visual of my uterus.

I nod. "I don't even know where to begin. It's like my blood hunger possesses me. This morning, I nearly drained Mikkalo."

"You should've heard her. She growled and everything," Jameson says. "It was so hot. I want her to get possessive over me like that."

My cheeks heat with embarrassment. "Jamie..."

"Anything else?" Rio takes his com device back from

Everett and taps the screen a few times. "How is your nau-sea? You had some food aversions last week. What about now?"

I shrug. "It's not that I don't like the human food—I mean, Jameson and Mikkalo are excellent cooks—but I just want blood. All the time. And sex."

"Lucky for you, we can keep up," Mikkalo teases, tak-ing a spot on the bed behind me. He pulls me closer to sit between his legs to use his chest as a backrest.

"And none of us are afraid to call for backup." Jameson tips his head back with a laugh. "I'm always prepared to make you cum."

Ohmyfuck. "Seriously, Jamie! Keep it up and you're going to have to wait outside through this portion."

"Maybe you should all wait outside. Gwen might have concerns that she doesn't want to discuss in front of you. While pregnancy is beautiful, it has some things women find unpleasant." Rio remains expressionless with his words.

My guys all stare at me, waiting for my response. I know they'd give me privacy if I ask, but I can tell it would bother them. And honestly, I don't care right now. "I think I'm okay for now. I don't have any other complaints. Just the blood hunger and lust."

"Uncontrollable attacks, too," Everett adds. "She bit someone in the stairwell."

Rio rubs his beard. "How much is she drinking?"

"I can't be certain since she no longer drinks from a

cup." Everett slides his hand over my ankle and squeezes my leg. "She said it tastes weird that way."

I nod and purse my lips. "It does."

"Then let's go ahead and double your blood consumption but not in one sitting." He turns to Everett. "Double up how many meals she gets and see if it makes a difference with her blood hunger."

"And the sex?" I ask.

"We'll quadruple that." Everett smiles at me. "It should do the trick."

I raise my eyebrows at his playfulness. I know he's kidding, but the idea totally and unexpectedly turns me on. "So, what? Am I never to leave the bed?"

"What are you talking about, dandelion? We have the shower, gym, kitchen, and hundreds, if not thousands, of places across the city to spice things up." Bronx glances to his brothers. "Right?"

I play-smack his shoulder. "Enough."

"Just think of all the fun, Gigi." Jameson combs his fingers through my hair, twisting my strands.

I flush. "Oh, I am."

Mikkalo rests his chin on my shoulder, his body arousing against mine. "Me too. So let's check on the mini-beast and take care of our girl before the dinner gathering."

Rio nods, still remaining stone-faced toward my guys' comments. I'm tempted to ask him how he does it— remaining so steely while my face bursts into flames—but he has Everett adjust the sheet across my lap so that he can roll up my dress to put the belt in place.

Silence draws between the six of us as Rio and Everett dim the lights and get the machines situated. Mikkalo hugs me close to his chest while Bronx and Jameson each grip my fingers so tightly that my hands numb. But I don't mind. Their reactions every time get me in the best way. They're all as excited and anxious as I am.

The projection screen lights up, and I suck in a small breath at the sight of what looks more like an itty-bitty human than even last week. And then the most musical sound thrums through the air—a heartbeat—one as sweet and melodic as the collection now pounding around me.

Rio runs his finger across his com device and magnifies the view. "You're measuring right on track. The fetus has a nice, strong heartbeat."

"Fuck, Gigi. Look at the fingers and toes." Jameson kisses my hand without taking his eyes from the screen.

"What do you think it is?" Mikkalo asks.

"Besides a mini-beast?" I bonk my head on his shoulder.

"Would you like to know?" Everett asks me, twisting his lips into a half-smile. "I might've asked Rio to include it in the blood work. We can narrow down the presence of male chromosomes or lack thereof through DNA-based tests. I figured it would be beneficial to know in advance."

I narrow my eyes at him. "And Rio told you, didn't

he?"

His smile only widens. "Yes, but if you don't want to know, I'll keep it to myself. I don't trust Jameson to keep the secret if you prefer it to be a surprise."

"I want it to be a surprise," I say.

Jameson releases the loudest groan in existence. Mikkalo smacks him in the back of the head. I tip my head back and laugh. He's as bad as I am. There is no fucking way I'm waiting to find out.

"But surprise me now." I scoot forward and hold my arms out to Everett.

Leaning in, Everett links his fingers through mine and hugs my hands against his heart. He brushes his lips against the skin just below my ear, showing me his affection, getting me ramped up with excitement. Because he's so calm, it has to be a boy. If it's a boy, the chances of him being a symptomatic carrier vanishes. Males don't show symptoms. Even if it's a girl, the chances are still not a sure thing...

I release a deep breath. "I'm so relieved it's a boy. He'll at least have a chance at some normalcy."

"A boy?" Bronx asks, his voice echoing through the room.

Mikkalo claps his hands once. "Hah! You owe me half of your next day, Jameson."

Jameson growls. "There must be a mistake. No way is our girl so insatiable not to be carrying a symptomatic female dhampir."

I swivel in my seat to clasp his hand. "I guess it's all just me."

Everett clears his throat. "Actually, Gwen. Jameson was right." He cups my cheeks between his hands and grins at me. "Surprise, it's a girl."

A cool wave cascades over me with his words. "You're joking with us. You wouldn't be so calm if it were really female."

Meeting his lips to mine, Everett kisses me sweetly. "I'm not calm. I'm ecstatic. I never thought I could be happier."

"And freaked the hell out," Bronx murmurs. "So a girl?"

Mikkalo tugs me back to him, engulfing me in the best hug. Everett, Jameson, and Bronx all join us and take turns kissing me. Jameson scoots down and whispers quietly to my belly too softly for me to hear, but I don't think I've ever seen him so happy.

But it doesn't last long.

The door to the exam room flies open.

Rio charges toward it from his quiet place in the corner.

I launch from the bed at Rio, crashing into his back.

Declan yells.

3

GHOSTS

"RESTRAIN HIM," BRONX COMMANDS, snatching me away from Rio.

Rio hops to his feet with Declan pinned against his chest. Mikkalo quickly shuts the door and takes my brother from Rio. Everett intervenes, flashing his fangs, getting my other human health keeper to back away.

"The asshole was eavesdropping," Rio says, linking his fingers to the back of his head. "You need to find out what he heard. If my coven finds out that I've been lying—"

"Leave us!" Bronx yells. "I will handle it."

"Bronx—"

"Do not argue. You're scaring Gwen. Now, leave!" he roars, his loud voice startling me. "Mik, follow him."

Mikkalo bolts from the room behind Rio. Jameson locks Declan in place even though my brother remains frozen. Declan's eyes remain glued to me in Bronx's arms, a dozen thoughts flickering through his eyes. I wiggle in Bronx's embrace until he sets me on my feet. He stays on my heels as I jog across the room and hold my arms open. Jameson doesn't let my brother go, so I sandwich him between us.

"I still can't believe you're here. Ashton will be so relieved to know you're okay." Tears blur my eyes, and I squeeze my eyes shut in an attempt to keep my shit together.

Declan exhales a long breath, his tense muscles relaxing. "He's okay? Fuck. Thank God." Tipping his head forward, he rests it on my shoulder. "What about Grayson? Silas and Porter?"

My stomach twists in knots at the mention of my other brothers. I wobble on my feet a second before Bronx relocates me to sit on the edge of the bed with him. Jameson decides Declan isn't an immediate threat and pulls up a chair for him. Everett remains in his spot by the door, ensuring we don't have any more surprises.

"We have so much to catch up on," I say, reaching out

to grab his hands.

"So they know about you." Declan lowers his voice to try to keep the conversation between us, but even if he whispered, we'd all be able to hear him. "What you are. Your needs. Fuck, I can't believe you're pregnant, Gweny. And with a girl." I was hoping he didn't hear everything. Now, I know what Bronx will want to do, even without asking him. I'll let him. Manipulating Declan to forget that information is for the best. It would be too easy to steal that information from his mind.

"It was unexpected," I say, sucking in my bottom lip. Inhaling a small breath, I try my best to calm my tense nerves. This wasn't how I wanted Declan to find out. I should've been the one to tell him. It sucks. "I had no idea it was even possible."

He frowns, his eyes crinkling in the corners. "Why wouldn't it be?"

"Because—"

Bronx covers my mouth with his hand, stopping me from spilling my heart out. I nip his palm. He doesn't relent, refusing to uncover my mouth. He says, "Because Gwen was worried about our possessiveness. She didn't know of the different ways to procreate without the physicality of being with a male human."

I glower at Bronx. I can't help it. "Are you ki—"

Jameson looms over Declan. "You and the rest of your brothers really left her at a disadvantage, not educating her on donor sexuality. She mentioned at least half of you were greatly experienced in that department."

Swinging my hand out, I clock Jameson in the arm. I don't even know how to respond to his remark—about my supposed and untrue naivety toward sex or my brothers' sexual experience. "That's enough. You can blame Grayson and the Barons for that bullshit. But right now, I just want to tell my brother the truth. I could use him on my side." But who am I kidding? I need to suppress my urge.

Bronx shakes his head. "No."

His response makes me want to argue more for the sole purpose that he doesn't even try to reason with me against it. But tonight now has me on edge. "What do you mean *no*? He's my brother." I cross my arms over my chest, trying to keep my anger in check. I knew this is how Bronx would react, but I was still hoping that maybe he'd give in to my request to include my family in my life at least a little bit.

"I know. And I'm sorry. It's just that he's the blood source of Macon, and we're not allies yet. Even so, it's better that your brother doesn't know anything that could be used against us. If I thought he was capable of giving away our secret about what you are, I'd wipe his mind right now. Locking his memories was probably one of the only good things Laredo ever did for your family apart from keeping you away from the Baron assholes." Bronx tightens his jaw, waiting for me to argue.

"I agree with Bronx, Gigi. He can't know anything,"

Jameson says.

Bronx touches my cheek, getting me to look at him. "So please just give us this. We'll figure out what is okay to tell him when we have more time to think it through. We don't want to jeopardize Declan. Not with what happened to Kyler."

He's right. Corona managed to break the block on Kyler's mind, and it led to his death. It caused all sorts of problems for us. Declan doesn't deserve such a fate. It's bad enough that he keeps my dhampir secret. But anything about the baby? I have to change my thinking. She must come first.

"I also think we should manipulate his mind to erase the fact that we're having a girl. The last thing we want is for the news to get out if the Barons manage to snatch up Declan like they have with Silas and Grayson," Bronx adds. "Yours and her safety is the most important thing."

Once again, he's right, as much as I don't want him to be in regards to the situation.

"Again, I agree with Bronx," Jameson says.

"Same." Everett takes my hand. "Vampire households don't share this sort of information anyway unless they have plans like Vienna and Rome. Their coven is small but powerful, and with the future plans for a permanent alliance using their mates' children as liaisons is rather brilliant. They could very well get invited onto the board to head a region in a couple decades."

I blow a breath through my nose and turn my gaze to Declan. He remains calm and collected, not bothering to fight. Grayson and Silas would kick his ass if they knew he wasn't going to try to get himself out of this situation, but unlike them, Declan has always been more reserved. He was never about the fight as much. He was more concerned with our safety as a family.

"Gweny, I think you should allow them. I've learned a lot over the last few weeks, and the last thing I ever want to do is jeopardize our family. The only request I have is that I get to keep the knowledge of your pregnancy. I can't believe I'm going to be an uncle. I always thought Silas's dumb ass would be first." Declan tightens his jaw at the thought. "But you? Fuck. You're going to be an excellent mother."

My bottom lip trembles at his comment. It was the last thing I expected for him to say. He and Ashton were always worried about what the Blood Rebels wanted from me. He worried about me getting used. Dad took us away from the elders for a reason.

Throwing my arms around Declan, I hug him. "I'm so scared, Decky. Everything is so messed up. Silas and Grayson—they've changed. They've made a deal with a coven without my consent, and now we're facing a war." It's been years since I've called him by his childhood nickname, but something inside me yearns to turn back time just a little so that I could appreciate everything he's done for me growing up.

"The region takeover?" he asks. "Macon told me about it. I hadn't realized you were involved."

I open my mouth to spill my guts about everything, but Bronx rests his hands on my shoulders. He leans in and nestles his chin on the crook of my neck. I tilt my head slightly to glance at him in my peripheral vision. His eyes spark with silver, and he kisses my jaw.

Silence falls over us. Declan shifts nervously on his feet in front of us, probably weirded out that no one responds to him.

After another minute of silence, I finally look back to him. "I want to tell you all about it, Declan. I really do. But it involves all of us. Just know that we're not going down without a fight."

"Gwen..." Fear pinches Declan's brows.

I take a breath and spin to face Bronx. "Be gentle, okay? I can't stay here and watch. It hurts too much."

Bronx engulfs me in a hug and whispers that he will take the best care of Declan. He nudges me toward Everett, and I let him pick me up in his arms. Jameson follows us out of the room and to the elevator.

"No celebrating without me, Gigi," Jameson murmurs through a kiss. "We'll do something fun later."

I bob my head. "Okay."

Everett snuggles me close. I catch sight of a few people watching me, so I rest my chin on Everett as the elevator doors start to shut. A figure appears in the reflective wall from across the lobby. My heart slips into my stomach as recognition sinks in me. I'm fucking hallucinating. Laredo is dead. He couldn't possibly be here.

I shift to look over my shoulder and into the room, but he's gone and the doors close.

"You all right, Gwen?" Everett asks.

"No. I just saw Laredo," I say.

"What?" His voice lowers.

"I think I'm going crazy."

Everett pulls out his com device and motions for me to cover my ears.

The shock alarms blare through the air.

I stare at the still image captured from the video feed. This is fucking nuts. There is no possible way that this could be Laredo. He's dead. I saw him die. My hand slid into his empty chest cavity, where Bronx had ripped his heart out.

"I'm sure there is an explanation to all of this," Everett says, stealing his com device away from me. "Just try to relax. My brothers are out there now. We'll find him."

I scrub my hands over my cheeks. "Is it possible to heal after losing your heart? What did you guys do with Laredo's body?"

"If he hadn't lost his heart completely, his body would've regenerated, but this isn't the case. Laredo is dead. Whoever that guy is can't be him. Laredo was cremated in the sun pit outside of the city." Everett scoots closer to me and pulls me onto his lap. "We have the records to prove it, including a visual."

I shudder at just the thought. I never dwelled on what happened to the bodies of the dead before now. "Oh."

"Try not to think about it. You're under enough stress already." He stands up with me in his arms and strolls across his room and to our bed. "How about you let me feed you and then we can workout for a bit?"

I puff out my bottom lip. "Can't we just cuddle in bed and watch a movie instead?"

Everett yanks off his shirt and tosses it to the floor. "Rio did send me some movies to help prepare you for what's to come."

I scrunch my face and whip my head back and forth hard enough to pelt him with my hair. He chuckles and kisses my frown until I give in to his affection. I slip my tongue into his mouth, deepening our kiss. His soft lips feel so good and taste even better that I never want to break away from his mouth.

Trailing his fingers over my shoulders, he nudges the straps of my dress off, tugging the fabric from my breasts instead of pulling it over my head. I gasp at the cool sensation of his hand touching my back to unhook my bra, letting it fall between us. He glides his hand to my breast and gently grazes his fingers along my curves until he massages my excited nipple, drawing a moan from me.

"Fuck, that feels good," I say, arching my back. My body devours the gesture, begging for more. It's like every nerve-ending on my body buzzes in a state of hyperawareness, more sensitive than ever.

He hums under his breath and kisses down my jaw while lowering me onto my back. Gliding his tongue over my heated skin, he kisses my nipples next, twirling his tongue around them and blowing a soft breath to make me shiver at the sensation. Goosebumps prickle over me, and I cradle his head, squirming under him.

He works his way lower, dragging his hands down my body as he positions himself between my legs. The simple stretching of my body feels amazing, my muscles yearning to be worked up and over. My lust and hunger collide, and Everett doesn't get the chance to kiss me where he likes, because I sit up and practically throw myself at him.

He catches me with a laugh, his back hitting the rug. Rolling me over, he tries to move lower again, but I push him back to climb on top. I want my mouth on him more. I need more. I'm on the verge of losing control, my emotions running rampant.

Everett bends his neck for me, his eyes flashing silver with his desire. Usually, he'd test my restraint, but I think tonight has him wanting to give me anything I ask for. My body hums and tingles, my dhampir nature taking over with his offering of his body and blood. Bowing forward, I sink my teeth into Everett's shoulder. His blood fills my mouth, and I swallow, the taste satiating my burning need.

"So incredible," I murmur, stroking my fingers over his hard pecs. "Just what I needed."

"You want more?" The way his voice lowers, I know he doesn't mean more blood.

I nod and kiss him hard, sucking his bottom lip into my mouth. "I don't only want it. I need it. So desperately."

"Mmm." He arches up to meet my eyes. "Anything you want."

Pushing up on one hand, he gets to his feet and moves me to the bed. This time he laces his fingers through mine, pinning them at my sides. I arch my back with a laugh, squirming beneath him. Everett manages to hook his fangs to my panties and rips them off me. I gasp and catch his head between my thighs, loving every second of teasing him and not letting him get what he wants.

I use my dhampir strength to roll him over. Scrambling down, I don't let him pull my body to his face. "Me first," I say, wagging my finger at him.

Everett play-growls and tries to snatch me again, but I shift beside him and fumble with the button on his pants. I'm so worked up that I end up yanking the button off in my attempt to pull them down. Everett chuckles and props up on his elbows, unfazed by my mad rush to get him naked. I drag off his pants and boxers and drink in the sight of him for only a few seconds.

"Do I need to brace myself for you to devour me?" Everett teases. "You look starved."

"Not starved." I rub my hands up his legs, crawling my way to situate myself in front of him. "Just...I want my mouth all over you. I want to take care of you."

Everett moans as I rest on my elbows and lace my fingers around his erection. I guide it into my mouth, twirling my tongue over his tip before sucking my way down. His sweet, smooth skin makes my mouth water, and heat builds between my legs with Everett's soft moans. He whispers my name and runs his fingers through my hair, pulling it up to get the best view he can.

"Let me turn you around," he murmurs, drawing his hands along my sides. "I want to take care of you too. I need to. It's all I can think about."

I slowly ease my mouth away and lick my lips. "What if I want you to cum first for once?"

He cocks an eyebrow. "Not going to happen. Always you before me."

"Not this time." I cup his balls with my hand and lower myself again, gliding my tongue along the underside of his boner until I reach the top. Pursing my lips, I slowly suck him into my mouth again, fully set on seeing this through.

Everett releases the sexiest sound from his throat, a mix between a teasing growl and a purr. He digs his fingers into my sides and surprises the hell out of me by flipping my body up too quickly to react. I hang upside down and facing away from him with my legs on his shoulders. He leans back so I straddle his head. Holding me in place, he sucks my clit into his mouth, stroking his tongue over me with enough pressure that I brace against the wall.

Holy fuck.

My mind turns to mush, my whole body exploding with a pleasure so intense that he remains true to his word. My intense orgasm leaves me breathless and buzzing, and I'm nearly certain it might never stop. I scream out and clench his head with my knees, unable to do anything except moan through it. My legs shake so hard that I'm not sure I'll even walk again.

Everett slides me down, his cocky-ass grin making me smile. I pat his cheek and shake my head, scooting lower until I feel his shaft between my legs. But I don't let him enter me. I slide up and down, teasing him with my slick heat, hoping to drive him crazy. He captures me with his stare, clutching my hips to pick up my pace as I slip and slide on him, enjoying the sensation he creates.

"You're so sexy, Gwen," he says, biting his bottom lip with his fangs, enticing me to bend forward for another kiss. "Everything about you, about this moment, about us and what's ahead. I'm the happiest man in the universe."

I smile and kiss him, letting him roll me off so he can get on top. He kneels between my legs and hooks his hands under my thighs, lifting my body to his. Snagging a pillow, he props up my ass and stretches my legs wider until I'm nearly doing the splits. His first thrust penetrates me so deeply that I can't stop my loud-ass mouth from screaming in ecstasy. He rocks into me while also pulling me to him. My moans come in loud, quick bursts with his rigorous movements. I feel so hot and sexy under the weight of his gaze.

I clutch the blankets in my hands and close my eyes, savoring every amazing sensation created from our bodies meeting. Everett enhances my pleasure with his hand until I climax again.

With a few more thrusts, he finishes with a moan. I arch forward and hold my arms open, wanting nothing more than to feel the weight of his body on mine.

"You should drink more," he whispers, twining our fingers together.

"I'm afraid I'll drink too much. My whole body—fuck, Everett. I want you again and again." I cover my eyes with my hands, trying to suppress my desire.

"I'll gladly give you what you want, but let me feed you. Just...open your mouth. I'll make sure you don't drink too much." Everett's fangs click as he extends them, the sound doing nothing for the ache inside me that craves his bite. I never knew I'd miss such a thing so much. The intimacy—being able to fulfill his needs—I miss it.

I part my lips, keeping my eyes closed. If I look, I'll grab his arm. If I grab his arm, I know he'll let me suck to my heart's content.

The scent of his sugary blood overwhelms my senses.

Everett gently hooks his free hand to my wrists and locks my hands in place, stopping me from reaching for him. It drives me crazy in a good way, but all I do is wiggle and move in anticipation. Warmth blossoms across my bottom lip until his blood drips into my mouth in a stream that sends tingles down to my belly. I groan in my throat, wanting so badly to break free. It takes everything in me to let him give me blood this way.

"I wish you could bite me," I say, licking my lips as the stream of blood turns into a trickle.

"Who says I can't? I have a lot of restraint. If it's what you want, I can do so without drinking...but don't test my brothers." He shifts my hair from throat and kisses my sensitive skin. Grazing his fangs lower, he nips the top of my breast hard enough to make my body buzz. He glides his tongue softly over my skin, and I moan and cup his head, the memory of all our previous blood exchanges flitting through my mind.

"I won't lie. It's torture to tease you like this," he murmurs, staunching the tiny drops of blood with his fingertips before licking them clean.

"You think you're the only one tortured? I want more. All of you. I can't get enough. My control...just one more taste." I tip my head up. "Please."

"You better give our girl what she wants before I do." Jameson's voice sounds through the door.

Everett releases a soft growl, and I cover my mouth to

muffle my laugh. He shakes his head, his annoyance over Jameson's arrival quickly disappearing.

"I know it's my time, but if you keep smiling at me like that, I just might let him in," Everett says, nestling by my side. "But you can't hold me responsible if he gets carried away."

"You think he'll be the one to get carried away?" I ask, laughing again.

Everett grins. "You're right." Sitting up, he calls, "Come on in, brother. But I'm warning you. If you prod out the feisty side of our girl, I'll let her devour you."

"Only if I get to go out with the best bang of my life." Jameson swings the door open and tugs his shirt over his head. He kicks it shut behind him, fully ready to proceed without an ounce of caution. His bravery toward my dhampir nature never fails to amaze me. He's always been all in, which I love.

"All right, Gigi. Have at me." Jameson plops on the bed on my other side. "Pick your position."

Heat blooms up my chest, and I crawl on top of him, kissing him with enough passion to make him moan.

"Don't bite him, Gwen," Everett says, sitting up. He eases me between his legs, not even caring that we're both naked with Jameson. "Let him feed you. I can gauge how much you get this way. If we know how much you need to remain in control, we can plan accordingly."

"That's no fun," Jameson and I say in unison.

"It is if I hold her down for you." Everett pulls me between his legs. "I think it's safe enough to drive her a little wild. It's only fair since she'll drive you crazy later."

I raise my eyebrows. "What's that supposed to mean?"

Jameson bites his arm and hangs it above me to let his blood stream into my mouth. "Your highly anticipated performance."

"The perfect stress relief." Bronx taps on the door. "Which we might all need...because we caught Laredo."

I freeze, forgetting to swallow Jameson's blood. Coughing, I spit it everywhere, my mind whirling at Bronx's words.

"That can't be," I say with a gasp.

Bronx eases the door open. "I need you to confirm it, dandelion. He won't talk to anyone but you."

"I—I can't." I shake my head, my heart ricocheting around my ribcage. "It's a trick. He's dead. You killed him. We were all there."

Bronx closes the space to me. "I know this is a lot to take in, but we're all here. We gotta figure this shit out."

I inhale a deep breath. "I'm scared."

"We'll protect you." Jameson slides his fingers through mine.

"I know. It's not that." I lick my lips. "It's everything else."

Because for the first time ever, I'm not sure I want answers.

I want to leave the past in the past.

But I don't think I can.

The Barons—whoever this new asshole is—they're dead-set on controlling my future.

4

PREVIOUS BLOOD SOURCE

MY HANDS TREMBLE AT MY sides as I stand outside the metal door of one of the testing rooms. Laredo's imposter sits in a chair with his arms chained behind his back. He doesn't twist to look at me through the window cutout, but I know he's aware of my presence. His posture changes the longer I peer at the back of his head.

"I can't do this," I whisper, trying to stop my voice from shaking. A dozen memories break free as I recall past moments with Laredo, but especially the last one of his death. He can't be here. He can't.

"We're right here, dandelion," Bronx says, preparing to open the door. He stands ultra-close, so it feels as if we're connected by invisible strings. The feather-light sensation of his sleeve against my skin helps ease my nerves. He's just a touch away, as strong as ever.

Mikkalo takes my hand and turns me toward him. His dark eyes search mine as he studies me. He takes care to remain emotionless, which I can't blame. My guys do it so often that any sign of concern freaks me out. I hate that they think they have to stay emotionless in times like this for me, but it is what it is. As long as they don't turn into hard asses all the time, I don't mention it. Their happiness, love, and desire are the things I cherish the most.

"I don't think she should do this. Listen to her heartbeat. The stress is too much," Mikkalo finally says. "Look how hard she's shaking. She doesn't get nervous like this often. She can spit in a Barons' face and stay steady. But this? She doesn't have to face him. There are other ways to extract information."

Other ways? Yikes. That's a side of regional power I don't want to think about.

"He's right, Bronxy." Jameson puffs out his bottom lip at me. Combing his hand through my tresses, he ruffles my hair and kisses my temple. "This can't be good for our baby girl. It's not a risk I want to take."

"Gwen and the baby will be fine." Everett slides his arm around me from behind, hugging me. "Not facing him might be worse for her. She won't stop thinking about it. I don't know about you, but I want her mind to focus on better things."

"Listen to your misters, my beautiful dhampir." The vampire's voice trickles through the metal door to me. He sounds exactly like Laredo, down to the way he says the nickname he gave me. And shit. I used to love it, but it ignites a new level of fear. I'm going to be sick. "You don't have to be afraid, Gwen. This must be strange for you, but I'm neither a ghost nor Baron, and I'm sure you have a lot of questions. So please, come in. It feels like forever since you've graced me with your beauty. I've missed you more than I knew possible. This has been the longest we've been apart in years. Do you miss me too or have I been so easily replaced?"

His words make my guys tense and crowd closer around me. I'm nearly certain they've all changed their minds after hearing him speak to me. To them, he was my dead blood source. He was someone from my past. He was never a threat. That's one thing Bronx used to struggle over every time Laredo was brought up. But now? It's just as hard for them as it is for me.

It doesn't help that Laredo's just as charming as ever.

His familiarity engulfs me, and I step toward the door and press my palm to the lock screen. It turns green under my touch and swings open. The vampire still doesn't turn to meet my gaze. Each of my footsteps feels heavier than the last, and my body slows like I'll sink into the floor before I even get to him. Maybe it's my subconscious's way of warning me to turn around and leave.

Everett and Mikkalo each hold onto me with Bronx and Jameson remaining a foot behind. The door clicks closed, locking us in the room. My heart bangs like crazy, thudding hard enough that I worry it might bust through my ribs to splatter on the floor.

"Fuck," I whisper. "I think I'm going to die. I need to leave."

Mikkalo tries to scoop me up, but Everett stops him.

The vampire sighs. "Wait. Please stay."

Instead of walking in front of the vampire to face him, I stop a foot behind him. From my spot, I can smell the freshness of his skin, more powerful than I've ever smelled it before. It reminds me of the late nights of Laredo carrying me through the orchards, stopping to pick fruit. I can envision the crisp air, the glittering stars in the sky, and how his blood tasted flooding my mouth with my bite.

A hundred stolen moments come crashing back to me—moments he ensured stayed locked away with mind manipulation. Moments that have yet to come back to me, even after Everett removed the block from my mind.

"My dhampir, let me take a look at you. I hear congratulations are in order." The vampire's deep, velvety voice snaps me from my thoughts. "I guess I should've expected such a thing. I knew you wouldn't be able to resist your nature forever. You were on the verge of giving in the last time I saw you. So close. I have so many regrets."

I squeeze Everett and Mikkalo's hands so tightly that I'm sure their hands are probably numb. "Who are you?" As much as I want to comment on his admission, I don't want to open a door to something like that. It takes everything in me to ask even the simple question, because a huge part of me knows the answer. It's undeniable. But how?

"Gwen, I know this is hard on you, and I apologize for everything I've done. Only your brothers were supposed to get captured and put in the system. You were to be free." The vampire shifts on his chair. "Will you please face me? I'd like to explain."

Anger bursts through me, and I break away from Mikkalo and Everett. Instead of stomping in front of the vampire, I grab his shoulders and yank him back, sending his chair crashing to the floor. He doesn't move or fight or complain, even with his arms crushed beneath him. All he does is stare at me with a strange expression crossing his face.

Our eyes meet, and I freeze. His familiarity overwhelms me. My hurricane of emotions collides through my chest, attempting to shatter the wall I've built around my heart. And then tears cloud my vision, and no matter what I do, I can't get them to stop. They pelt the vampire's forehead and cheeks, but he doesn't move. He doesn't react.

"Who are you?" I ask again, my voice cracking. It hurts

to even speak.

"You know who I am, my dhampir." He keeps his gaze locked on me, despite my guys surrounding us. It's almost like he refuses to acknowledge they're truly here, being the only ones who can manage to hold me together as I fall apart.

"I don't. You look like my previous blood source, but he's dead. I watched him die." I wipe my hands across my cheeks, managing to pull myself together.

Everett uses his sleeve to finish drying my eyes in silence. I swallow the knot in my throat, my stomach twisting and threatening to expel all the blood I drank.

I straighten my shoulders and purse my lips before adding, "You're not him. You're not Laredo."

"Or perhaps the vampire who died on your behalf wasn't me. I'd never go down so easily." Laredo's words hang in the air. I want so badly to deny the truth, but I know it in my very being that the vampire chained to this chair is Laredo. "You don't think I'd actually get us caught by accident, do you? I've managed to avoid the Barons for three years. I've kept you safe like I had promised. And I plan on continuing to do so. These new circumstances have changed things. The Barons sneak too close, and your misters are failing to do the job I had entrusted them to do for me...then again, you've always been my weakness. I could never truly stay away."

I slam my hands into his chest, pushing myself up. Laredo heaves a breath at my strength, but he doesn't continue. He remains placid on the floor. And it's a good thing he does. I'm a second from losing control, and he will disappear from my life once again. My blood hunger will ensure it. My guys wouldn't stop me.

"This is bullshit!" I scream, twisting around. "Total bullshit!"

Mikkalo holds open his arms for me first, and I fall into them and press my face into his hard chest, inhaling a breath of his scent. It helps calm my shot nerves. It's like the universe loves to just keep throwing one thing after another at me to kill my excitement about my future.

I tilt my head up and peer into Mikkalo's eyes. "I don't understand any of this. Do you think he's lying? I need you to help me work through this. You're the strategy expert. Why would he do this?"

"I had my reasons, and I've never lied to you, Gwen," Laredo says, answering my question I failed to keep between Mikkalo and me.

Fury whips around me, slicing me open with a dozen memories. I fly back at him and grip his shirt between my fingers. I scream in his face, my frustration, confusion, and anguish unleashing my dhampir side.

"But you fucking manipulated my life!" I can't stop myself from tearing into his throat, my emotions setting off my blood hunger in the worst way possible. He should feel the pain he put me through. He should pay for all his games. Laredo needs to learn that my life and my future are mine, not his. He can't get away with this bullshit.

Bronx drags me up, holding me out as I kick and punch and flail in an attempt to escape. My vision shadows with my rage. I can barely see. Barely think. Jameson and Mikkalo lift Laredo to his feet, keeping him restrained but out of the way of my wrath.

"Let me go, Bronx!" I yell, bucking uselessly in his arms. My strength diminishes the longer he grips me to his chest. I haven't felt his strength like this ever before.

"No, dandelion. We can't risk you ripping his heart out. I know this is a horrible situation, and I promise, I'm going to deal with it so you don't have to, but I need this asshole alive for now." Bronx adjusts me to face him, meeting my eyes. His jaw tightens, his gaze flicking over my face. "I've known since the moment you told me how you ended up in Crimson Vista that something didn't add up. Remember how we had gotten a call about Blood Rebels?"

"How we thought you were set up," Everett adds, moving closer.

I inhale a few sharp breaths through my nose. "But you thought it was because Laredo was trying to separate me from my family."

"And it worked, but there was more to it." Laredo draws my attention back to him. "Your brother ruined my plan by accidentally shooting you. I knew once you got a taste of someone new, you'd have them enchanted. But that doesn't matter now. I won't hold it against you. If you please just control yourself, I will tell you everything, Gwen."

"No, you will tell *us* everything," Jameson says. He straightens his back and narrows his green eyes.

Laredo's eyes flash silver at Jameson's effort to intimidate him. "If that's what Gwen wants, then fine. I recognize her bond to your coven and respect it as much as it pains me."

"Good. Because I do want them here." I look at Jameson, wishing I could hug him instead of watch him restrain Laredo. A part of me doesn't want my guys anywhere near him. "They're mine. Anything you say affects all of us. I belong to the Royale Coven now. I've accepted a Blood Vow."

Laredo's mouth tightens, his eyes flicking across each of my guys. He doesn't admit as much, but my revelation bothers him. I understand why, considering all of the moments we've spent together. He was clear with his feelings of wanting something with me, though I always denied him.

"Then perhaps we can go somewhere more comfortable," he finally says after a quiet moment. "You can leave me in chains and bound. But I think it's best if you sit down, my dhampir. We have a lot to discuss. Arrangements to make. Enemies to pursue."

Mikkalo stiffens, losing his composure. One second Laredo stands a few feet away, and in the next, Mikkalo thrusts him into a wall and aims a dagger at his heart. He growls, the low, threatening noise reverberating through my bones. But I don't rush to stop him. I don't react. All I do is watch in silence.

"You will not refer to our mate as yours," Mikkalo says, flashing his fangs. "She is ours. *Ours.* Do not act as if you belong here."

Laredo trains his stare on me. It's like he can't stop looking. The weight of his intensity burns through me, and I close my eyes just to cut myself off from him. "My sincerest apology, Misters Royale. I've overstepped my boundaries. Gwen is yours. She chose you."

It's enough to get Mikkalo to chill out. He releases Laredo and returns to my side. I grab his hand and tug him closer, standing on my tiptoes to brush my lips to his. Mikkalo sucks my bottom lip into his mouth, savoring my affection.

I think he purposefully shows off my love, wanting to make a point. And I don't mind. I love it. There's something about his claim on me in this moment that gets to me in a good way. He has every right to threaten Laredo and make his place clear. I'd do the same if I were him in this position. This is all so...fucking insane.

"Laredo." My voice comes so softly that I'm not even sure I say his name. If my guys didn't look at me with indecipherable expressions, I'd clear my throat and try again. "I know we have some history, but as far as I'm concerned, you fucked up. You played with my life. You destroyed my family. You bit me with venom and—abandoned me? I was so confused about what was happening to me. I was lucky that it was the Royales to capture me. Without them, I'd be caged or worse."

"You'd have been fine with or without them, my dham—Gwen. Don't underestimate your capabilities." Laredo risks stepping closer, his hands remaining behind his back. "You are a powerful being with an exquisite bloodline so strong that the Barons recognize it. They believe you will change the world."

I touch my belly. "And apparently bear some incomparable power."

He smirks. "Who will be as beautiful and fierce as you are if raised right. With my help—"

"With *your* help? Are you fucking kidding me?" Jameson growls, cutting off Laredo's words. If Everett didn't step in front of him and raise his palms, Jameson would attack.

Laredo nods, keeping his chin up. "You'll need me."

Bronx stomps forward, his muscular frame towering over Laredo. His muscles flex with his clenched fingers as he refrains from touching Laredo. "Get it fucking straight. No one needs you. Not Gwen. Not us. And especially not our heir."

Holding up his hands in surrender, Laredo finally turns his eyes from me to acknowledge my guys. I release a breath in relief, the lightness from his lifted gaze feeling like the weight he presses on my soul diminishes. "But you need answers. Gwen chose you as her protectors. She chose you to mate with. You obviously don't understand the way of dhampirs like I do. If you had, you would've been better prepared. You wouldn't have wasted your efforts on this pitiful region and weakened territory. Instead, you'd have put all your efforts into Gwen."

Bronx shoves Laredo back, his fury palpable enough to heat my skin. Tension bunches my muscles, and it takes everything in me to move forward. My shoes squeak on the tiles, and Bronx extends his arm, blocking Laredo, even though he doesn't attempt to move from his spot on the floor.

I shift under Bronx's arm and hug him, nestling into his side. "It would be in your best interest to watch what the hell you say, Laredo. We've been fine figuring things out on our own. No one's getting comfortable. If you don't want to meet your final donation, I suggest you tell me everything. If and only if we find it worth our time will I consider not punching your heart out for everything you put me through. Start with who the hell died if it wasn't you."

Laredo releases a long-ass sigh and shuffles to the chair, plopping into it. "It was my brother, my biological twin, and the one helping me protect your family from the Barons."

"You *are* a Baron," I snap, clenching my jaw.

"I was what I had to be. Donor Life Corp cast me out for an unauthorized transformation with my brother, Livorno, after The Divide. He was given my place in the Duchanne Region before its downfall." Laredo shifts his gaze from mine. "I found the Barons not long after. It turned out that Thaxton bit me and had been searching for me. The Barons can hack all the systems, and when I was cast out, Thaxton saw the notification and found me. Several others too. They never knew of Livorno's existence."

"Why?" I find myself moving closer, my curiosity getting the best of me.

"Because I had intended to use the Barons as leverage to regain good status in the Donor Life Corp Territory once my banishment was lifted...but then I met Gwyneth." His voice lowers, his handsome features turning into a scowl. "She was enamored with Rochester. A Blood Rebel from a human line that managed to escape both the uprising and the divisions."

"Yet she fell for that asshole," I mutter under my breath.

"Not exactly. She was taken by the idea of immortality. She wanted a life different than the one she was born into." Laredo rolls his shoulders. "But the rebels weren't as charmed by Rochester as he was with her. So they used her. Promised her she'd get her eternity if she convinced Rochester to start a dhampir line."

My stomach twists at the thought. I knew rebels did everything in their power to fight against vampires. I knew why they believed dhampirs to be important—supposed gifts to humanity—but to do something like this? It's horrible. I can't imagine what my ancestor had gone through. I can't imagine why she agreed to it.

"And then they killed her before Rochester could take what he thought was his." Laredo falls silent, his eyes searching over my face.

Strong arms wrap around me from behind as Everett scoops me off my feet. A dozen thoughts flood through my mind. I always thought it was the failure to transition because of being bitten while pregnant that killed Gwyneth, but all along it was Blood Rebels. She never even had a chance.

"I'm sorry, Gwen," Laredo says softly. "I tried to stop them. Rochester and the Barons ended up annihilating many soldiers. They took control of the rebel cluster and used it as a way to keep the dhampir line hidden. And then you came along."

"And Rochester wasn't going to risk the rebels taking me," I whisper.

"No. He wasn't going to risk them using you against him, not when he knew of your capabilities...which I'm sorry for." Laredo stretches out his legs and shifts to look at Bronx. "Gwen isn't the first dhampir to survive to adulthood but many don't survive long thereafter."

I knew this. I think my dad told me this. Maybe an elder. That's why I was always prepared for a short life.

"How do you know so much?" Jameson asks. "You're

younger than I am, and I had to scour old documents and still came up short. It's all hearsay."

"My sister was a symptomatic carrier. My mother was bitten with venom during the uprising. It wasn't supposed to happen, but the humans in our town...they weren't going to bow to vampires. I was part of a rebel nest and my sister convinced an outcast to transform me. That's how I found my brother again. He was caught and registered as a donor. So I bit him."

This is so much to take in. I hate how fascinated I am. Laredo had a dhampir sister. A fucking dhampir sister. But what happened to her?

"This is how I know rebels have no idea how to properly care for these magnificent beings," Laredo continues, glancing to each of my guys. "They got my sister killed. They sent her to war. They didn't fulfill her needs." Laredo closes his eyes as he falls silent. Ah, hell. This is the kind of moment I'd have hugged Laredo before. But I can't. Not now.

I find my footing and shuffle closer, caught up in his familiarity. Everett remains by my side and doesn't say anything as I touch Laredo's shoulder, getting him to look at me. "That's why you never returned to the city and remained with the Barons? Because of the Gallagher dhampir line?"

He twists his lips. "Something like that. I made a promise to Gwyneth. She knew how much I knew. She wanted me to watch her heirs because rebels don't know shit. Hell, they don't even know dhampirs have seasons or their procreation capabilities. They muddle bloodlines and are careless. They have no idea—like most everyone who treats dhampirs as a myth—how powerful these women really are and how much they continue to grow as long as they have a coven powerful enough to help them rise."

"You said women. So no males at all?" Everett asks.

Laredo shrugs. "As far as I know. It's part of a dhampir's evolution because of how many males outnumber females. It's why she claimed your whole coven."

Jameson heaves a dramatic sigh. "Yeah, no. Gwen thinks of us beyond a coven and what we offer."

I shift and smile at him. "You're right about that, Jamie."

Laredo's eyes flicker with sparks of silver. "Either way, none of that matters. What matters is that you understand what you're dealing with and can keep Gwen safe. Which is why I'm helping whether you like it or not. My brother didn't fall by your hand for nothing. I didn't give up my comfortable life just to entrust you with a job that had been important to me long before Gwen was born."

Anger crashes over me, killing my curiosity. "There has to be more to it. What do you get out of it? What do you want?"

"You, of course," he says.

All four of my guys growl.

"Perhaps the chance to start a new coven for your daughter if my first demand isn't possible."

It's my turn to react.

I slam my hands into Laredo, knocking him to the floor again.

My fury controls me, and I jab my fingers into his chest, feeling his blood trickle over my hand, the feeling of his heart thrumming the oddest sensation. It doesn't beat out of control or anything, remaining as calm as he does.

"You can't and won't make those crazy-ass demands," I say, my voice sharpening.

Something strange crosses Laredo's face. His features soften, and he says, "Okay."

I furrow my brows. "Really?"

"Yes."

Well this is weird. I wonder what changed his mind. I blink a few times and loosen my grip. "Why are you agreeing so easily?"

"I have faith you'll change your decision. Now, please, if you don't mind." He motions to his chest.

Swallowing my anger, I slowly slide my fingers from his chest. I automatically lick the blood off like my dhampir side refuses to waste a drop, even if it's not from my guys. They all watch me in silence, and heat floods my face. I end up wiping Laredo's blood on his shirt and pushing off him to get to my feet.

I press my lips together and look to Everett. "I feel

weird. Take me back to our suite? I think I need to rest for a bit."

Bronx turns to Mikkalo. "Lock him up and meet me in my suite."

Laredo laughs from the floor. "Don't worry, Misters Royale. I'm not going anywhere as long as Gwen is with you."

I turn away and hold my hands out for Everett to lift me into his arms.

"I promise you, Gwen. I won't leave you again," Laredo says.

I hate that I believe him.

5

FRAGMENTED MEMORIES

"WHY ARE YOU BEING WEIRD?" I place my hands on my hips, giving Laredo a long once-over. "You look like you're expecting Grayson to throw you into a sun cage."

Laredo materializes in front of me, tilting his head to gaze into my eyes. His muddy-brown irises flash silver the longer I trap him in my stare, though I know it's him who could trap me. But he wouldn't. He promised me.

"Actually, I'm expecting you to sink those perfect teeth of yours into my throat," he murmurs, reaching up to touch my jaw.

I whack his hand away. "Shhh! My brothers will hear you. They'll stake you if they knew how much I enjoy sucking your damn neck."

"It'll be worth it." Laredo flicks his gaze to the bedroom door behind us. "Maybe just this once." It sounds like he's talking to himself. What gives?

I frown. "Once? No. You know I despise the damn cup." Grabbing the front of his shirt, I pull him closer. I expect him to resist and tease me, but he shuffles into my space willingly and leans in so close that I expect to have to punch him in the gut if he tries to kiss me.

Instead, he tugs down the collar of his shirt. "Come on, Gwen. Show me what it's like."

"Laredo...you know what it's like." Confusion washes over me.

He brings his finger to my lips, cutting off my words. "Just play along, my dhampir. I hear your brothers nearby. We can pretend this is the first time."

I slide my fingers into his soft, black hair, holding his head in place. "You're so strange today, but whatever. Don't think this role-playing bullshit is going to be a regular thing."

He chuckles.

"Now take a breath. You're lucky I'm so fucking starved."

A deep grunt, followed by a soft purr of a moan, pulls me from sleep. Bronx's sugary blood fills my mouth, and I swallow and snap my eyes open. His fingers comb into my hair, holding my head in place.

He stops me from pulling away and uses his free hand to tug my hips closer as our legs entangle. "I look forward to waking up with you sucking my neck like this for eternity, dandelion."

My heart thrums against his, his words suppressing my ever-present fear about the possibility that forever might never come if the Barons have their way. Instead of murmuring the thoughts on my mind, I suck his throat a bit longer and roll on top of him.

He graces me with a bright smile, one that lights up the dark depths of his eyes. It feels like it has been forever since we've had a moment alone even if it's only been a couple of days. Bronx hasn't stayed in bed with me long, always up before nightfall and keeping busy until well past dawn. If it's not preparing for the fight for the board seat, it's helping assure that we have everything we need...in case.

I hate it. I hate thinking about it. This wasn't how I wanted to wake up. One second dreaming—remembering a weird-ass moment with Laredo...fuck. That wasn't a memory about Laredo. It was his brother. It had to be. And now that I know that I've been manipulated and tricked, I can think of a dozen other memories where I thought Laredo was being strange. And now it makes sense.

"Easy, Gwen. It's taking everything in me not to bite you back," Bronx murmurs, dragging me from the thoughts

I would prefer to forget.

It's enough to get me to pull back. "You just taste so good."

He releases a rumble from his throat. "Fuck it. I'll accept this torture for you as long as you take a minute to kiss me."

I smile and brush my lips to his, giving him as much affection as he craves. A million things swirl through my mind, but I shove them away and focus on Bronx. He deserves my full attention, especially after everything.

"I'm going to need more than that," he says, shifting me on top of him. "I can't waste the extra time Everett gave me while he met with Rio to discuss your health and...this little baby girl." He draws me closer and kisses my stomach. "Who I want to know that I love her as much as I love her mom."

I bite my lip between my teeth, my eyes watering at his words. "Bronx..."

His brows furrow on his forehead. "Hey, whoa. No. Don't do that. I was trying to be romantic and sweet, not make you cry."

I laugh and blink like crazy, trying to get my eyes to get their act together. "I'm sorry. It's just—I love you too. So much. But I'm scared."

"Aw, dandelion. You shouldn't be. I got this. I have more to fight for than the Baron asshole. I won't let you or our coven down." He sits up and engulfs me in a hug, resting his chin on my shoulder. "And you know what?"

I rub my fingers over the taut planes of his muscular back. "Hmm?"

"This will be for the best. We'll get the chance to re-form the region with people of our choosing and not the ones Zaire felt he could control. We'll have real allies, who won't let us down. Our region will be a place we can raise children. A place where everyone wants to live. All because of you." Bronx tips his head back to meet my eyes. "I promise."

I smile and clutch his face in my hands, kissing him deeply and desperately with everything amazing he elicits inside of me. I repeat his words in my mind again, feeling and savoring the possibility of such a place, risen from our fight and desire to change things. "I promise to fight with you too...for our *children*."

He grins at me. "You caught that."

I run my fingers through his hair. "I did. And I think I could get on board with that...if it's possible. With the Blood Vow and everything—"

"We will figure it out." He kisses me again. "I had no idea this was something I wanted. Something that helps me look more at the future than planning and preparing for what happens now." His eyes search mine, his hope and desire so prominent that I can feel them in my soul.

I smile and scoot closer, feeling his arousal at my closeness. "The future...I can't wait. With everything going on—

fuck, Bronx."

Gently grasping my chin, he stops me from burying my face against his shoulder. "Hey, no. We got this. You're the most powerful being I know, and with you by my side, I can face anything. No more stressing, okay?"

I puff out my bottom lip. "I can't help it."

"Then let me help you." His eyes flash silver with his desire, his need to be near me drawing me closer to him like a gravitational pull that will save me from losing control and spiraling adrift with my all-consuming thoughts.

Leaning in, I caress my lips to his, savoring his sweetness for a moment before giving in to the carnal need that has me ripping off his shirt. Bronx releases a playful growl and reciprocates, bunching the fabric of my dress in his fingers to tear it off my breasts. He flips me off of him and onto my back. Bowing down, he uses his teeth to drag my bra straps away from my shoulders. He kisses the supple skin of my cleavage, and works his way lower, shredding the lacy fabric of my bra with his fangs. He nips me, making me moan, and it takes all my willpower not to beg him to bite me.

I arch my back as he grazes his tongue over my nipples, ripping the rest of my bra free. He adjusts my legs to nestle between them and works his way lower to my panties. Lifting my hips, I give him easier access to drag them off me. He flings them with his desperation and sinks his fingers into my sides, yanking me to the edge of the bed so he can rest on his knees.

He slides his big hands from my knees and to my thighs, spreading my legs wider to fit his hulking frame where he wants. The second his mouth sucks my clit, I moan so embarrassingly loud and squirm to grab a pillow. Bronx snatches it away and throws it across the room, not letting me muffle any of the sounds he's determined for the whole building to hear.

My body trembles at the electrifying sensations he creates with his tongue. He kisses and sucks and licks so fervently that I feel like I'll explode at any second. I can barely stay still under his attention as he works me up until my whole body tenses with my orgasm. Bronx moans at just the sound of my pleasure and pushes to his feet to kick out of his pants and underwear. He aligns his body to mine, holding me by my hips, so that I arch back, letting him have complete control with how he wants my body.

Gripping me by my ass, he thrusts into me, his desperation and need turning his movements hard and furious, rough, but in a way that I enjoy. I gasp at our bodies connecting and how his pelvis slaps against me with each of his movements. His eyes capture mine, his pleasure clear in his expression as he rocks faster and faster until I can barely catch my breath. I can't breathe without gasping, the intensity so incredible, so hot, that I cum a second time. The feeling rips through me, my whole body feeling it from my core and to the tips of my fingers and toes.

I blindly extend my arms to Bronx, wanting to hold onto him through the wave of pleasure. He sinks onto the bed with me, never stopping in his powerful thrusts, though his mouth explores mine softly, lovingly. I nip his lip, getting him to pierce it with his fangs to give me a taste of his blood.

The drops of sweetness set me off like crazy, and I scratch my nails down his back, breaking from his kiss to suck his shoulder. But I don't bite him. It takes everything in me not to, because I know if I do, he might lose control and bite back. Even if I want it. Even if I know nothing bad could ever come from our passion. I know he'd beat himself up over it, because he is afraid of doing anything that could jeopardize me and the mini-beast.

Bronx moans with his climax, thrusting a few more times before rolling me on top of him. I rest my cheek to his broad chest, listening to the thrumming of his heart beating, his rapid breathing, his contentment of just being close like this.

"Dandelion, I want so badly to keep you here with me for the rest of time." He strokes his fingers up and down the length of my back. "But if I'm going to be true to my promise, we must meet with our potential allies for dinner."

I groan and rock on him a few times. "I need more. I don't want these feelings to disappear just yet."

He moans, his body fully ready to give into my desire again. But instead of letting me have my way with him on the bed, he scoots off, holding me by my ass to take over, and heads toward the shower. He kisses me tenderly without stopping, blindly turning on the hot water to send steam through the air. My back hits the cool wall, making me gasp.

"You really test my capability to multi-task," he murmurs, gripping me with one hand while reaching for the shampoo with the other. "I'll never hear the end of it if I drop you or if we're late."

I laugh and kiss him, enjoying how he bounces me on him hard and fast. I barely manage to wash his hair, our bodies slipping and sliding with the soap. This was one way to cure my disappointment of having to leave bed, and I can't stop smiling at how determined Bronx is. He never does anything half-assed, especially in regards to me.

Soft voices trickle through the door, but it doesn't stop us.

Mikkalo knocking doesn't stop us either.

"Need help, brother?" Jameson calls through the door.

Bronx surprises the hell out of me by calling out, "Yeah."

I tip my head back in the water, the short bursts of my moans echoing through the shower. Jameson cracks the door open, drawing my attention to him for only a second to watch him strip out of his clothes to join us.

Fuck. Me.

They weren't joking earlier with their teasing about

backing each other up to satiate my desires.

"She needs more blood," Bronx says, panting against my shoulder. "She's insatiable. Bit me in her sleep."

Jameson chuckles. "My favorite."

Jameson bites his arm and steps behind me, sandwiching me to Bronx. The two of them act like this is so normal that it's easy to just sink into this bonding moment and let them give me whatever they think I need.

"Is everything in order for the gathering?" Bronx asks Jameson, totally acting like he's not fully set on making me cum.

"I oversaw everything myself. The donor feeders just arrived and the guests are settling in their r—"

I bonk my head playfully into Jameson's chin. "Shhh. This is not a meeting. Save that kind of talk for outside the shower. Your next words better be dirty and hot."

He nips my shoulder. "I'm trying not to steal your sexy ass from my brother before he finishes."

"Her first," Bronx says.

"And I'm not sure how you feel about...other things," Jameson adds.

I raise my brows without comment. I don't know how I feel either. But I can't help releasing a surprised laugh. My giggle turns into a moan, and silence falls between the three of us as Jameson works me over with his fingers. Who knew I'd enjoy this so much? The thought used to intimidate the hell out of me, but I love how close we've all become. How none of this is awkward, and the only thing hard about the situation is my guys' muscles and cocks.

I reach my peak before Bronx, and Jameson offers me more of his blood again. Bronx slows his thrusts, and Jameson takes me and spins me around. I laugh and hug onto him, resting my chin to his shoulder while I catch my breath.

"Again?" he asks, his face stretching with a teasing smile.

I graze my teeth along his throat. "Whatever makes me late."

He laughs and kisses me. "You know that has already happened."

"Seriously, Jamie?" Playfully shaking him, I wait to see if he can resist me.

Bronx shuts off the water. "Later, dandelion. The sooner we get this over with, the sooner we can return to our suite. You owe me a little show, anyway."

"Us a show," Jameson teases.

"And if I have to continue to stand out here, I'm going to ask to join." Mikkalo peeks his head in and beams me a fangy smile.

I wiggle my fingers at him. "How about you give me a bit more of your blood, so we can ensure I'm not going to lose any more bets tonight?"

Mikkalo meets me with a kiss and wraps a fluffy towel around my shoulders. Bronx excuses himself, taking Jameson with him, and I follow Mikkalo into the bedroom to find a beautiful sapphire gown with long sleeves made of lace, a low-cut bodice to accentuate my cleavage, and a train on the skirt that'll flow behind me.

"What do you think?" Mikkalo asks, swinging the flouncy fabric back and forth. "The delicate material is easy to rip off if we need to."

I gather the soft material between my fingers. "Need to or want to?"

"I guess it depends on the situation." Mikkalo motions for me to turn around, and he helps me into the dress. His hand rests on my hip as he zips it up, taking a moment to shift my damp hair from the back of my neck to kiss my warm skin.

Spinning around, I laugh as the skirt sweeps across the floor. "I feel like a princess."

"You're more stunning, though. Like a goddess with incomparable beauty," Everett says as he swings the door to Bronx's suite open. "I wish it was my arm you'd cling onto through dinner."

I extend my hand out, motioning for him to close the distance. When he's within reach, I wrap an arm around Mikkalo and Everett, squishing them to me. "I wish I could be paraded around by all of you. I hate that a Blood Vow can't extend to our whole coven."

"While technically it can since it's a vow of loyalty, it's best if Bronx takes the lead with you because it'll be his name on the contract and his venom bite as the head of our coven to turn you into a true Royale." Mikkalo snuggles his face into the crook of my neck. "Tonight, we must show unity and complete loyalty, which means pretending that you're Bronx's. We'd rather not have people question our willingness to share."

I guess it makes sense. "As long as you're all on board. I don't want this situation to mess things up."

Everett takes my hand and spins me around, watching my dress sweep out with my twirl. "Nothing can. You're our girl. We love you, and we know you love us, Gwen."

"More than I knew possible." I grin. "So, let's go. You can show me off as your future coven mate, and I'll do my best to make every damn person in here jealous of the lot of you."

Mikkalo laughs and takes my other hand. "Exactly how I want."

The two of them stroll with me from the suite, and I try to listen for Bronx and Jameson, but they were already gone when Mikkalo and I came out of the bathroom. Our private floor of the Blood Match Center is as quiet as always, and I can't help but wonder what's happening on all the floors beneath us. I wonder where Mikkalo took Laredo. I wonder if my brother will come to the gathering. I can't stop praying to the universe that everything goes smoothly, and we'll be one step closer to claiming our region for good.

We take the elevator down to the second floor, and

Mikkalo holds it to keep the doors from opening. Everett pulls out the small box with the contacts he made for me. I glare at them, wishing they'd disappear.

"Please, Gwen," Everett murmurs. "Your eyes are already flashing again."

"Because I'm nervous." I exhale through my nose. "Just give me a moment."

"Come on, ball kicker. If you don't want to do it for yourself or for us, do it for her." Mikkalo grazes his fingers over my stomach.

I narrow my eyes at him. "I can't believe you went there."

He smiles and grabs my hands to stop me from reflexively batting Everett's hand away. "Damn straight."

Everett manages to pop in the contacts faster than I can blink, and the two of them wait until my eyes stop watering. Hitting the button to open the elevator door, Mikkalo peers into the hallway before stepping out. Everett guides me with him, taking his position behind me to watch my back.

Soft music trickles through the air, increasing in volume the farther we stroll down the hallway on a floor I've never been. The hallway leads into a luxurious lobby with rainbow bouquets of flowers. A few people sit on the leather couches and speak quietly to each other. Two armed guards stand tall in front of a set of open doors. Colorful lights flicker to the sound of the music, the grand room bursting with life and excitement that stirs something inside me. The last gathering I attended was at Corona's, and I didn't enjoy much of it. But this one? I had no idea this was what the guys meant.

"Whoa," I whisper, peeking over Mikkalo's shoulder at the packed room. I hadn't expected so many vampires and donors to mingle together. "This isn't a gathering."

Bronx materializes in front of the double doors with Jameson behind him. They each grace me with handsome smiles, looking hot in their tuxedos. Vampires turn in our direction, and I straighten my shoulders, keeping my eyes on Bronx. He bows to me like he would to a board member. I laugh and close the distance, yanking him upright.

Scooping me up, he kisses me so passionately that I gasp for breath. "You're right about this not being a regular gathering. It's a celebration, dandelion."

I frown. "A celebration? For what?"

"For our news from earlier...and for this." Bronx pulls out a box from his pocket and snaps it open to reveal the most dazzling necklace I've ever seen.

Diamonds and rubies glitter from the princess-style necklace with a pendant in the shape of the Royale crest. Each petal of the blood root flowers sparkle, sending rainbow light dancing across Bronx's fingers.

Lifting my hair, I show off my neck for Bronx to fasten the necklace on. It hangs heavy on my chest, now a constant reminder of my guys. Because the pendant includes all four of their crests that come together as one, a bouquet of sorts with four teardrop-shaped vials of blood just like the humans who Blood Vowed to Vienna and her brother.

This is real. A real Blood Vow proposal.

"I know we've already made it official in front of the Donor Life Corp board, but I never did get a chance to propose." Bronx takes my hands into his. "And with this proposal, I promise to take care of you and our coven to the best of my ability. I will treat you as my equal and assure you a life as incredible as you are—not only for the two of us, but for our coven and future heirs. Always."

My heart thrashes with excitement, and I beam a smile and kiss him, whispering how much I love him. Jameson, Everett, and Mikkalo surround us, each taking a turn to hug me despite the onlookers.

"This was exactly what I needed, you guys," I say, trying to smother the four of them to me. "I'm so happy."

Bronx suddenly growls, tightening his arms around me. I don't get a chance to react before Mikkalo and Jameson unsheathe their blades. Other vampires shift and move around us, clustering together in their covens. I twist and look behind me at the open doors, spotting the guards blocking someone from entering.

"I suppose congratulations are in order," Corona says, flashing his fangs at me. "It's a good thing I've come bearing a gift."

Shoving through the guards, Corona drags a hooded figure with him. The man falls to the floor, dripping blood.

"The Barons thought you might like to return this law-breaker to his appropriate region." Yanking off the hood, Corona reveals Ashton. He lies limply on the floor, his throat gushing with a fresh bite.

Corona disappears.

Vampires growl.

I lose my shit.

6

BLOOD BONDS

BRONX RUSHES ME FROM THE room before I can chase after Corona at vampire speed. If I try hard enough, I can outmatch Corona, and I plan to. Seeing him with Ashton opens up the wounds he inflicted all over again, stabbing through the scar tissue, making my heart ache worse than ever. The fucker has to die.

"We'll get him, dandelion. But you have to let me subdue him. I won't risk you getting hurt in a fight." Bronx's words surprise the hell out of me. I thought for sure we were going on lockdown instead of pursuing Corona. "He won't get away with this."

The shock alarms blare, stealing my hearing. If Bronx wasn't carrying me, I'd fall to the ground from the noise. Bronx pushes through it, not letting it affect him, and he races toward the stairwell to go to the first floor.

"We'll cover the other exits." Mikkalo's voice echoes through Bronx's com device.

"Do not end him. The kill is Gwen's," Bronx says.

Bronx flies into the stairwell at vampire speed, effortlessly jumping down the flight of stairs. He slams his hands into the metal door of the first floor, but it doesn't open. Setting me on my feet, he rams his shoulder over and over into it until it bends under the force and soars off its hinges across the lobby. Bronx freezes in his tracks, blocking my way. I can smell the vampire blood without having to see it. And fucking hell.

Bronx growls. "Do not force me to fight you, sister. I will do so if you try to stop me."

Brooklyn glides closer, her dark hair swaying with the skirt of her dress. Her brown eyes, the same color as Bronx's, spark with flickering silver. Her pursed mouth hides her usually full lips, stealing away some of her beauty.

"Brother, please. Just stop. I'm not here to fight." Brooklyn's eyes dart to look at me as I hide behind Bronx. "I want you to think about what you're doing. I know my father has messed up, but he's only doing what he has to.

The Barons will kill him otherwise. This was their doing, not his."

Anger collides into me, turning my vision red. How dare she try to place the blame anywhere else. This isn't the first time Corona has done something to my family. I'm sure he was bowing to the Barons the second Freeport saved his life by challenging Bronx for the board seat.

"You have ten seconds to get out of our way," Bronx says. "Corona must be held accountable for his actions. This is not his first offense. I'm still in control of the region until the challenge, and I've found him guilty of treason. He will pay for his crimes against us."

Brooklyn straightens her shoulders. "Crimes? Are you kidding me? You cannot tell me you wouldn't do the same thing in his position. You act as if your blood source is on the same level as us. But get it straight. She is not. She will be the ruin of you. But you can save yourself and the Royale Region. All you have to do is return her to where she belongs and be done with this wretched madness."

Bronx charges forward and grabs Brooklyn by the shoulders. He pushes her into the wall and snaps his fangs in her face, releasing a deep growl that reverberates through my bones. Brooklyn scowls but doesn't fight him, keeping her eyes trained on me as I shuffle from the stairwell.

"Gwen, talk some sense into him," Brooklyn says. "I know you're not a selfish bitch. I see your bond to my brother. It's undeniable. But letting him do this? Letting him challenge a coven who surpasses his power? What will it accomplish apart from ending his life? He doesn't deserve such a fate. You know this."

Her words stab into my chest, sending sizzling pain through my heart. Of course Bronx doesn't deserve to be in this position. He deserves an uncomplicated, powerful life—one that he fought and worked hard to get. But he also deserves more. We both do. If he bows down to the Barons, our lives together will be over. The Royales will lose everything. As much as I hate the idea of the challenge, at least he has a fighting chance. Because I will not let Freeport defeat him. I won't. I'll reveal my true nature if I have to. Everett, Jameson, and Mikkalo will stand by my side. If we fall, we will fall together. Same goes for if we rise.

The world might be cruel. It might feel impossible to survive in. But the same world still has good in it. The fact that I now carry a piece of one of my guys, building a life I never imagined, proves it. My dad did not die protecting me just to prolong my freedom. He died so that I could learn to fight for myself. So I can change things. So I can be the change in the world.

"Please, Gwen." Brooklyn's soft voice draws my attention away from my all-consuming thoughts and back to her pleading gaze. "I can't lose him. He's my brother. You have brothers. You understand."

"And Corona killed one of them!" My rage clouds any sort of sympathy I could ever have for Brooklyn. My dhampir nature ignites, sending me charging toward Bronx. "He ruined everything!"

Brooklyn breaks free of Bronx's hold, and the two of them blur in a fight. The scent of Bronx's blood wafts through the air, and he freezes with a dagger lodged in his stomach. Brooklyn disappears, choosing to run instead of fight.

I jog to Bronx and automatically hold out my arm for him to bite. "Fuck. Are you okay?"

Bronx denies my offer of blood and yanks the dagger from his gut. Pressing his hands to the wound, he tries his best to staunch the bleeding. His blood splashes the floor, blending with blood from...ah, hell. Now that Brooklyn isn't stealing my attention, I finally get a good look around.

Two vampire guards' bodies slump on the floor, their heads missing. Bullet holes ravage everything from the walls to the ceiling. Broken furniture sprawls across the lobby, and shattered glass from decorative vases sparkles under the overhead lights.

The door leading outside swooshes open, startling me. I nearly fly to attack the intruder, but Mikkalo steps inside. Blood drips from his split lip, and stains pepper his white dress shirt. It's enough to snap me out of my haze of fury.

"Corona's gone, but I killed both remaining Anderson sons," Mikkalo says, slumping his shoulders. "They took out four of my security personnel."

Bronx scrubs his hands over his face. "Check all the

feeds. Send everyone we can to the gates. I want the city in lockdown. No one goes in or out."

Mikkalo nods his head. He steps closer to me and gives me a long, quiet look. "You okay, Gwen?"

I bob my head. "Just pissed off."

"Take Bronx back to the gathering. Make sure he gets blood. Everett took Ashton to your medical suite. Rio is with him as well." Mikkalo leans in and brushes his lips to my forehead. "Jameson and I will handle it. We'll catch the bastards."

Mikkalo disappears, leaving a cool spot on my cheek with his whisper of a kiss. Turning to Bronx, I trail my gaze over him, trying to remain expressionless. If I lose control, he'll let me, and his blood is seriously prodding at my nature.

He licks his lips. "If you continue to look at me like that, we'll never make it back upstairs."

His words surprise me, catching me off guard. I release a breath and shake my head, really pulling my shit together this time.

"Maybe you shouldn't smell so damn good. Or taste even better." The more we pretend like this shit didn't happen, the easier it is on the both of us.

Bronx struggles with talking to me about his feelings, and I don't want to test him right now. We have a room full of potential allies, and the last thing I want to do is mess this up for him. It's bad enough that Corona got in here in the first place.

Bronx extends his arms to me. "Come on. Let's go check on your brother."

I hike up my dress and motion for him to turn around, so I can climb on his back. "You heard your brother. We're to take care of you first. If Ashton is with Everett, I know he'll be fine."

He clears his throat and doesn't move. "They'll expect me to take from the feeder donors."

I try not to react. "Then you will do as they expect."

He cocks an eyebrow without saying anything.

"But I'm picking who," I add.

Bronx breaks out in a smile and chuckles. He motions for me to come closer but doesn't turn his back on me so I can hop up. "This will be interesting."

"And weird." I try to stroll around him to his back.

He grabs his wrist. "In my arms this way, dandelion. Don't argue. And I plan to hold onto you the entire time, so you know."

I scrunch my nose. "You're bleeding."

"When has that ever stopped you?" He hooks his hands around my waist, pulling me to him.

"Fine, but if I do this, I can't promise not to lick your wound."

"Whatever you want."

The world blurs around me as Bronx scoops me up and heads to the stairs. It only takes a few seconds to return to the gathering, where the vampires and donors continue to party like Corona didn't interrupt.

I find it fascinating how easily vampires can just move on from certain things while holding onto other things forever. I'm far too curious to acknowledge that things might not be my business.

"It's a shame that you can't properly care for your mister, isn't it?" Vienna appears before us, cutting off anything I could possibly say to Bronx. "That's always my brother's biggest complaint with choosing to allow our mates to procreate together."

"I think it bothers me more," I say, meeting the woman's gaze.

Her lips split into a beaming smile. "Might I suggest a little extra bonding? Pick someone you both like and join them."

My eyes widen at Vienna's suggestion. That sounds weird as hell. I wasn't planning on watching Bronx at all.

"That's an excellent idea," Bronx says. "Thank you."

"Perhaps you'll join us for a dance after? Rome's mate would love to get to know Ms. Royale better." Vienna motions to her brother dancing with Noelle and Henrique. The three of them acknowledge us with smiles.

I can't stop myself from smiling back. I don't know what it is, but I kind of like the idea. It's not often that I get a chance to talk to other humans, and especially never anyone pregnant. "I'd like that."

Bronx nods in agreement. "We will join you shortly."

"Perfect." Vienna bows and motions for her mate to come to her side. The two of them return to the crowd and disappear among the mass of dancers.

Setting me on my feet, Bronx laces his fingers through mine and silently guides me around the dance floor and to the back of the room, where two dozen feeding tables rest in neat rows. Only a handful of the tables have donors lying on them with vampires getting a taste. From my last experience, I know the humans get to join the party. They find it fun.

"We'll take this to a private room, dandelion," Bronx murmurs, flicking his gaze to mine. "Just in case. If you feel jealous or uncomfortable at all, just say something. I never want that. I'd much prefer to grab gen. pop., you know. I'm still willing to do it."

"I'll be fine. I'll just wait outside," I say. "You need blood, and I know it's best to come fresh. People are watching. There is nothing sexual or intimate in you drinking blood from a feeder."

Bronx stops short of the tables. "I'm not leaving you alone."

I frown. "Then just drink out here."

He rubs the back of his neck. "I thought Vienna's suggestion was a good one. I'll feel less guilty."

"Guilty?" I scoff and shake my head. "Don't be ridiculous."

His fangs peek out from beneath his lip. With his gaze, a dozen thoughts pass between us as I realize that Bronx is serious. And it might bother him more than me.

So I suck up the weirdness and bob my head. "Okay. If this is what you need to comfortably feed on a donor, then I'm here for you." Shifting on my feet, I peer around the room to look at the feeders. "And how about that guy? He's the only one without a boner."

Bronx chuckles. "Come on. This way."

The older human follows us to one of the doors along the back wall. Various noises sound above the music, coming from the closed doors. It sounds like several people have one helluva good time, and now I can't stop thinking about if that's what I sound like.

"You okay, dandelion?" Bronx asks, stopping in front of an open door to a room that looks like one of the guest suites.

"Just struggling to push out the weird-ass noise." I bare my bottom teeth in a grimace.

"It is weird, right? Sounds like a couple has agreed to a blood exchange, and it might be the human's first time." He chuckles, his whole face lighting up. He makes it so easy to forget the world around us, and especially with the bullshit we're currently dealing with. "You're far sexier, so maybe you'll let me give you a bit?"

"But your injured," I argue.

"And I'll be fine."

The feeder donor clears his throat. "I'll ensure your mister gets what he needs, Ms. Royale. Neither of you have to look at me. This isn't my first time supplying to the mate of someone with a Blood Vow, carrying a future heir."

Does everyone in the region know my business?

I don't get the chance to ask because Bronx tugs me into the room and closes the door. He remains expressionless as the donor takes a spot on the bed. Seeing him there makes me wish this small room had a damn couch.

Bronx doesn't give me time to think about it and pulls me in for a kiss. His lips brush mine, stealing my attention completely. The world shifts, and I continue to kiss him until he breaks away first. The sound of his fangs clicking excites me enough that I open my eyes to meet his gaze. His eyes flash silver with his hunger and desire. He bites his arm first and holds it up to me, getting me to drink.

And then shit gets real.

Like it's the most normal thing, the human feeder kneels behind Bronx and slides his arm in front of his mouth. Bronx bites the guy and sucks, never taking his eyes from mine. I straddle Bronx's lap, feeling his desire for me.

He releases the feeder's arm and says, "Thank you. You are excused."

The man exits without a word. If Bronx's com device didn't chirp from his pocket, I'm sure he'd unzip his pants and shift my panties out of the way to make love to me this very second. I almost tell him to ignore it, but Bronx pulls the com device out too fast for me to say anything. My body tingles, a strange feeling prodding at my nature.

He answers the call, and Jameson's projection lights up the wall. "Please tell me you found him."

Jameson tightens his lips. "No. They're either hiding or escaped through one of the tunnels. But that's not why I'm calling. Laredo's gone."

Bronx growls. "What?"

The door to our feeding suite opens and a figure rushes inside. Laredo slams the door and rests his back to the wood. "We have to go."

Bronx launches at Laredo and grabs him by the throat. "Was this your doing?"

Laredo flashes his fangs. "No, I swear." He turns his attention to me. "Tell him we have to go. Get everyone out."

Fear squeezes my heart. "What's going on?"

"There's going to be another attack."

Bronx releases a scary-ass growl. "Tell me everything."

"We have to go," Laredo repeats. "Please. Gwen has to get out of here."

I stride forward to face Laredo. "No. I'm not going anywhere. This is my home. Now, tell Bronx everything. We can strategize. We will fight back."

Laredo stiffens, flaring his nostrils with anger. "Gwen."

I shake my head. "If you ever want me to trust you, then you'll help us now. If you help us, I'll let you stay."

Bronx jerks his attention to me.

I hold my hand up to him. "But there will be a lot of conditions."

Laredo gives me a sharp nod. "Fine, okay. But we have to move."

7

FAMILY REUNION

EVERETT SITS ON THE EDGE of the bed we use for my check-ups. The scent of unfamiliar blood trickles through the air. My eyes dart to Rio, and I can't help but stare at the two circular wounds on his arm. Ashton lets Everett hold the cup of Rio's blood to his lips to drink. I hesitate in the doorway, my feet quitting on me.

Bronx nudges me forward into the room. "Go to Everett, dandelion." Swiveling on his feet, he flicks his gaze to Laredo. "You're coming with me. If you think for one second that you can use Gwen to get your way, you're mistaken. This is my city. Gwen is a member of my coven and my mate. We, along with my brothers, are a team. You're an outsider. Got it?"

Laredo flares his nostrils. "Understood."

Bronx and Laredo disappear without a word to anyone else. Everett doesn't give me the chance to close the space to him. Handing the glass of blood to Rio, he abandons my brother's side and engulfs me in a hug. His lips crash into mine with fervent desperation like he'll die if he doesn't taste my mouth or feel my body against his right this second.

"Are you okay?" Everett asks against my mouth, refusing to pull away. "What the hell was that about? Did Bronx let him out?"

I graze my lips to his without responding. I suddenly feel threatened by even the air around us. I'm afraid an inch of space between us will send the world crashing and burning down. Everett strolls with me toward one of the plush recliners and sits with me on his lap. Rio and Ashton remain silent, but the weight of their gazes bores into my back.

"I don't know how Laredo got out, but he claimed there was a threat—the Barons. He swore to help us deal with it." I rest my forehead to his without meeting his gaze. "If he does, I told him he could stay."

Everett releases a guttural noise from his throat. "What?"

I clutch his face in my hands, trying to minimize the space he puts between us. "I'm sorry I didn't discuss it with you. We didn't have time. I was worried about—"

A knock raps on the door, cutting off my words.

Everett holds his index finger to my lips, stopping me from continuing. "Rio, will you answer that?" He leans into me, caressing his lips to my ear. "We'll talk about this later. You're too worked up, and I'm afraid someone will hear you."

I groan and rest my chin on his shoulder. "Remind me to practice more."

Everett sits straighter, tightening his hands on my waist. "Macon, this room is off-limits right now. Please go find one of my brothers if you need assistance."

"Bronx sent us here." Macon's smooth voice catches my attention. "He thought Gwen would appreciate knowing Declan's okay."

"D-Declan?" Ashton's words echo through the room, and I twist on Everett's lap.

Declan slides past Macon into the room and runs to Ashton's side. The two of them fall into a hug unlike anything I've seen them do. My heart pounds like crazy—both happy and sorrowful over this reunion. Having my brothers together like this digs deeply into me. I wasn't sure it would ever happen. I just wish it could be the seven of us together—not just three. But that's impossible now...

"Everett," Ashton says. "Can we please hug Gwen?"

It's weird to hear Ashton say Everett's name, but it's weirder that he asks for his permission like Everett would ever deny me the chance. The world blurs, and Everett sets me on the edge of the bed.

"Careful, Gwen. Ashton is still healing," Everett says softly. "Corona did a number on him."

Anger blasts through me at his comment. If Declan and Ashton didn't embrace me between them, I might've screamed in frustration that Corona got away.

"Fuck, I'm so relieved you're okay, brother," Ashton says, his voice low.

I know he wants to speak to Declan in private, but I don't think they'll ever get the chance. Without super hearing like me, they'll never be able to converse low enough at a pitch that vampires use when they want to keep things a secret.

"What happened to you? Who was that vampire?" Declan's question hangs unanswered in the air.

Ashton looks at me. "It's complicated."

Everett's com device chimes, and I turn my attention to him. He taps the screen a few times, keeping his gaze indecipherable. I can't stop myself from flicking my attention to Macon as he leans against the wall, now in a quiet conversation with Rio.

Everett clears his throat. "Rio, Macon. Bronx would like you to join him in the lobby. Your covens are already there."

"Yes, of course. Anything for our future region head." Macon closes the space to Declan. "If Mr. Royale is okay with it, would you like to stay here? I trust you'll mind your manners and follow the rules we went over?"

"He can stay," I'm quick to say. "He'll be safe with us."

Macon nods and extends his fist to Declan. They knock their knuckles together, and a slew of questions swirl through my mind. I mean, what the hell? I've never in my life seen a vampire act so friendly without anything in return. Macon and Rio disappear, and I swing my head to look at Declan.

He smirks at me and taps my chin. "Jeez, Gwen. With the way you're looking at me, I'd think you were going to attack me and call me a traitor to humanity."

I wag my head, pushing away my awe. "That was weird as hell."

"Says the woman who's carrying a vampire's baby," Ashton whispers too quietly for Declan to hear. He breaks into a smile and holds his arms open to me. "Fuck, come closer. I've missed you, little sis. How's everything?"

I open my mouth to blurt the news about having a girl, but Everett touches my shoulder.

"Gwen is in good health and things are exactly as they should be." Everett massages his fingers into my muscles in an attempt to loosen them. "We can't say much else."

Ashton opens and closes his mouth, darting his gaze to Declan. "Oh, okay."

Declan doesn't miss a beat and scrubs his hands over his cheeks. "Fuck. I wish someone would tell me what the hell is going on."

Turning their attention to me, Ashton and Declan wait to see what I have to say. I tip my head back and look at Everett. He hides his lips in a line, his blue eyes roving over mine. I can tell he'd prefer to discuss it in private and also get his brothers' opinions on how to proceed, but he can tell my brothers are anxious. Anxiety leads to wild emotions, in his experience with me.

Everett clutches my hand. "I can't give you all the answers now, but you should know that we're doing everything we can to keep Gwen safe. Her previous blood sources were manipulating you because the Gallagher dhampir gene came from the Baron bloodline. They've tried to stake their claim on all of you."

Declan whacks Ashton with the back of his hand. "You knew?"

He shrugs. "Only for a few weeks. The Barons had captured me and turned me over to one of the cities, but things have changed."

Turning to me, Declan asks, "And you've been here?"

I nod. "The Royales and I have a good life as long as people stop fucking it up." Bringing my hands to my stomach, I can't help touching my belly. "All I want is a safe place to raise my child, and that's what we're trying to do."

"But Grayson and Silas want the opposite for Gwen.

They've given up our family name. Made a deal with the Barons that will ruin Gwen's eternity." Ashton sighs and leans his elbows on his knees. "Fuck, Declan. There is so much more I want to tell you."

"Possibly when everything settles," Everett says, resting his hand on Ashton's shoulder. "There is just too much at risk now."

"Which is why I want you to wipe my mind." Ashton's comment surprises the hell out of me.

I open my mouth to try to say something, but the door flings inward and clatters against the wall. Bronx takes up the frame, his shirt worse than when I last saw him. I scramble to my feet to rush to him. He meets me halfway and envelops me in a hug only to swing me toward Jameson. Mikkalo shoves Laredo into the room.

Both my brothers gawk at him.

It's Ashton who launches to his feet.

Bronx intercepts him and restrains him. Turning to Everett, he says, "Grab Declan. We're leaving."

"Leaving?" I meet Jameson's gaze, looking for the answer.

"Midnight Valley," he says. "We caught a Baron breaking Donor Life Corp law on the feeds. We're taking him to the board."

"Was all this security necessary, Misters Royale?" Viorica

Vaduva stands in front of the open gate to Midnight Valley with all her daughters surrounding her. Even more security personnel hide in the shadows, waiting for their call.

It takes everything in me not to retort with the same question.

"We were having a gathering of sorts and a few other covens wanted to show their allegiance to the Royale Region," Mikkalo says. "While the security measures were not necessary, they were appreciated. The Barons have no regard for Donor Life Corp law. They've even stolen one of your gen. pop. donors and left him in our city."

Oh, shit. He's referring to Ashton.

Viorica flashes her fangs. "I see."

"Another was caught stealing females from Crimson Vista. Six of them in total. One pregnant. She had bite marks." Everett hangs his head out the window. "We have him with us."

I still have yet to see the mysterious Baron as my guys would never let the bastard get within a foot of me, but I am curious as hell. Shifting in my seat, I peer at Bronx in the rearview mirror. Jameson hugs his arms around me. He hasn't let go of me since we got in the car, and I'm not sure if he will. I don't mind though, especially if he keeps hand-feeding me cookies from the container of human food he packed.

Viorica closes the space to our vehicle and meets my gaze. "Ms. Royale, that must've been disturbing for you." Is she trying to empathize with me?

I shrug. "I didn't know until now. How...awful." I force my mouth to pout, giving her the response she expects. But in all honesty, all I can think about is how much I miss feeding my guys and taking care of them.

She rests her hands on the doorframe and turns her gaze to Bronx. "Why don't you and Ms. Royale join me at my home while my daughters help your coven with the lawbreaker? I'm sure you will both be more comfortable there while we wait for the rest of the board to arrive."

"Thank you, Viorica," Bronx says. "We'd appreciate it. I fear the Barons will continue to retaliate against us out of jealousy, and I want Gwen nowhere near any possible danger."

"Perfect. Come along."

Bronx exits the vehicle and opens the door on Everett's side. Everett slides out to give me a chance to exit the car. Jameson hugs me from behind and kisses my shoulder, and I force myself to move. It's not that I don't want to go with Bronx. It's just that I'd prefer it if we all stayed together.

"We'll see you in a bit, Gigi," Jameson says, flicking my ass as Everett helps me to my feet.

I jump and try to smack his hand. "With more food."

He chuckles. "You bet."

Mikkalo squeezes my hand without comment, and Everett nudges me to Bronx. He opens his muscular arms and sweeps me off my feet, cradling me like a blushing bride.

The world blurs around us, the cool wind blowing my hair from my neck. I shiver as goosebumps prickle over my skin. I wish I could see more of the city apart from the fuzzy lights from our fast pace, but I understand why we don't spend much time outside. Even with the best security, the Barons seem to infiltrate everywhere we go.

Bronx slows as we come to a massive hillside mansion that overlooks the city. I only get a few seconds to take in the glittering lights before Bronx follows the Vaduvas into the grand estate. A glittering chandelier sparks rainbow fractals of light across the tiles in the foyer. Half of the Vaduvas disappear without a word, leaving Bronx and I standing with Viorica, Merrick, and Sammy. I haven't seen any of them in a few weeks. I don't know if it's the time apart or I just didn't pay that much attention before, but I'm taken aback by how beautiful each woman is.

Viorica shifts closer and touches my stomach without even asking. It catches both me and Bronx off guard that neither of us reacts. Usually, he's the first to growl and threaten someone for intruding on my personal space, but Viorica smiles, the gesture lighting her face so much that I can't stop smiling right back at her.

"I'm assuming all is well with your pregnancy?" Viorica tilts her head a bit to meet my gaze.

"It is," I say, gently extracting her hand from my stomach before she starts rubbing it. "Everett says we still have a bit of time until anyone will be able to feel it kick." I purposefully keep the sex to myself, knowing that such information isn't something normally shared.

Viorica steps back, realizing that she's making me uncomfortable. Unlike most vampires I've encountered, she's far more aware of my feelings. "Oh. I suppose you're right. It's just been a while since I've been around children. My household is made of an all-male staff. We prefer it that way. Men should always serve a woman, in my opinion."

"Are you serving Ms. Royale, Bronx?" Merrick says, speaking for the first time. "If you cannot fulfill her needs, I have the perfect companion who can help."

Bronx growls. "That is not necessary."

"I suppose your brothers probably help you...if I recall correctly." Merrick laughs at her own comment and bumps her shoulder with Sammy's. "We should introduce her to Jewel, don't you think?"

I frown. "Which one of your sisters is Jewel?" My. Mouth. I know better than to open a line of communication with Merrick, but I just couldn't help myself.

Merrick twists her lips. "Jewel isn't a Vaduva. She didn't have the good sense to accept my mother's offer."

"Oh."

Sammy sighs. "Merrick, quit it. Jewel is far better as a Divine."

Bronx releases a grumble from deep in his throat. "As much as I'd love to listen to your gossip, we'd like to get situated in our room. It's been a long night, and dawn approaches."

"Very well, Bronx," Viorica says. "A staff member will show you the way. As soon as the board arrives, I'll summon you. Until then, please enjoy the amenities we have to offer."

The three vampires disappear without another word, leaving me staring at the archway to a long hallway ending at a staircase. Bronx doesn't have a chance to say anything to me before heavy footsteps slap against the tile, and a naked man waltzes from a room and greets us with a friendly grin.

I gawk at his boner first, before flitting my eyes to the several healing bite marks peppering his body. Bronx groans under his breath, but he remains composed despite the ridiculous sight.

"Well, they did say their all-male staff was here to serve them," I comment to Bronx.

He chuckles and shakes his head. "You know he's going to offer me a taste."

"I guess you're lucky I packed some gen. pop. blood in my suitcase for you guys. I had a feeling this might happen, and the weird-ass moment at the party...yeah, I don't want it to be a regular occurrence." I snap my teeth at him. "I envied the guy a lot. All I could think about is having your fangs in my skin instead."

Boner guy clears his throat, drawing my attention to him. He doesn't say anything but stands there and waits to be acknowledged. It's so hard for me to keep my eyes off his naked body. It's not like I want to look at him. My guys are far sexier. But having a cock point in my direction is impossible to ignore. It doesn't help that when I look at the ceiling, the mirrored window gives me an aerial view of the guy.

"We need a suite that will accommodate my coven," Bronx tells the man without looking at him.

"Yes, sir," he murmurs, turning on the balls of his feet. "Right this way."

The man's bare feet slap the ground with his hurried footsteps. I can't even hear Bronx's movements, his ability to move without a sound a little bit weird when next to someone so loud. Laughter trickles through one of the doors, and I can't stop from looking as we pass. Just as quickly, I jerk my gaze away.

"Have you never seen someone have sex before?" a feminine voice calls out. "You may watch if you want."

Fuck. Me.

"Perhaps they'd like to participate, my love," a masculine voice says.

"It would be no fun. I can't bite her."

Their conversation fades as the naked guy leads us up a staircase and down a long hallway with dozens of doors. Silence fills the air. I don't think anyone is in this section of the house, which is probably a good thing. I don't know if I could survive the day with the extra noise. It really makes me wonder about me and what others hear. My guys love me being loud, but damn.

"Would you like me to join you, so you can have a taste?" the man asks, opening one of the double doors to a room at the end of the hallway. "I can also provide other entertainment. Ms. Merrick thought Ms. Royale would enjoy my company. I'm excellent at massages...among other things."

I grimace and shake my head. "You're excused."

The man nods without comment and swivels on his feet to dart in the direction we came.

Bronx enters the room and kicks the door closed, burying his face into the crook of my neck. I laugh and clutch onto him. He speeds through a large sitting room with several couches and to the archway to the sleeping area with a four-poster bed with a canopy made of sheer lace. Meeting me for a kiss, he gently sets me on the bed and nestles his body between my legs, guiding me to lie down.

"I want nothing more than to enjoy you for as long as possible. This night has been rough," he murmurs, hooking his fingers to the hem of my dress.

I raise my arms and allow him to tug it over my head. "It's a good thing I know how to change things."

A soft whistle sounds through the air.

One second Bronx is on top of me, and in the next, he lifts Laredo off his feet and holds him by his neck. The two of them growl at each other, but Laredo darts his gaze to me on the bed, and his eyes flash silver. I snatch a pillow and cover my sexy lingerie the best I can.

"Sorry to interrupt," Laredo says, his voice low and breathy as he struggles to say the words. "But I can't exactly ask for my own suite."

Bronx drops Laredo and returns to my side. "Get out of our sleeping quarters, asshole."

Laredo gets to his feet and smiles at me. "Join me, Gwen? I'm sure you're hungry. How about I feed you just like old times."

I close my eyes and flop back. Bronx growls and shoves Laredo again, pushing him out of the small room. I should intervene—I mean, I really should. Bronx looks ready to rip Laredo's heart out like he did to Laredo's twin—but I just don't have it in me. I'm still bitter and confused, especially after the last memory I had.

"Hey, Bronx," I call, propping up on my elbows. "You might want to keep it down. Gag him or something. Don't spill any of his blood either. The only one I want to taste is you, and I'm kind of hungry."

Bronx materializes at the end of the bed, the door to the sleeping quarters now closed. Laredo groans from the other room. I smile at Bronx, wiggling my fingers for him to come back to me.

"You were supposed to end him." I shift my gaze to the door. "End all those who dare intervene in our possible sexy time."

"Seriously, Gigi?" Jameson's familiar thud of him bonking his head against the door sounds through the air.

"When did that become a rule? Last I checked I always got to join."

I tip my head back and laugh. "Not always."

He play-growls and taps his fingers to the door. "Is this one of those times?"

Meeting Bronx's gaze, I search his expression for a reaction. He glances from me and to the door, and then back to me. Twisting my legs under me, I crawl across the bed to where he is and link my fingers to his belt, pulling him onto the bed.

He chuckles and rolls, so I straddle him. "Brother, I need backup. She looks starved."

"Thank-fucking-fuck." The door clatters open. Jameson has his shirt unbuttoned before he reaches the bed. "I was going to kill that asshole if I had to spend another minute with him."

"Which is why you're taking care of Gwen. It's your time, anyway. I have a few things I need to discuss with Laredo." Bronx sits up and kisses my forehead.

I gawk at him sliding me off as he gets to his feet. He flicks his attention to Jameson, who bounces on the bed next to me. He traces his fingers along my bare stomach, attempting to get my attention, but I burn daggers at the back of Bronx's head.

Scrambling to grab my dress, I try to tug it over my head. Jameson rips it from my hands and tears the fabric in two. I whack him in the shoulder and reach for the blankets next. He flips me onto my back and pins my hands over my head, playfully wrestling me.

So I stretch up and bite him.

He purrs deep in his throat, loosening his grip on my wrists. I manage to flip him to his back and break away from his shoulder to work my way down. I trail my lips lower and lower, teasingly unbuttoning his pants. He watches me yank them halfway down with a smile.

Snatching his discarded shirt, I make a run for it toward the door. He trips and falls off the bed and yells for Bronx to brace himself. I fling the door open and run into the sitting area in my lingerie, trying to tug Jameson's shirt around me.

I slow my steps under the weight of everyone's gazes, including Laredo's. Flicking my hand toward him, I say, "Either close your damn eyes or face the wall. I'm not yours to look at."

Laredo sighs and shifts on the couch to stare at the wall. "You act like I haven't seen you in less."

My eyes widen with anger, and I march over to him. He senses my presence, his attention focusing on me, though he continues to keep his gaze elsewhere. I clench my fingers to stop myself from slapping him.

"I hope you realize none of that matters. I don't care if you've seen me before. That time isn't now. The games you and your brother played with me—you should've been honest. You shouldn't have messed with my head."

"Then you should've just abandoned the Gallaghers like I wanted," he snaps. "I told you this would happen. I warned you a dozen times that you might be blood, but blood doesn't matter to many once they transform. Look at Silas. Look how fast he put himself over you."

I silently beg for someone to speak up. I want Bronx, Mikkalo, or Everett to intervene. I need Jameson to come out here and throw me on his shoulder to carry me back to the room. Something about Laredo's words stab into me so wicked-hard that it steals my breath.

And then my damn eyes begin to leak.

The second a tear splashes across my cheek, Mikkalo reacts and punches Laredo hard enough to send him flying off the couch. Everett intervenes before the two of them break into a fight, which will surely cause enough noise to bring the Vaduvas to our suite. Jameson spins me around and engulfs me in a hug, stroking the length of my back with his hand.

"Come on, Gigi. Let's go back to the room. Let my brothers deal with this," he says, lifting me up.

I shake my head. "No, I need to. This is our lives together."

"But you're crying," he whispers. "I hate seeing you so sad."

"Or perhaps you don't want her to know what you are all planning," Laredo says, flashing his fangs from Mikkalo's grip.

Mikkalo growls. "Shut up. We will get to it with her, but she's been under too much stress."

I jerk my attention to them. "Mikkalo, what is he talking about?"

"Not now, dandelion." Bronx gets to his feet and blocks my view of Laredo. "Laredo, if you say another word, this is over for you."

"Or do you mean you?" Laredo has a lot of nerve to speak to Bronx like that. "I think you're more afraid for yourself."

I furrow my brows. "Someone better tell me. Now."

Bronx flies toward Laredo, but I break free of Jameson and grab the back of his shirt, stopping him. Laredo sucker punches Mikkalo and dodges around him. He closes the space to me and lifts me off my feet, using me as a shield.

"Do you want to know which Baron your misters have brought here to face the wrath of the board?" Laredo asks.

I try to remain calm, my heart thrashing like crazy. "Who?" I don't know why I ask. I already know the answer.

"Gwen, we can explain," Bronx says.

Laredo breathes against my neck. "Explain that you'll be responsible for the death of another one of her brothers? I'd just love to see you try."

8

REMINDER OF LIFE BEFORE

I DON'T KNOW WHAT TO think or how to feel. Silas is my brother, but he also chose another family—traded my eternity for a chance to have one of his own.

"Gigi, come here. We still have a bit of time, and I think you should eat some food. Drink some water." Jameson taps a fork to the full plate from my breakfast. We were invited to join the Vaduvas and their staff, but my stomach was in knots, and I kept getting sick just thinking about everything.

Bronx, Everett, and Mikkalo wanted to stay, but I sent

them off, because I feel smothered. We're all conflicted over the situation. Laredo's presence doesn't help. I don't know what he expected—that I'd suddenly hate my guys and run to him or something, but I'd never. I know they have their reasons. We have more than just ourselves to look after now. It just sucks.

"What about a bath?" Jameson asks, dropping the fork to pace along with me. He takes my hand and swings my arm. "Or we could do some proper exercise. Maybe watch the movies Rio sent me about donor births."

I stop in my tracks. "I'm not ready for that shit."

He chuckles. "That's why we should prepare. It's never too early."

Touching my fingers to his mouth, I say, "Oh, but it is."

Narrowing his eyes, Jameson gives up on trying to convince me to do something other than pace the room and scoops me up. My nightie falls away before my back hits the bed. He crashes his mouth to mine, his last-ditch effort to distract me now in full force. My body loves the hell out of his determination, and I give in to his affection and kiss him back, stroking my tongue across his while dragging his shirt over his head.

"That's my sexy dhampir," Jameson murmurs, breaking our kiss to travel his lips down my throat. "I know you're not exactly in the mood, but I—"

I reach between us and slide my hand into his boxers.

"I'm so in the mood...so be quiet and let me taste every inch of you."

He releases a grumbly sound but doesn't roll over. "Not happening this time. You tricked me once already."

I giggle into his shoulder. I don't think I'll ever hear the end of that. "I'm sorry. I want to make it up to you."

"And all I want to do is make you scream and orgasm so hard that everyone in the city can hear how much I satisfy you." He gently pinches my hip, ripping the string on my panties. Moving to my other hip, he does the same and throws the torn fabric on the floor. "I want you to let me have my way."

"What if I want to see you cum first?" I ask, grazing my teeth to his shoulder.

"Not happening." Jameson scoots lower and kisses the top of my breast, sending tingles blooming over my heart. "Now, no moving. If you do, I'll tie you to this bed."

I rub his hard cock in long, slow strokes. "You've been talking to Everett."

He stops his exploration of my nipples. "Mikkalo. You know Everett doesn't tell me shit."

"You two broke the rules," I tease, tightening my fingers a bit, feeling his body throb under my fingers. "You know what that means."

"I get exactly what I want." Jameson drags his fingers down my torso and slips one between my legs.

I moan at the sensation. "So do I."

Jameson increases the pressure with another finger, working me over enough that I try to move his hand to guide him inside me. He groans and catches my wrist with his free hand. Adjusting his hand over mine, he gets me to continue stroking him while he rubs me.

I lose myself to the pleasure he elicits and enjoy the sensation of his hand and mouth. He waits for me to stop playing with him and kisses my breast one more time before mapping a line down my stomach with his tongue. Shifting my legs open, he nestles between them and nips me on my pelvis just hard enough to make me moan in anticipation of his bite—but he won't. He's teasing me, instigating my deep-seated nature.

"Fuck, I can't wait until I can give you what you really want," he murmurs, digging his fingers into my ass cheeks to raise my body to his mouth. He hums under his breath, slowly grazing his tongue over my clit before sucking it.

I moan so loud, my body feeling more sensitive than ever. Jameson adjusts one of his hands, fingering me while his mouth gives my clit all its attention. And then he does something that surprises me, tracing his finger somewhere new.

"Is this okay?" he asks, looking up to me. "Remember how I said I didn't know how you felt?"

I swallow and bob my head. "Yeah."

"I'd like to find out. Nothing crazy. If you don't like it, I'll stop."

Fuck. Me. I'm always down for some adventure, and he's never asked anything like this before. And I always have a good time with him. He knows exactly what to do to drive me wild.

I suck my bottom lip between my teeth. "Whatever you want."

His eyes flash silver with his lust, and he slowly continues to kiss my clit while pleasuring me in a new and unexpected way. I close my eyes, enjoying all of his attention until my body hums with my oncoming orgasm.

I arch my back, the intensity causing me to stiffen and tug the short strands of Jameson's hair. He eases away and grins at me. Wiping his face on his arm, he adjusts my legs down and slides up next to me.

"One down. I think I can get you to cum a hundred more times before it's time to go." He chuckles at himself.

I roll toward him and groan into his shoulder. "You're crazy. I don't think I can survive so much pleasure."

"I'll prove you wrong."

I hook my leg over his hip, aligning my body to his. "After I get what I want now."

Jameson puffs out a breath as I guide his tip inside me, not letting him push in all the way. I rock a couple times against him, just teasing him until he can't take it and pulls me on top. With a moan, I sink all the way onto him, and he sits up so that we can face each other. He kisses me lovingly, letting me savor the softness and sweetness of his lips.

Jameson holds me close, guiding my body to his, slow and deep, making love to me in the way I need in this moment. I want nothing more than to relish being with him, losing myself in his love and letting him lose himself in mine.

While adventure and a bit of roughness excite me, I also crave being cared for like the most precious being in the universe, and Jameson always treats me as such—even more so now.

"I fucking missed you, Gwen," Jameson murmurs, only allowing a few millimeters of space between our mouths. "Every time we're apart, it feels like my heart abandons me to stay with you."

I smile at his words, kissing him again. "I promise to always bring it back."

He hums, his voice vibrating against my mouth. Sinking his fangs into his bottom lip, he sweetens our passion, inviting me to deepen our kiss. I suck his lip and stretch it for a moment, suddenly yearning for more. I break away and graze my teeth to his shoulder until he bends his neck in silent permission.

I bite him, sending my body humming. Taking over our movements, I quicken my pace while sucking his neck, bouncing fast enough to make him pant and scratch his fingernails into my back. I moan at the sensation, my skin tingling and warm. Jameson slides his hands lower to my ass and thrusts me against him, hitting just the right spot to make me scream in pleasure, begging him not to stop as I reach my point of release.

Pushing me back, Jameson stretches my legs up and uses them to brace against as he slides in and out of me faster and deeper, shorter thrusts that let me feel the softness of his balls slapping my ass with his movements. His face scrunches in ecstasy as he cums, and he spreads my legs to lie on top of me.

"Two down," I say, nipping his ear. "Don't tell me you need a break already."

He chuckles and lifts his hips enough to bring his hand back to my clit. "Pshh. I can do this in my sleep, Gigi."

I laugh and swat his shoulders, linking my fingers to the back of his neck to kiss him again like it's all I ever want to do. A heavy sigh comes from the living area, drawing my attention toward the door. Jameson grazes his fangs to my throat to pull my attention back to him, not wanting me to give Laredo even another thought.

"If you intend for my time to feel torturous, it's working, Gwen," Laredo says, his voice growing in volume. A soft thunk thuds against the door. "I always knew you had a ravenous libido but this is unlike anything I imagined. Do the Royales ever give you a chance to do anything else besides eat and pleasure them?"

Jameson growls.

I gently pinch his chin and pull him back to me. "Ignore him. He's trying to ruin our time together."

Another thump sounds on the door. "Don't you remember how much fun we used to have exploring? Or training. Playing hide-and-seek from the world."

This. Fucker.

"I bet you get exhausted from always having to give the Royales all your attention. When was the last time you got to be alone? That used to be your favorite thing—alone time. You hated how crowded it felt with your brothers always around. I bet this doesn't feel much different."

"I'm fucking certain as hell that this is nothing like her imprisonment under the Baron Coven's psychotic leader," Jameson snaps, unable to ignore Laredo any longer.

I reach to grab his cock, but the moment between us slips away. Jameson can't enjoy his time with Laredo trying to manipulate the situation to get a reaction. Groaning, Jameson rolls off me and gets to his feet.

"Perhaps it's not, but I highly doubt it's as good as her time with me and my brother."

Ah, hell.

Jameson abandons me on the bed and yanks the door open. Swinging his fist, he punches Laredo in the stomach too fast for him to react. I grab the blanket and pull it around me, getting to my feet to follow Jameson into the living area.

"I want you out of here. Go hang out under a damn tree or some shit," Jameson says, shoving Laredo toward the door leading to the balcony. "Gwen has had enough of your games. Whatever it is you're trying to do isn't going to work. We unlocked the block you put on her mind. Gwen knows everything, and your presence will summon all the horrible shit you did to her."

Laredo has the nerve to smirk. "Or perhaps it'll rouse everything she liked about me. We always had a good time."

"Laredo, enough!" I rush between him and Jameson, stopping them from punching each other. Their deep, threatening growls vibrate over my palms as I keep them apart. "You both need to chill out. You're going to draw attention to us, and you're not supposed to be here." Shifting on my feet, I meet his gaze. "You don't have to go outside, but you better keep your mouth shut. This is my time with Jameson, and I refuse to waste it. He's my mate and my confidant, and I really need him right now. All this bullshit with the Barons makes me want to do something incredibly dangerous and stupid, and I have far greater concerns than your dumb ass right now."

Jameson takes my hand and pulls me closer to him, getting me to stop touching Laredo. Laredo's eyes flash silver, his features softening under my words. And then he takes a breath and steps back.

I meet Laredo's gaze again. "I'm sorry this isn't how you imagined things. I'm sorry that your brother died, and that the Barons ruined everything. But that's all I'm sorry for." I touch my stomach. "If you cared about me even a little bit, you would respect the men I've chosen as my mates. You'd respect that I'm pregnant and in love and no longer the same person you left. And you can't blame me. You purposefully set me up. You tore my family apart. You did all of this yourself, and now I'm having to deal with the consequences. So, if there is anything you want to tell me, it better start with an apology to me and Jameson. After that, I'll consider hearing you out but don't expect anything from me. Understand?"

Laredo flares his nostrils and glances from me to Jameson. "I'm sorry. I've overstepped my bounds. Please forgive me for my oversight. I will not disrespect you or your mates again."

I thought for sure Laredo would growl and disappear. I thought he'd continue to play stupid games. But I didn't expect this.

"Thank you," I say quietly. "Now, please excuse us. We have to get ready for the night. If I finish early enough, I'll allow you ten minutes of my time to talk with me, but Jameson has to agree to give it to you, and he will be with me. I don't keep secrets."

Jameson turns me around and leans in, whispering in my ear. "I'll do whatever you want. Your time is your time, and I'm lucky that you share it with me. You're not a possession to me. You're my girl, and if you want to hear Laredo out, then I accept it. I know you have a lot of questions for him."

I pull back only to meet him for a kiss. "I love you, you know. Thank you for saying that."

Laredo disappears from beside me and plops down on the couch. He rests his elbows on his knees and scrubs his face with his hands. I try not to stare at him long, knowing Jameson watches me, but it's still so strange to see him alive and in front of me. I mourned him. I felt lost when I entered the Blood Match Program against my will because of him. I was pissed the hell off too—not only because he bit me but because he was gone.

After three years, I was used to him always being around. He was more than my blood source no matter how much I deny it. Exactly what he was to me? I have no idea. I don't even know how much of our time was him or if it was his twin. I think that's what bothers me most.

Jameson strokes his fingers across my cheek, and I realize he does so to wipe a tear away. Fucking shit.

I pull myself together and tug him with me back into the bedroom without looking at Laredo. The second the door closes, and I meet Jameson's worried gaze, I break down. I don't know what comes over me, but I hate it.

Jameson engulfs me in a hug. "I'm sorry, Gigi. This sucks. I know."

"I'm just—everything is catching up to me...and it doesn't help that I'm already an emotional mess. All I want is to go home and put this bullshit behind me. I don't need the reminder of my life before. I don't. All I want is to look at our futures."

He hugs me tighter. "I know, and we'll get through

this...but maybe you need to confront Laredo. What he did...you deserve more than the bullshit answers he's given you. I'm here no matter what, okay? Nothing he says will make me go anywhere. You had a life before me just as I had one before you."

I sigh a long breath. "I don't like to think about that life. It's too confusing. I have too many sets of memories. I just want to get them sorted out. Laredo and his brother—ugh, Jamie. I can't decipher who was who."

"Then ask. Come on. Let's do it now. Maybe you'll feel better."

I nod my head. "And if not, I'll just junk-punch him. That'll make me feel better too."

With a laugh, Jameson opens the door again. "Hey, asshole. Gwen decided she wants to talk to you now. I swear if you—"

Jameson frowns and looks to me. I peer into the living room.

Laredo's gone.

9

SEVERED BONDS

"WHERE'S THE DICKWAD?" MIKKALO ASKS, standing just inside the door to the suite.

His face softens when his eyes meet mine. I remain resting my head on Jameson's shoulder, running my fingers through his soft hair. Closing the space, Mikkalo sits next to his brother, and I scoot onto his lap, hugging my arms around them both.

"I missed you," I tell Mikkalo, tipping my head to kiss him. "You were supposed to be back hours ago."

Mikkalo groans and snuggles me. "I'm sorry, Gwen. Shit is complicated, but things have settled. Are you hungry? Can I feed you?"

Jameson flicks his shoulder. "What kind of question is that? Our girl only ever flips between hungry, starved, and damn right insatiable."

I laugh. "Hopefully it's not like this forever. It was a real struggle not to drain Jamie."

Mikkalo grins and shifts me on his lap, unbuttoning his shirt, choosing to offer me a bite instead of giving me his blood from his arm. I don't argue and kiss his cool skin, taking a minute to leave a hickey just to work him up.

"You're going to have to make it quick, dandelion." Bronx's voice draws my attention for a second, but I continue with my mission to suck Mikkalo's neck.

Mikkalo tightens his hold on my hips and moans at the pressure of my bite. Bronx steps up behind the couch and kneels down to get to my eye level. His eyes flash silver as he watches me drink from his brother. Sweeping his finger across my forehead, he combs stray strands from my face. His fangs peek out, and he nips his bottom lip, enticing me to release Mikkalo to kiss him.

I take his bait and push up higher on my knees to kiss him from over Mikkalo's shoulder. Mikkalo laughs and buries his face in my breasts, taking advantage of my boobs being so close to his face.

His amusement lightens the rock currently replacing

my heart, making my chest feel heavier. I love how much he enjoys playing around with me. Bronx reaches over and hooks his fingers under my arms to pull me up. Mikkalo catches my waist, sticking his head under my dress while adjusting my thighs on his shoulder. I tip my head back with a squeal, his unexpected interception sending tingles exploding through me.

Cool arms catch me and pull me away from Mikkalo and Bronx. Everett flips me in his arms, expertly hiking up my dress to wrap my legs around his waist. I hum through his passionate kiss that leaves me breathless.

"I hope Jameson took good care of you," Everett whispers. "If you need a little extra love, I can take you in the bedroom. We won't even have to undress."

I giggle against his lips as he strolls with me toward the door to the sleeping quarters. Mikkalo materializes in our path and holds out his arms.

"It's technically my time, brother. If anyone's taking Gwen in for some fun before..." Mikkalo's words trail off. He rubs the back of his neck, turning his attention to Bronx, which makes me look in his direction.

"Is the board here?" I ask when no one is quick to respond.

Bronx tightens his mouth and looks around the room. "Where's Laredo?"

I squirm in Everett's arms. "Oh, no you don't. Answer my question first. I know you don't really care where Laredo is."

Bronx sighs. "They are and currently interrogating Silas."

"Interrogating?" My stomach twists in knots. "Fuck. You make it sound bad."

"His cooperation determines his punishment." Stepping closer, Bronx takes my hand. "I did what I could to persuade the board against execution."

"And it took everything in me to allow him to do so," Mikkalo says. "I'm sorry, Gwen. I am. But your brother—"

I raise my hand. "You don't need to justify your feelings. I understand. Silas severed our familial bond, remember?"

"But he's still your brother," Bronx says. "Those memories just don't go away. Trust me." Out of everyone, he'd know and understand because of Brooklyn.

Pressing my lips into a thin line, I bob my head. "Not without help."

"Dandelion..." Bronx closes his eyes and shakes his head, denying me before I even ask the question on my mind.

I sigh. "No, I know. I wouldn't ask that of any of you now. It's just—I'm still struggling to deal with all this. Sleeping is the worst. It's like my mind refuses to allow me any reprieve."

Mikkalo clears his throat. "I can do something about that next time. You don't have to relive your life like that."

I swing my gaze to him. "Are you saying you'll help me sleep?"

He smirks. "Not exactly."

Jameson groans. "Damn it. I wish I were better at mind manipulation. I'd give you fantasies every single one of our days."

My eyebrows peak on my forehead, and I can't stop the blush warming my cheeks. "That sounds far better than memories that don't include any of you."

"Or perhaps you'll let me properly fix what the Royales broke in your mind. Breaking a block is far worse than having the person who put it in place unlock it. Things get jumbled and mixed up. You'll be in a near state of confusion for who knows how long."

Before anyone can stop me, I spin on my feet and charge Laredo, shoving him into the wall. He doesn't react apart from inhaling a breath. My guys surround me, preparing to intervene if they need to, but they let me get in Laredo's face.

"Act like a creep again, and you'll wish you hadn't." My low, threatening voice surprises even me. "How long have you been here?"

"A few seconds." Laredo leans closer, bringing his lips to my ear. "What you said earlier...I know you needed space. I just struggle with knowing you don't need me, my dhampir." His words sound too quietly for anyone else to hear.

I release his shirt and step back. "Stop assuming what I need. Don't you get it? If I need something, I'll tell you. What I needed earlier was fucking answers, Laredo. You just don't get it."

I hold my hands out, waiting for Mikkalo and Jameson to take them because they stand at my sides. They don't say anything, realizing that what I need is their support. And maybe that's why I'm so annoyed with Laredo. My guys don't have to assume things they know. It proves just how little Laredo knows me. After three years—fuck. I can't think about that now. I'm still too angry that he tries to come in here and pretend like he didn't mess with me.

"Then explain it, Gwen. Because you're right. I don't know you anymore. You've changed." He flicks his gaze to my guys. "For the better. That's something I'll admit."

Squeezing Mikkalo and Jameson's hands, I stare at Laredo. I search his face, starting from his brown eyes to the stubble peppering his cheeks. I trail my gaze lower to his lips and to his fangs extending out from beneath them. I try so hard to find something good to think about, but every time I think of my past, it's now completely ruined. If it wasn't Laredo manipulating my mind, it was something stupid my brothers did. It's the grief of my dad's death sneaking up. It's constantly moving and sneaking and hiding. A life apart from the world. A life I feel like I lost.

"Is she going to try to devour him?" Jameson whispers under his breath. "Should we let her?" His comment snaps my attention away from Laredo and to him. He narrows his eyes at me and straightens his shoulders. "What do you want us to do?"

I swallow, my nerves twisting my stomach. "I don't know."

"We'll do whatever you want," Everett says, speaking up. He's been quietly standing nearby, always less reactive than his brothers. "This is...complicated for all of us, and I don't want you to feel like you have to do anything because you're afraid of how we'll react. I just want you to know that I'm—we're—here for you."

"And you can process this in whatever way you need," Mikkalo says, hugging me.

"Except for being alone with him." Bronx lifts his chin. "I will not allow it as coven leader."

I don't argue. I don't need to. The last thing I want is to be alone with Laredo. I don't trust him.

"But if you need space," Jameson says, "we can sit over there."

He whacks Bronx on the shoulder, knowing that his way of pulling the I'm-the-boss card might not go over well with me. But this isn't about control or who has the power. It's about respecting our feelings of the situation, and even if I wanted a moment alone with Laredo, I wouldn't ask. I wouldn't put my guys in that position. They are obviously uncomfortable, and we can figure out a way to get through this together.

"No space," I say. "I no longer want to deal with this right now. Can I see Silas instead?"

The four of them look at each other in silent conversation. I can feel the weight of Laredo's stare on me, but I ignore him. He's not the only one who can do as he pleases, and right now, I'm over talking and thinking. I need to deal with more important things than my hurt feelings. He's obviously not going anywhere, but my brother might. I have a feeling that the Barons will come to collect him to flex their power against the board.

"I'll make a call," Bronx murmurs, tugging out his com device.

"Can you arrange for my other brothers to join me?" I know it might be asking too much, but they both deserve a chance to see and speak to Silas. I might also need their support. I thought I lost the bonds I shared with my family, but knowing that Ashton and Declan remain by my side proves that the whole world outside my guys isn't against me. It gives me hope that all of this will eventually work in our favor. That my brothers and I will get a life outside of rebels and outcasts—outside a life my dad died trying to keep us from.

Mikkalo puffs a breath through his lips. "I'll see what I can do. We'll need permission from Declan's mister and approval from Viorica about Ashton. She was not happy to discover him in our care. Luckily he couldn't give Viorica much information."

"Because the Barons messed with his mind?" I ask, knowing it's the truth without confirmation.

"Thaxton is rather good at that particular skill, but not nearly as good as me," Laredo says, speaking up. "If you'd like, I can visit with Ashton and—"

I jerk my attention to him. "No fucking way—"

Bronx drapes his arm over my shoulder. "Wait a sec, Gwen. I want you to think it over before shutting his offer down. If he can gather information from Ashton, it could benefit us."

I squeeze my eyes shut and twist to bury my face against his chest. "You can't try to do it first?"

Everett touches my back. "We can, but from how difficult it was to unlock your mind, I believe Laredo is truthful about his capabilities. He also knows your brother and can use that connection to his benefit. It's harder otherwise. Humans are less open."

I bounce on my feet, thinking over Everett's words. "I don't want this decision to be in my hands. I want to take a vote. If this is what everyone wants, and Ashton agrees to it, then okay. But I want to be there."

"Dandelion, you—"

"No, Bronx. That's my term. I know you worry about something setting off my dhampir side, but this is something you can't protect me from. I need this. We all do." I slide my hands up his chest to lock around his neck. "Please. You can be in charge of my wild ass. I know how much you like to wrestle if I get caught up in my emotions."

He smirks and kisses me. "I only enjoy where it leads."

"Me on top of you?" I play with the hair on the back of his head.

"Only because I let you."

Before I can open my mouth to respond, Mikkalo says, "I vote yes."

"Agree," Everett and Jameson say in unison. I know they purposely interrupt mine and Bronx's conversation to keep us from distracting each other. We both make it far too easy, especially when it's something we want.

I nod and turn to Laredo. "If you try anything stupid, I will drain you."

Laredo cocks an eyebrow, his gaze shifting to my mouth like my words get to him in a good way. Warmth blossoms up my neck, catching me off guard. My body is a traitor...or maybe it's because it's out of control with my pregnancy, and I really just love to drink blood.

"By a knife to the throat. Into a glass," Jameson says, nudging me with his hand. "She wouldn't give you the fun kind of sendoff."

I remain expressionless. "Just don't prove my thoughts and memories of you right. It's hard enough looking at you already, Laredo."

"I promise to be the good, obedient blood source your brothers thought me to be," he quips. Yeah, right. I seriously don't believe him.

"I expect you to be even better than that. You will follow orders like you belong here, even if you don't." Mikkalo jabs him in the shoulder. "Understand?"

Laredo purses his lips. "Yes."

Bronx's com device beeps, stealing everyone's attention, and he taps the screen. "Looks like it'll have to wait. We got approval to see Silas, and your brothers will meet us there."

My heart bounces around my chest in erratic beats. I thought it would be longer. "Fuck. I'm nervous."

"Don't be, little dhampir," Laredo says. "I'll ensure all goes how you want. The Royales aren't the only ones with power around here. It's time you realize mine."

Throwing my arms around Declan and Ashton, I pull them to me. I think this might be one of the few times my guys haven't growled or reacted to someone who isn't them touching me, and I automatically glance in their direction to make sure they didn't suddenly disappear.

"How are you holding up?" I ask my brothers, easing away to give them each a look.

"Don't worry about us, Gweny," Declan says, hiding his lips in a thin line. "My mister allowed me to stay with Ashton. His place is far nicer than anything we've ever lived in before. His hot neighbor was rather excited to see him back."

I raise my eyebrows and look at Ashton. "A hot neighbor, huh?"

He smirks. "Who will remain as such, considering who I am."

I frown at his statement, realizing that how my life has turned out must have changed his perspective on what he wants with his future. All my brothers had wanted to form a union and have families. They all thought I'd need the protection a greater number of Gallaghers could provide. But now? I bet all Ashton thinks about is how he doesn't want to risk passing on the dhampir gene with the possible chance of having a daughter who is symptomatic to the mutation.

My lip quivers for a split second before I bite it and get my face under control. My wild emotions are ridiculous lately. Everything just seems more intense. "Oh, Ash. The chances of you-know-what are so slim. You shouldn't worry about it and let it stop you."

"Especially considering who your future heirs' aunt is," Mikkalo says, stepping closer. He hugs me from behind, joining our small circle.

Bronx, Everett, and Jameson disappear into one of the rooms without a word, giving me more time with my brothers.

I tip my head back to rest it on Mikkalo's shoulder. "Or their uncles. You know we'd help you out. You're family."

Ashton lifts and drops his shoulders. "Maybe someday."

"I'll take you up on the offer," Declan says. "I already know Macon expects it."

I reach out and touch his shoulder. "Do you like living there? Is his coven good to you?"

Declan bobs his head. "Macon's cool, Gweny. He's nothing like the vampires we were raised to fear."

His words help ease the anxiety clenching my heart. If only Kyler had been so lucky. And Porter? Fuck, I pray to the universe that he's okay. That it's not too late. Without Corona, locating him has been a bit tougher. As long as the Barons don't get to him first, things might be okay between us. But if they do...Porter had always looked up to Grayson, and he still blames me for his best friend's death.

"All right, dandelion. Everything is set. Did you tell Declan what to expect?" Bronx materializes next to me and links his fingers with mine.

Shit. I haven't. I never got the chance to tell him that Silas was transformed.

Bronx studies my face and then dips his chin. Turning to Declan, he takes initiative to break the news for me. "Declan, you're probably wondering why the board deems Silas a Baron."

"I know he transformed," Declan says. "Ashton told me of the deal he and Grayson made."

"And you know that whatever happens now—"

"Don't worry, Mr. Royale. I will not do anything stupid that could jeopardize Gwen, my mister, or you. My only intention is to say goodbye and to support my siblings." Declan drapes his arm over Ashton's shoulder. "I was never much into the rebel life."

"Okay," Bronx says with a nod. "That's what I needed to hear."

The huge metal door at the end of the hallway swings open, and Jameson steps forward to let us pass into a new section of the building, secured and protected by several vampire personnel who work for the Vaduvas. The last time I was in the Midnight Valley Blood Match Center, I only saw a few floors. I had no idea they had an entire vampire prison below ground.

"Keep your eyes on the floor the best you can. There are a few criminals here awaiting their punishment." Bronx pulls me in close, tucking me safely under his arm, so I hold onto his waist. Mikkalo guards my back while Jameson leads the way.

At the end of the hallway, Everett appears, his eyes meeting mine but his face remaining expressionless. He rolls out a rack of black clothes, and I gawk at the protective gear. It's been a while since I've worn it, but I guess no one will take any chances.

"These are for your brothers," Everett says, pulling an outfit off a hanger. "It will ensure not only their safety but also help identify them if something happens and security gets called."

Jameson opens a door and ushers my brothers in to get

changed. I stand with Mikkalo, Bronx, and Everett in the hallway. The three of them cage me in with their muscular bodies, ensuring that no one could dare get to me.

Bronx leans in, hooking his hand to my hip to keep me close. "So far he hasn't said anything about you. I think he expects that the Barons will save him any minute."

I rest my hands on his shoulders. "Do you think the same?"

He shakes his head. "No, I don't think they even consider him a brother. They're only using him. Now that they know even a familial bond won't bring you to them, they'll turn on your family."

"Which means he might try to take you down with him, Gwen," Mikkalo says. "We can't control what he says, so we need to be on guard if he tries to use your nature against us."

Fuck. I didn't think about that.

I tense. "What do we do?"

Bronx sighs, his sweet breath caressing the nape of my neck. "We want your permission to do what is necessary before that can happen."

"You want my permission to kill him?" I ask, needing to hear him confirm my suspicions.

"We will be swift and humane," Mikkalo says quietly. He shifts on his feet and rubs his hands together. He doesn't like confirming it as much as I hate hearing it.

Ice travels from my heart to slide through my veins.

What the fuck am I supposed to say or do or think? A part of me says good riddance. Just because we share a blood bond doesn't mean we're family. Silas made his decision, and he can accept the consequences. I have not only my life and my guys to worry about now. I'm going to bring a beautiful, powerful daughter into this world who will need me. Need her Royale family and the protection that comes along with the ones who love her so deeply and truly already. If that makes me a horrible person, then it is what it is.

"I just...this sucks. My heart and mind are at war. I feel sick even thinking about it. I don't want any of us to be in this situation." I rub my hands up and down my arms. "It feels worse than with Kyler, and he betrayed me too."

A dozen thoughts cross my mind, blips of fragmented memories from my past. From the times Laredo eased the pain and grief inside me. Before, when I realized it, I was so pissed off. I couldn't believe he'd go so far to manipulate my feelings...but now? Fuck. It sounds better than the alternative.

"We will be here for you in any way you need as well." Bronx straightens his shoulders. "I will take it upon myself to do this. If you need space from me after, I'll accept it."

"I never want space from you, Bronx, no matter what. Even if it hurts. Even if it tests my strength. I know you're not doing this because you want to." I take his hand. "But if this does happen, I need you to agree to something." Can I really ask this of him? I know his feelings after the first day I threatened him to never try to mind manipulate me. And it could be too much.

I shift on my feet and pull Bronx a few feet away from his brothers. Reaching up, I graze my fingers over his jaw, feeling the prickle of his stubble. He covers my hand with his, pressing my fingers deeper into his skin. We lock each other in an intense gaze that penetrates my soul. His too. I can nearly see the beautiful, powerful essence that makes him flashing in his eyes along with the spark of silver.

"If it gets to be too much for me, I want you to help me," I whisper. "I know you said you would never again, but I don't want to feel horrible every time I think of this. I want to be able to be strong for everything to come. You need me, and I'm terrified that this will jeopardize my ability to stand tall and powerful by your side."

Bronx closes his eyes, breaking my stare. Hooking his arm around my back, he pulls my body to his, allowing my heart to beat against his as he lifts me up completely to hold me close. To feel my body curl around his. To be close enough that we share the same sweet breath.

"Gwen, I love you. I love everything about you," he whispers. "If this is what you need from me, then okay. I never want you to feel the agony others bring to you. If I could take your pain, your fears, every bad thing that dares touch you, I would. I'll carry your anguish for eternity to ensure you never have to. You're my dandelion."

He smears a tear from my cheek with his thumb and brushes his lips to mine, kissing me tenderly, sweetly, just letting me feel his love and devotion. It fills me with everything good in the universe to give me the strength to ease away from him. It helps me straighten my shoulders and stand on my two feet.

Holding out my hands, I motion for Mikkalo and Everett to join me. I hug and kiss each of them and let the three of them sandwich me between their bodies until Jameson returns with my brothers.

The seven of us stroll in silence down the long hallway until we reach a door with two guards standing in front of it. They move out of the way for Bronx and give slight bows. My chest tightens as the door swings inward. Silence greets us. Bronx and Mikkalo enter first. Jameson scoops me up to carry me across the threshold because my feet stop working. My brothers trail behind us, and Everett finishes our line.

"My siblings," Silas says from his spot chained to a chair. "I assume you're not here to rescue me."

Something snaps in Ashton, and he pushes past my guys.

No one stops him.

No one has time to react as Silas's chains fall away.

Extending his fangs, Silas hops up and grabs Ashton.

The shock alarms blare.

10

TREACHERY

SILAS DROPS TO THE GROUND with a thud, not used to the high-pitched screeching that sends my head spinning. Bronx covers my ears, muffling the sound the best he can. Ashton shoves Silas off him and gets on top. Silas manages to push the sound away and extends his fangs.

"Mik, grab him!" Bronx shouts. "Venom!"

Mikkalo locks his fingers to the back of Ashton's body-suit to drag him away. Ashton yells, Mikkalo's strength stretching him out because Silas refuses to let him go. I shriek, terrified that Ashton will get ripped in half. It's enough to get Mikkalo to push him forward to throw Silas off balance. Silas snaps his fangs with a growl over and over again, yanking Ashton closer.

Jameson locks his hands into Silas's hair, but he's not fast enough to stop him from sinking his fangs into Ashton's shoulder. Ashton yells again, and something wild snaps inside me. I thrash and launch forward, my dhampir nature refusing to be rational, and I tackle Mikkalo in an attempt to get to Silas.

Bronx hooks his arms around me and spins me away. I land in Everett's arms, where he smooshes my face to his chest, trying to restrain me. Growls sound through the room, and the shock alarms finally shut off.

"Gwen, calm down," Everett says, adjusting me tighter. "Ashton will be fine. That suit protects him from bites."

But it doesn't protect my guys.

Silas somehow manages to break his arm free of Jameson, and he locks his hand around Jameson's wrist, yanking it up to his mouth. He sinks his fangs into Jameson's arm. Jameson punches Silas in the back, knocking him forward into Ashton and Mikkalo. Silas snags Ashton and spins him around, using him as a shield. He grips one hand to his head and the other around his neck.

Everyone freezes.

"I will kill him if you step closer," Silas says, flashing his fangs.

"Silas, what the fuck?" Declan's sharp voice echoes through the room, drawing my attention to him. I hadn't even realized he stands behind Everett, letting him act as a shield. "What does this accomplish?"

Silas releases a threatening growl. Not at Declan, but at Mikkalo and Bronx as they inch closer. Jameson holds his bleeding arm, the sight enough to send my heart crashing around my ribs like crazy.

"Nothing," Silas snaps. "I don't want to do this, but I don't want to die either. That's what these assholes will do to me. All because of Gwen."

Silas's glower narrows on me. I stiffen under his scrutiny, the weight of his fury stealing my breath.

"Because of Gwen?" Ashton says, grinding his teeth together. "No. All of this is your own damn fault, brother. You put yourself in this position. You made a deal with the very vampires that dad wanted to protect Gwen from. The ones that killed Mom. So don't you fucking dare put this on Gwen."

Silas snarls and squeezes Ashton tighter. "You don't get it. Gwen doesn't belong to them. Her future is with the Barons whether she likes it or not. They're the only ones powerful enough to protect her and all our future heirs."

"*Our* future heirs?" My voice rings through the room. "*Ours?* You lost the right to be part of my family the second you transformed. You're delusional if you think I'll let you even within a mile of my baby."

"You're wrong, Gwen. You'll see. The Royales won't be here forever because of you. Don't make this difficult. You can end this impending war now." Silas's eyes flash silver.

"Mik, get ready," Bronx says, stepping another foot forward.

Silas roars. "I said, stay back!"

He tightens his hold on Ashton, causing Ashton to squeeze his eyes shut. Declan pleads with our brother, begging him to let Ashton go. My whole body trembles in fear. I never imagined we'd all be put in this position, choosing sides. I never thought Silas could dare hurt any of us. But there are a lot of things in my life I never imagined possible. Jameson has always been right in his thoughts of nothing being impossible.

"Tell them to back up, Gwen," Silas growls, extending his fangs longer. "Five seconds."

"No, Gwen," Ashton says. "Don't listen to him. This isn't your fault. Whatever happens now—I love you."

Bronx and Mikkalo share a look. Again, they step forward, preparing to get to Silas.

"I love you too, Dec." Ashton turns his gaze away from me. "Be there for Gwen."

Silas snarls and bends Ashton's neck, making him holler. Jameson flies at him, taking advantage that Silas stares at Mikkalo and Bronx. Snatching Silas by the neck, Jameson stops him from trying to kill Ashton. Mikkalo drags Ashton away and pushes him toward the corner. Racing to Ashton,

Declan kneels beside him. Bronx aims his dagger at Silas, preparing to take his heart.

"That's enough, Misters Royale." The feminine voice hums from the doorway. Viorica stands between the two guards that never bothered to come in. They probably wouldn't have, leaving it up to my guys. "Save it for the rest of the board."

"Ash, fuck. Ash." Declan's pleas snap everyone's attention away from Silas.

My heart sinks into my stomach at the sight of Ashton convulsing on the floor. Everett rushes with me to my brothers, holding me tightly as he kneels on the floor. Declan cradles Ashton on his lap and rubs his hand over his forehead.

"Guards, please take the outcast to the boardroom," Viorica says. "Mr. Royale, escort them." She motions to Jameson.

"What's wrong with him, Everett?" I wiggle until he sets me down.

"I'm not sure. I need to take him to the Human Health Center." Everett twists and looks at Bronx. They share a silent, indecipherable look. "Possibly a seizure."

"Bronx, do you trust your coven to handle this? I'd like a moment of your time." Viorica acts like none of this is happening—like this is all a mere inconvenience.

Turning to me, Bronx presses his lips together. He looks ready to deny Viorica, but she waves her hand toward the door. I don't think she'll take no for an answer.

"Yes," Bronx finally says. Turning to Mikkalo, he adds, "Stay with Gwen. Follow Everett and get the Gallaghers situated in the Human Health Center. As soon as they're settled, join us in the boardroom. All of you." By all of us, he means Everett, Mikkalo, and I.

"Yes, brother," Mikkalo says, tugging me to my feet.

Viorica nods and disappears. Bronx gives us one more look and vanishes after her, leaving us in the small cell. Everett slides his hands under Ashton and lifts him into his arms. It's a strange sight to witness, and my stomach twists in knots. Declan laces his fingers on the back of his head. I close the space to him, and he engulfs me in a hug, doing his best to keep his shit together.

"Mik, bring them both. I'm going to rush ahead." Everett disappears with Ashton, leaving us behind.

Mikkalo waits until Declan releases me and quietly motions for Declan to climb on his back. When Mikkalo picks me up next, I rest my head to his chest and listen to the sound of his heartbeat. The soft thrums thump in my ear, helping to calm my racing heart.

"Gwen," Mikkalo says softly. "I'm sorry I fucked up. This shouldn't have happened, but my focus was on you. I thought Ashton would be safe in the suit."

"Man, it's not your fault," Declan says from over Mikkalo's shoulder. "Silas has always been a selfish asshole, even before all of this."

I touch Mikkalo's cheek and lean up to brush my lips against his cool skin. "He's right. You can't blame yourself. This whole situation is fucked up. I'm sure Ashton will be fine. Everett is the best."

Mikkalo doesn't respond as he slows down. Everett materializes in the hallway outside a room. He meets my gaze, his blue eyes searching mine before running over the rest of me to be sure I'm okay. Mikkalo tenses, his muscles flexing and tightening. I half expect the Barons to charge from another room, but the place is empty.

A strange, strangled noise rips through the air, coming from the room Everett stands near. I squirm until Mikkalo sets me on my feet. Declan rushes forward before us, but Everett blocks his way.

Unsheathing his dagger, Everett offers it to my brother. "I need you to stay out here for a moment."

Declan takes the dagger. "What, why?"

Everett ignores him, turning his gaze to me. "I need to speak with you, Gwen." Shifting his gaze to Mikkalo's, he adds, "Mikkalo, I need you to double check something for me. I'm having a difficult time confirming my suspicions about Ashton's condition."

I suck in a sharp breath. "Is he okay? Just tell us, Everett."

He shakes his head and glances at Declan. "In a couple minutes. I'd like to wait for the rest of our coven. Now, come in. Try to stay calm."

Declan steps forward, but Everett stops him. "Wait here. It might not be safe for you, and I don't want to risk it until Macon approves it. He'll be here shortly."

I purse my lips and hug Declan again, whispering to stay safe. He doesn't argue and lets me follow Everett into the room with Mikkalo behind us. My fear instincts go off like crazy, and I stop in my tracks. I try to scramble back a few feet but hit Mikkalo's solid body. He steadies me on my feet, releasing a soft growl.

"Fuck," Mikkalo mutters. "Fuck, fuck."

"So I'm not crazy," Everett says, holding his arms for me. "I can't find the bite, though."

My eyes widen, my heart stalling only to kick up in overdrive. I turn my attention from Everett to Ashton, now restrained and thrashing on the bed. Deep, guttural noises escape his mouth, but his eyes remain closed. He looks like he's in agonizing pain, his body writhing and moving. His back arches, and he looks almost possessed. I can't stop the panic rising in my throat, threatening to make me sick.

Everett cups my face with his cool hands. "Hey, hey. It's going to be okay. Ashton isn't sick. This state is only temporary."

"Temporary?" My question comes out so softly, I'm not sure Everett even heard it over my brother's yells.

"Gwen, Ashton is transitioning into a vampire," Everett says, locking me in his blue gaze. "Somehow, Silas managed to bite him with venom."

Ohmyfuck.

Ah, hell.

Holy shit.

I snap my attention away from Everett, pushing my hands against his shoulders. He backs up but doesn't let me go, staying between me and Ashton on the bed. Mikkalo hovers over him, holding the sheet up to inspect my brother's body. I can't stop myself from doing the same, roving my gaze across his bare chest and shoulders.

"I need you to prop him up," Mikkalo says, flicking his attention to Everett. "I think I know where he got him. There is a bit of blood on the pillow."

Everett shifts me to stand at the foot of the bed. He takes a place on Ashton's other side and hauls him forward, pinning him in place. Ashton fights against his hold, gnashing his teeth. And then he yowls and throws his body back. Everett nearly loses his grip and forces Ashton to arch all the way forward.

"I know you're scared and in pain, but I need you to try to calm down. We'll get you blood soon enough," Everett says, rubbing his hand over Ashton's back.

"Just kill me," Ashton spits out.

I tense at his words. Despite Everett's pleas, I waltz around to the head of the bed. I gingerly touch Ashton's back. "Don't talk like that, Ash. I know what venom feels like, and I promise you it'll get better."

"But Gwen, I know what happens to a coveless vampire. I know what happens to unauthorized transitions. I can't turn into an outcast. You know how they are. They're monsters." Ashton finally stops fighting, his muscles relaxing the longer I rub his back.

"Found it," Mikkalo says, combing the strands of Ashton's hair from the back of his head. "Right through his skull."

"Damn. Ouch," Everett says, leaning closer to inspect the puncture wounds.

Neither of them comments on Ashton's fears, which makes me a bit nervous. Laredo said he was outcast for transforming his brother and not the other way around.

"Ash, I'd never let that happen, okay? I don't think it works like that." I bump into Everett, grabbing his attention. "Tell him."

Everett doesn't respond to me, leaning Ashton back up. Ashton snaps his eyes open, the silver sparkling in his irises startling me. I brace myself, begging my body to chill the hell out. The last thing I need is for Ashton to think I'm suddenly afraid of him. Because I'm not.

Everett grabs my brother's face and lifts up his top lip. "Here come the fangs, Ash. Watch your tongue and bottom lip. They're going to extend completely before you can retract them."

Ashton groans and bares his teeth. "Get Gwen out!"

I brush my hand over his head. "I'm not going anywhere."

"Get her out!" he yells again.

I don't have the chance to argue before Mikkalo scoops me up. The world blurs as he relocates me into the hallway. I groan in frustration and bonk my head to his shoulder a couple of times, gently grazing my teeth across his jacket.

"Mr. Royale, is everything all right?" The familiar voice draws my attention to Macon, now standing with Declan.

Mikkalo composes himself, hugging me more tightly against him. "No. Please take Declan with you. We will call you with an update in a bit for his peace of mind."

Declan opens his mouth to complain, but Macon disappears with him, his voice fading in the air. Strolling a couple of feet away, Mikkalo opens another door and locks us in the room. He sets me on my feet and shrugs from his jacket. I watch him in silence as he unbuttons his shirt next.

I gawk at him. "What are you doing?"

He sits on the edge of the bed and motions for me to close the distance to him. I do as he silently asks, strolling forward. Mikkalo opens his legs so that I can stand between them. He brushes my blond hair over my shoulder and grazes his fingers over my jaw, staring into my eyes, just drinking me in for a few seconds.

I suck my bottom lip into my mouth. "What are we doing? Ashton—"

Mikkalo kisses me, cutting off my words. He doesn't ease back until I slide my hand to the back of his neck. "Ashton's experiencing the start of his blood hunger."

My mouth forms an O.

"And I don't know if we tell you enough, but you smell incredible." Mikkalo slides his hands down my sides, tugging me even closer. "It's best if he has gen. pop. blood to start. It'll help with his nature. If he accidentally got to you...well, for one, I'm not sure he'd survive. Neither of us would intend to, but it's possible that we'd kill him, and I'm not talking about just my brothers and me." He means me, too.

I groan and sink into his arms. "Fuck. What will happen?"

He sighs and buries his face into the crook of my neck. "I don't know, to be honest. All I know is that you and I will stay in here until I'm sure you can keep it together. The contacts are luckily holding up, but I know how reactive you get in stressful situations."

I breathe in his delectable scent. "I need to be there, Mikkalo. Even if it's just outside the door."

He shakes his head. "Not until you drink some of my blood and my brothers come to get us."

My brows pucker. "That's why you took off your shirt? You're trying to distract me with your body?"

He chuckles. "Actually, I didn't want to risk you getting my blood all over my clothes."

I crinkle my nose. "I'm not that bad."

"You're wildly messy. Sexy, though. I love seeing my blood all over you." Mikkalo tilts his head to the side, exposing his neck. "I love your mark just as much."

A dozen thoughts flit through my mind. "Maybe I shouldn't. I feel okay."

Mikkalo tightens his mouth. "Just take a little. Please. I don't know when we can give you more next. Once the board calls us...it might be a shit show."

I groan and hug him tighter. "Okay, you're right...but maybe I should lose my dress."

"That's probably a good idea." Mikkalo's eyes flash with his desire as he says the words. Hooking his hands to the hem of my dress, he slides it up and over my head.

His eyes roam over my body, drinking in every inch of me. I shift on my feet, my skin buzzing under the intensity of his stare. It's far too easy for me to go from blood hunger to blood lust, but I can't help it. I'd do anything to forget what's going on outside these walls, even if it's only temporary. And Mikkalo looks ready to ensure I forget the world outside us.

Stretching out his arms, he pulls me to him by my waist. He lifts me off my feet and scoots back on the bed a bit. My legs curl around his waist, and he takes a moment to brush his lips to mine.

"Whenever you're ready," he murmurs, bending his neck to the side.

I kiss his throat, tasting his skin, and explore my way to his shoulder. Fuck, I didn't realize how much I needed this, just being with Mikkalo. Instead of biting him, I suck his skin hard enough to leave a hickey. Reaching down, I un-buckle his pants and rub my hand over his hard cock. He moans, the sound of his fangs extending clicking in my ear. And damn does it make me want him to bite me. It's going to be a long pregnancy with a bite craving my guys will struggle to give in to. They have to have complete control not to drink.

"You have no idea how much I want your mouth on me. I miss taking care of you," I murmur.

"You're taking care of me now." He leans in and kisses me. "Your attention is more than enough."

"I want to do more."

Nudging him back, I slide off his lap onto the bed next to him. He doesn't let me rest on my hands and knees for more than a second before hooking his fingers to my legs to pull me back on top but facing his cock. I laugh and squeeze his sides between my thighs, shifting to smile at him.

"Can you resist me for a bit?" I ask, shaking my hips. "If you can't, I'm turning around."

He play-growls and swats my ass. "No promises. You underestimate my restraint, especially wearing that sexy lace."

I smile again and turn to focus on his body. He traces his fingers up the backs of my legs, massaging his hands into my hips and thighs, outlining my panties without exploring further. I run my hands down his pelvis and clasp his boner between my palms, tightening them around the base of his shaft. Bowing down, I lick his tip, tasting his building sweetness, just teasing and testing him, listening to his reactions to see what he likes best.

I take my time working him up, loving his soft moans and the exploration of his hands up and down my legs from my hips to my knees. It doesn't take long for him to graze his fangs over my panties, catching them in his teeth to tug them without letting me go. Pulling me a few inches closer, he brushes his lips to my skin, sending my body buzzing.

He hums under his breath, licking and sucking me a bit harder. I moan and pick up my speed, determined to get him to cum before me. Mikkalo takes my silent challenge, ripping my panties off completely. He flicks his tongue over my clit, holding my body still against his face. I don't know who's more desperate—me or him, but it turns our foreplay into a mind-blowing moment with only one way I want it to end.

Mikkalo grunts and stiffens with his orgasm, sinking his fangs into my ass cheek. And holy fuck. It sets me off with the most intense climax that I scream in pleasure and bite Mikkalo on his thigh.

"Fuck, Gwen. I didn't mean to bite you." His cool fingers press into his mark on my ass, sending tingles through me.

I suck his leg for a moment, forcing myself to ease away. "I wish you'd do it again. I miss it. It felt amazing."

"But—"

"You didn't drink," I say cutting him off. "Now, shhh. I'm not ready to stop enjoying you."

He releases a soft chuckle and lets me drink for a minute longer before he sits up and flips me forward so that I sit between his legs. Shifting my hair, he kisses my shoulder and makes his way to the back of my neck. I can't handle facing away from him, so I spin and meet him for another passionate kiss that quickly turns into exactly what we both want and need.

Mikkalo lifts me up a bit, sliding inside me, the pressure so good in this position. I grip his shoulders and lean back, bouncing on my knees while he guides my movements with his hands, digging his fingers into the sensitive bite mark he left on my ass. A wave of ecstasy rushes over me, and I gasp and moan, our lovemaking turning harder and more passionate, rough and intense as we allow our deep-seated nature as a dhampir and vampire take complete control.

He nips my shoulder, kissing the tiny tease of blood drops, and I bite him to drink again, my blood hunger and lust crashing through me like an unstoppable hurricane that leaves the both of us breathless.

"I love you, Gwen," he murmurs through his panting breaths, enjoying my body as much as I enjoy his. "I hope I tell you that enough."

I smile and meet his gaze, lifting my hands to cup his cheeks. "I love you too, Mikkalo. You make me so incredibly happy. I hope I tell *you* that enough.”

“Mmmhmm.” Mikkalo slides his hand between us to play with my clit, making me orgasm first.

He nips me again, sucking my lip into his mouth. We stay kissing until he cums. Lying back together, Mikkalo pulls the blankets around us, and I hug his side.

If it weren’t for the muffled voices humming through the door from the hallway, I could pretend we were back in Crimson Vista on our night together instead of in Midnight Valley with the shit show the Barons created with my family. I could pretend that Laredo is still dead and gone, that Bronx isn’t up to challenge Freeport for a board seat, or that Ashton isn’t in the process of transforming into a vampire—bitten and betrayed by our brother, not even getting a choice in his future and now his eternity.

“Come on in, Bronx,” Mikkalo calls without getting up. “Now’s probably the best time to give us the bad news.”

I frown at his words and flip over to lie on my stomach. The door creaks open, and Bronx’s familiar footsteps tap lightly across the floor. I don’t move, keeping my face buried in the pillow. The bed shifts next to me as Bronx sits on the edge. He rests his big palm on my lower back for a second before rubbing smooth circles.

“Dandelion, I’m sorry. I’m so sorry I let all of this happen,” Bronx murmurs.

Mikkalo scoots over, pulling me with him to make more room on the bed. The blankets lift, letting in cool air, and I shiver until Bronx lies beside me and wraps his arms around me, pulling me in closer. I shift on my side to meet his gaze, and he uses his sleeve to wipe my mouth, still stained with Mikkalo's blood. Leaning closer, he kisses me tenderly, brushing my hair from my face.

It takes me a moment to gather myself, my words stuck in my throat, the passion and good feelings Mikkalo rose in me still clinging to every molecule in my body.

"What's going to happen?" I ask, my voice quaking.

Mikkalo rolls closer, fitting his body to mine to hug me from behind, enveloping me between his and Bronx's bodies. I savor the sensation, the love, the tranquility they encompass and share with me through their presence alone.

Bronx groans under his breath and meets my gaze, his eyes blinking with silver. "I can only guess, but I believe the board will show compassion toward Ashton in his new state."

I sigh a breath in relief. "This is all so crazy. What about Silas?"

"I've heard talk of execution," he says, remaining expressionless. "The board considers the Barons unpredictable and will flex their power to show them that even if they've come in to try to take a piece of the Donor Life Corp territory that it doesn't mean they're above our laws or invincible. They'll treat Silas as a warning and an example."

A pit settles in my stomach. I knew this was coming. I expected it. A part of me is relieved, especially after everything Silas has done. But the loving part of me that still considers Silas as my brother mourns. I wish I understood what was going through his head. I wish I could have a chance to speak with him as his sister and not his supposed enemy. But I know by now that I don't always get things I want and life likes to test me over and over again.

"Will one of you be present?" I swallow the tears burning the back of my throat.

Bronx nods. "I'm heading over there now. I just wanted to be here with you for a couple minutes."

A knock taps on the door. "Sorry, Mr. Royale. Your time is up." The feminine voice sounds through the door. "Please gather your coven, including Ms. Royale, and join the region heads in the boardroom."

Bronx stiffens in my arms. "Ms. Vaduva, Ms. Royale will not be attending."

The door flings open, and Merrick stands in the doorway. Bronx hops to his feet to cut her off before she enters. She smirks at me from around his muscular body but doesn't comment that I'm lying in bed with Mikkalo.

"It's an order from the board," Merrick says, tightening her mouth. "I'm sorry. It's mandatory. You don't have a choice."

Bronx clenches his fingers. "Fine. We'll need a few minutes."

Merrick nods. "Have Mikkalo get her dressed and ready. I need you to take me to the unauthorized transformed Gallagher. His presence has been requested too."

"Why do you need Ashton?" I ask, sitting up. I know I shouldn't ask, but I have to. I have to know.

Merrick turns her attention to me, and I half-expect her to ignore me. Surprisingly, she frowns and says, "The board isn't so certain this whole thing wasn't a setup. I'm sorry, Ms. Royale. Your brother will face board scrutiny as well. If they deem him a participant, he'll face the same fate as the godforsaken Baron rebel."

My stomach twists.

If that happens, I won't only lose one brother.

I'll lose two.

11

VERDICT

I CATCH SIGHT OF ASHTON standing with Bronx outside of the double doors to the meeting room. Breaking away from Mikkalo, I rush my brother, flinging my arms open to tackle him in a hug. Everett materializes out of nowhere and cuts me off, lifting me off my feet.

He spins me around and squishes me against the wall. "I'm sorry, Gwen. You can't do that just yet. Ashton lacks restraint with his blood hunger, and biting a pregnant woman will not go over well."

"Oh...okay." I rub my lips together.

Mikkalo stands between us and Ashton, remaining expressionless to Everett's words. We both know he unintentionally bit me, and I wonder how much intervening I'd have to do if any of his brothers found out, but especially if Everett did. He didn't want me to test his brothers in the first place. They'll see it differently than I do, because Mikkalo's was a reaction to our passion and not giving into my request, though I would've asked him.

I blink my eyes a few times, suppressing my wave of emotions torn between seeing Ashton like this and trying not to think about it and instead thinking about Mikkalo's passion. It's enough to get my eyes to chill out before they start to leak tears.

Standing on my tiptoes, I peek at Ashton from over Everett's shoulder. "I don't care. I'm willing to risk it. He's my brother, and I highly doubt he'll hurt me."

Ashton jerks his attention to me, finally looking. His eyes flash silver, and his fangs protrude from beneath his top lip. "I can't promise that. So I'm not endangering you, Gweny. I wish they wouldn't even let you get this close. I can smell you from here. It's weird as hell. I don't want to bite you, but I also really fucking do."

"I bet." Jameson steps from the double doors and swings his attention from Ashton to me. "She smells even more delicious now. At least I still get to taste one of my favorite parts of her."

"Jamie!" I snap, sliding around Everett, who looks ready to join me on my quest to get Jameson to quit talking about me like that to my brother of all people.

Ashton releases a deep, guttural growl and gnashes his fangs, surprising me. I stop in my tracks and meet his silver eyes. I realize Bronx restrains Ashton with a pair of metal binds. Bronx's muscles flex, his jaw clenching. He looks as if it pains him to have to keep my brother away as much as it pains me to see Ashton like this.

"Get back, dandelion. I mean it. That's an order." Bronx spins my brother and shoves his front to the wall. Leaning in close from behind, he says, "Don't make me hurt you. We talked about this, Ash."

Everett abandons my side, only to have Mikkalo and Jameson silently fill it. Pulling a flask from his jacket, Everett offers it to Ashton, holding it to my brother's lips. Ashton's nostrils flare, his fangs extending longer, and then he opens his mouth and guzzles the blood Everett pours for him.

Everett straightens his back. "Bronx, go tell the board that it's unreasonable to have Gwen here. They should know better than to force her to bear witness to this."

"Yeah, Bronxy," Jameson says. "Ashton shouldn't even be around any donors for at least another few hours. He needs to experience blood bloat to get himself under control. Tell the board that refusing to give him what he needs is cruel. It's not his fault."

The double doors swing open. "That is still yet to be decided, Mr. Royale." Mr. Goldman from the board greets us with a tight mouth. His gaze flicks to me, and he zones in on my belly like he expects me to be showing already. "Now, please. Come in. We don't have all night. We've already wasted enough time on this nonsense as it is."

Bronx pulls Ashton from the wall and straightens him on his feet. "The fact that we have to be here at all is ludicrous."

"I have to agree." The sultry, feminine voice sounds from the meeting room, and I take a few steps with Mikkalo and Jameson at my side to get a better view of Zara, the head of the Aku Region. She's just as gorgeous as I remember with her flowing black hair, tawny complexion, pouty mouth, and high cheekbones. "Which is why I'll take temporary custody of Mr. Ashton Gallagher until the state of the Royale Region is organized."

Viorica clicks her tongue. "He was a donor in my region and city, Ms. Aku. I'd like to hear from the Royales before determining his fate, since Ms. Royale shares a blood bond."

A deep, guttural groan erupts from the other male board member's mouth. Mr. Woodsman rests his elbows on the massive table. "What about the criminal outcast? He also shares a blood bond to Ms. Royale. Are you going to allow her mister to plead on his behalf as well, knowing that Mr. Royale should've ended his life the moment he was caught trying to steal the untouchables from Crimson Vista?" Snapping his head in Bronx's direction, he flashes his fangs. "Why you'd go through the trouble of bringing him to the board is beyond me."

Bronx flies forward and towers over Mr. Woodsman in his seat. The vampire hops up and withdraws a blade, preparing to fight. My fear instincts trigger, and I step back into Mikkalo's arms. He pulls me in close, and Jameson slightly blocks me, shielding me in case.

Bronx unsheathes his own dagger. "I went through the trouble to show you that the Barons must be dealt with accordingly. You should not allow Freeport to challenge me for a board seat when his coven can't follow Donor Life Corp laws. Allowing this to continue will only open your regions up for war. Is that something you want, Mr. Woodsman? Your region is as new as mine, so stop acting as if you're better or more powerful than me."

Oh, shit.

I expect Mr. Woodsman to attack. I brace myself, praying that I can keep my dhampir nature in check with Bronx being threatened. Mikkalo squeezes me tighter like he knows I'm on the verge of losing control. But Viorica materializes between Bronx and Mr. Woodsman and holds her hands up to each of their chests, braving getting in the middle.

"Mr. Woodsman, settle down. Now is not the time to question Mr. Royale's judgement. I have the same reservations toward the Baron Coven. They're obviously hiding something, and we must proceed with caution."

"But it is in their right to test the Royales' power. It is our way." Mr. Goldman draws my attention to him. "They've done everything correctly under Donor Life Corp law. If the territory suspects we'll deny the power of another, they might try to test us. I think we should continue on accordingly. Who knows? Perhaps our territory will thrive with the addition of someone from outside our laws."

I don't believe what I'm hearing.

"Which is why we need to remain cautious," Zara says, standing beside Viorica. "And our ways are changing. It was necessary after the fall of so many regions in the last year, or have you already forgotten? This is more than about power. This is about cementing our regions' future."

"They will destroy us if we don't comply!" Mr. Woodsman bares his fangs with another deep growl.

Charging around Viorica, he launches at Bronx, wielding his blade. Bronx dodges out of the way and manages to trip the board member. Mr. Woodsman lands on his back with a grunt. I push against Jameson, my body going out of whack at the board member's audacity to start a fight like this.

Bronx kicks Mr. Woodsman and blurs at vampire speed to snatch him from the ground. Yanking him off his feet, Bronx holds the board member against his chest with his dagger resting on his throat. Several vampires materialize in the room, but Mikkalo abandons my side and cuts them off with a glower.

"Mr. Woodsman," Zara says with a smile. "Perhaps we should offer the Barons your seat on the board."

Oh, man. I can't stop my mouth from mirroring the beautiful vampire's smile. Because, hell yeah.

Mr. Woodsman growls. "That won't be necessary."

Bronx releases him and returns to the table without another glance. Mr. Woodsman slinks back into his seat, and I wonder if Bronx could actually threaten Mr. Woodsman's board seat.

I don't get the chance to whisper to Jameson about it, because a roar erupts from the hallway, and four guards drag Silas into the room. Ashton thrashes from Everett's arms, drawing my attention to the two of them for the first time since we entered.

"You asshole!" Ashton yells. "How could you do this to us?"

Silas only smiles. "You mean give you the life you deserve? You should thank me, brother."

"Thank you? Are you kidding me, Silas?" I tense at the sound of my voice echoing through the air.

All eyes fall on me, and I wish my dumb mouth would've just stayed shut. The last thing I need is to be under the board's scrutiny.

"Aw, come on, Gweny. You should thank me too, considering you're going to need us in your—"

Bronx rams his hands into Silas and knocks him into the wall. The two of them growl at each other, but Silas can't manage to fight with his hands bound behind his back. Viorica and the other board members watch in silence. So do my guys.

"Under the authority of the Royale Region I convict you of treason against Donor Life Corp, donor trading, and an unauthorized Blood Vow. Because of these severe offenses, you're hereby sentenced to death." Turning toward the board members, Bronx adds, "Does anyone object?"

"No," all four of them say.

I clench my fingers into fists, my whole body screaming in agony as a lifetime of memories flood back to me of my time in the bunker and growing up with Silas. Tears burn my eyes, and I twist and bury my face into Jameson's shirt. He engulfs me in a hug and rubs his hand up and down the length of my back.

I knew this was coming.

I knew that Silas's life would end.

But a part of me wishes it wasn't going to happen by Bronx's hands, despite his word on ensuring my brother's death comes swiftly and painlessly.

It still doesn't make this much better.

"Gweny! Gwen! Are you really going to let him do this?" Silas yells. His amusement suddenly shifts to fear. I think he realizes that this is really happening and none of his precious Baron brothers have arrived to save him.

I clear my throat, praying my voice doesn't break. "You broke Donor Life Corp law, Silas. You brought this on yourself. What did you expect?"

Silas growls. "Gwen! You traitor. You bitch! After everything I've done for you? After giving up years of my fucking life to make sure you had everything you needed? Kyler died because of you. Our family was separated. All because you couldn't just be a good dh—"

The shock alarms ignite, cutting off Silas's words. I startle and cover my ears as pain from the noise explodes through my head. Mr. Goldman and Mr. Woodsman both drop to their knees along with Ashton. My guys tense, but they manage to stay on their feet. Viorica and Zara tug out their com devices. Several figures blur into the room, and Mikkalo, Jameson, and Bronx materialize around me. Everett remains with Ashton.

Fear clenches my chest at the familiar faces of Freeport along with Thaxton. A few of their brothers linger outside the boardroom, waiting for their command.

A dozen thoughts cross my mind as Freeport turns his attention to me, managing to still see me even between the safety circle my guys create around me. Silence falls through the room, and I blink the haze from my eyes enough to get my shit together.

"Gwen, how glorious it is to see you," Freeport says, totally ignoring the fact that Merrick, Heidi, and an unfamiliar Vaduva sister all aim their weapons at him. "You look ravishing. Practically glowing."

I remain expressionless, choosing to keep my mouth shut. I will not give him the satisfaction of seeing that he gets under my skin. It's what he wants. From next to him, Thaxton trails his gaze around the room, staring from Silas with a glower and then to Ashton. He looks more pissed off than I feel about the whole situation. Like he senses I stare at him, he darts his gaze to me, inching closer. He has the nerve to wink.

"Mr. Baron, I see you've finally managed to respond to my call," Viorica says, placing her hands on her hips. Her voice drips with annoyance. "If you succeed in claiming a board seat, I expect far better from you and your coven. This is unacceptable."

Freeport twists his lips in a cocky smile, still not turning his gaze away from me. It's like his attention freezes my heart by the second until it feels as if an ice cube cracks behind my ribcage. "My apologies, Ms. Vaduva. I was in the middle of preparing my future city heads for our rise in power. Forgive me for believing you could handle such an unimportant situation regarding my brother."

Wow. I jerk my gaze to the board, half-expecting, half-praying that they get their act together and realize Freeport must be stopped now. Why they're waiting? Bullshit. Who cares about what the vampires in the territory will think. They can do better. For being such a powerful woman, I don't understand Viorica's hesitation. She's the head of Donor Life Corp. She survived when more than half the regions collapsed, apparently. She doesn't look like one to take shit, so I struggle to figure her out. There has to be more. She has to have a strategy I can't see. I'm almost afraid to find out.

Viorica glowers, finally reacting as Freeport's condescending tone sinks in. She closes the space a bit more to stand behind her daughters. "Do you think this is a game? We at Donor Life Corp take such offenses seriously. His conviction is one that could possibly start a blood feud. That might be something you brush off, but strict order and our laws are necessary to maintain peace."

Freeport waves his hand, acting like a total ass. I never expected anything less, but it pisses me off for Viorica's sake. He has the nerve to step closer to Merrick to force her back an inch to speak to Viorica. "You cannot tell me you haven't broken one of your own laws. What of your daughters? Do not underestimate my knowledge of the Donor Life Corp Territory. I've had more than a century to watch from the shadows as it rose. I've traveled from region to region and past the borders into other territories. You are far worse off and should concern yourself with other boards noticing you grow weak. You should be thankful I chose to register when I did."

A collection of growls vibrates through the air. I shiver at the deep noise awakening my fear instincts. Because holy shit. It's hard to imagine anything outside of Donor Life

Corp.

Zara materializes next to Viorica. "Mr. Baron, make no mistake. The Vaduva and Aku Regions can consume all others in our territory. We stand firm in our powerful alliances. To even consider that we grow weak proves just how archaic and naive you really are."

Freeport opens his mouth to retort, and Thaxton cuts him off with a touch to his shoulder. "Now is not the time to challenge, brother." Thaxton straightens his shoulders and shifts his attention to Viorica. "Please excuse my brother, but we don't take kindly to unwarranted threats and accusations against the Baron name. You act as if Silas stole from you, Ms. Vaduva. As far as I'm aware, the Royale Region is currently in limbo in regards to the population and transfers in and out have been permitted for both vampires and donors."

"Silas was not authorized for either," Bronx says, holding the front of Silas's shirt. He shakes him. "He tried to remove a pregnant donor. She was bitten."

"Limited blood donations from them are not harmful if done properly. I'm sure Silas would've never taken without permission." Freeport shifts his gaze to Silas. "It was consensual, was it not?"

Silas nods. "Yes."

"As a medical practitioner, I will confirm this," Thaxton adds. "From our studies, there is no adverse effects on donor or fetus." Medical practitioner? Yeah-fucking-right. I don't believe a word he says.

"Also, must I remind you that you've taken donations from your own blood source?" Freeport's eyes turn to me again. He extends his fangs a bit, teasing me in an attempt to get a reaction. "They taste better, don't you think? Intoxicating. I'm sure you haven't resisted a small taste in prior weeks. Especially if she begged—"

Bronx releases Silas only to tackle Freeport. The two of them blur in a fight, crashing into the far wall. Freeport shoves Bronx into the cracked drywall, but Bronx swings his fist and punches Freeport hard enough to send him flying back. Tension burns hot in the room, sending beads of sweat dripping down the back of my neck. No one tries to get between Bronx and Freeport, and a huge part of me fears that Freeport will try to end Bronx's life now.

I can't take it.

Sucking in a deep breath, I yell, "Freeport! Stop! Leave my intended alone."

My comment does the trick, and Freeport abandons Bronx to materialize a few feet away. Mikkalo tightens his arms around me protectively, and it takes everything in me to remain composed despite my heart thrashing against my ribs. Nerves tighten my muscles, and I wish I could take a few steps closer and surprise him with a kick to his junk. I want him to feel at least a fraction of the pain he put me through.

Freeport tilts his head, his gaze burning over every inch

of my face. My essence burns under his scrutiny, my insides threatening to expel just to get away. "If you agree to cancel your Blood Vow to someone beneath you, I'll consider it." Standing taller, he traces his gaze down my body, stopping on my stomach. "I can promise a life beyond your imagination and a brilliant future for your heir."

This fuckhead. He's worse than Laredo with his quips and ability to test me and my guys.

"Enough!" Viorica yells. She grabs the back of Freeport's suit jacket and hauls him away, the sight of her small frame pushing around a guy much larger than her impressive. I thank the universe for her interruption. I wasn't sure how much more instigation I could take. "I've had it with your interruptions, Mr. Baron. I don't take kindly to your manipulation. Ms. Royale belongs to Mr. Royale. His coven paid the fees, and she agreed to accept a vow into his coven. If she went through so much trouble to evade getting tied to you, then she obviously wants no part of your existence. I will not stand by and allow this poor behavior in my boardroom. If you cannot act in a civilized manner, you will be treated as an outcast. Do you understand? You will not speak to Ms. Royale again without her mister's permission."

Whoa. Her words shut everyone up. It takes everything in me not to cheer. If she didn't ruin her speech by making me feel like property, I'd have risked my limbs to hug her.

Freeport growls, tightening his hands into fists. "I understand, Ms. Vaduva. Now, if you would please release my brother, I will ensure he doesn't break another Donor Life Corp law. I'm asking you to show mercy due to the fact that he's young, born a rebel, and has not exactly had an easy life."

"No," Bronx says, stepping closer. "He knew exactly what he was doing, just as Corona knew what he was doing when you sent him to us, using Ashton as a warning by nearly draining him dry. This must stop."

Freeport has the nerve to bring his hand to his chest. "I did no such thing." He flicks his gaze to Ashton. "He looks well enough now."

"You dick!" Ashton yells, pushing against Everett as he blocks him. "You tortured me. Bit me a dozen times. If that bitch daughter of Corona's hadn't suggested using me as a message, I would have been dead."

Brooklyn suggested it? Bronx meets my gaze, remaining expressionless, though I know a dozen thoughts cross his mind. He thought Brooklyn was a traitor, but she's doing what she claimed Corona was doing—only trying to survive. A part of me knows she didn't suggest leaving Ashton as a message to get to me. She did it to save him. Bronx recognizes it as clear as I do. But still. She won't abandon Corona. It makes her dangerous.

Curling his lips into a smile, Freeport tries to lock Ashton in his gaze. "I'd suggest that someone open your mind to prove it, but it seems you got your wish to turn into a vampire—using your brother to do so. I always knew you were more intelligent, Mr. Gallagher. Using this situation to your benefit. How cruel of you to play with my brother's emotions and blood bond to you, getting him to break the law we both know he would prefer to follow. You know as well as anyone that there are no blood bonds allowed within a coven under the law. What were you expecting to get out of all this?"

It feels as if my heart plops into my stomach at his words. Silas's face morphs, his forehead crinkling, his lips puckering a bit. He's acting the role that Freeport paints for the board, trying to turn this situation into their favor.

And fuck. If I didn't know the truth, I might be slightly convinced.

Freeport shifts to look at the board. "I hope you take my pleas into consideration. You know many donors are desperate. If anyone should be punished, it should be the true rebel. Don't you think it strange for him to just show up in your system, Ms. Vaduva? No rebel would ever pur-posefully register without ulterior motives."

Ohmyfuck.

Viorica tightens her jaw and brings her gaze to Zara. She looks like she's considering Freeport's words, which scares the shit out of me. It was one thing to accept that Si-las was facing death, but it's another thing to think that it could be Ashton...not together with Silas but in his place. It'll destroy Declan. It'll destroy me.

"Those are bullshit accusations and you know it!"

Bronx shoves his hands into Silas to get him away, chancing to release him from his hold. He turns to Mikkalo. "Mik, bring up the feeds."

Mikkalo quickly taps his finger over his com device, scanning the security feeds from our property.

"I have the feeds that show Corona bringing Ashton and announcing the Barons' warning," Bronx adds, flexing his muscles.

I lick my lips, suddenly dying for a drink—blood or water. At this point, I'm not sure which my body craves more. Jameson must realize it because he sneaks a flask from his pocket and hands it to me. Inching in front of me, he blocks everyone's view of me, but I don't think they'd even notice. All eyes remain focused on Bronx and Freeport.

I swig the blood, wishing with everything in me that I could just bite Jameson. My body reacts to the blood, begging me for more. I heave a few breaths and clutch onto Jameson's shoulders, burying my face into his back between his shoulder blades. I suck in a few deep breaths, my whole body trembling in fear and trepidation.

"Ev, quick. Something's wrong with Gwen," Jameson says, his voice cutting over the argument.

I blink the haze from my eyes, realizing that Jameson spun around and now is the only thing holding me up. He lifts me off my feet completely and cradles me like a blushing bride to give Everett a better view of my face.

"She's losing color," Everett says. Turning to the board,

he says, "Please excuse us."

Mr. Goldman slaps his hands on the table. "She can wait five minutes. I vote that Mr. Baron can take his brother. We'll deal with the traitor Gallagher appropriately since he's covenless. There is no need to start any feuds."

"What?" I ask, my voice barely coming out a whisper. "No."

"I agree," Mr. Woodsman says. "This is wasting everyone's time."

"Mr. Royale, you have one minute to provide your proof, or I'll have no other choice but to agree." Zara's voice cuts through the pounding in my head, stabbing me hard with her words.

If Jameson wasn't holding me, I'd lose my shit.

"It seems someone hacked into our system and deleted the feeds," Mikkalo says, his voice remaining even.

"How convenient," Viorica comments with a sigh. At least she doesn't sound convinced.

"I have eyewitnesses," Bronx is quick to say. "We were having a gathering at the time."

"I don't care. My vote remains the same." Mr. Goldman's voice booms through the room. "It also seems all of this unnecessary arguing might not even serve a purpose, considering the Royale Region will fall in a few days."

All four of my guys growl.

I wiggle in Jameson's arms, trying my best to break free. I'm going to kill Freeport for this. I'm going to kill Silas too. How dare they come in here and manipulate the board into believing this is Ashton's fault. They've ruined enough already.

Viorica slaps her hand on the table, stopping everyone from getting riled up. "I disagree, Mr. Goldman. As head of the Donor Life Corp board, I'm overruling all decisions. I think a compromise is in order, considering how personal these accusations are to both parties. Because I hold great respect for the Royales, I will agree that Mr. Silas Baron must be punished."

Freeport materializes in front of Viorica. "Ms. Vaduva—"

She aims her dagger at his neck, her ever-silent daughters suddenly surrounding her protectively. "Do not interrupt me, Mr. Baron. I don't know how things are done outside of my territory, but I don't appreciate these games. I am not stupid. I've dealt with enough hot-headed, power-hungry men in my lifetime to know manipulation when I see it. So, I will proceed with Silas's conviction, but to satiate your need to protect him, I will only banish him from the territory. Starting immediately."

Everything happens so fast that my brain can barely process.

A team of security personnel in all black storms the room and restrains Silas and Freeport, separating them from each other. Viorica pulls a strange glass bottle from a cupboard on the wall and dips an ornate dagger into it.

Silas bucks and yells, thrashing against the guards' hold. It takes Merrick getting in front of him to grip his neck to get him to chill out.

Silence fills the room with Viorica's approach.

"Be brave, brother," Freeport says, flashing his fangs. "Do not embarrass the Baron line."

"You have to stop them, Freeport." Silas tenses, his eyes flashing crazy silver. "Thaxton, please. You guys are strong enough."

Thaxton disappears without response. Freeport only crosses his arms and nods to Viorica. Turning away, Ashton links his hands to the back of his head. I don't look away. I can't. Silas narrows his eyes on me, his face reddening.

"Freeport!" he hollers. "If you let them do this, I will share your secret. I will tell the fucking world!"

My heart stalls, my chest tightening. Silas continues to glower at me. Without having to hear his thoughts, I know the secret he refers to is me. Jameson adjusts me again, preparing to flee if we have to. He won't risk sticking around. Mikkalo joins us, getting ready as well.

But we don't get the chance to leave.

Freeport materializes in front of Silas and aims a dagger at his heart. "I should end you right here," he growls. "A Baron doesn't blackmail, nor do they cower in fear. If you even think about using my beloved against me, you're sorely mistaken. I've lived far too long to have things end right here with the likes of you."

His beloved? Fuck that.

Silas flares his nostrils but doesn't argue. Freeport steps away, fully prepared to intervene if he has to. Viorica proceeds with her mission and takes Merrick's place, gripping Silas's chin. My stomach twists and turns at the sight of her locking her hand into his hair to yank it from his face. In a slow, steady motion, Viorica runs the inked blade across my brother's forehead, giving him the outcast tattoos that will take who knows how long to fade.

Because Zaire had used the tattoos as punishment for Mikkalo and Jameson, I know the ink contains some sort of UV chemical that remains for years against a vampire's regenerative ability.

Silas hollers once before sinking his fangs into his bottom lip, spilling blood. The blue ink and his ruby blood blend into a nearly black concoction that drips down his face. He grinds his teeth and glowers at me, a dozen thoughts crossing his eyes. He looks like he wants to kill me. He looks like he might make it his mission in life to see me fall by his hands.

It's enough for me to break his stare.

"Mr. Silas Baron, you've been inked with ten outcast marks. If and only if you manage to survive outside the cities and the territory long enough for them to fade will you be welcomed to register. Crossing our borders is an automatic death sentence. You are not welcome even in the city your coven has acquired. Do you understand?" Zara stands tall next to Viorica while the other two board members remain a few feet back.

Silas retracts his fangs from his bloody lip. "Fuck off."

"Guards, escort him from the territory," Viorica says.

And before I can glance at Silas one last time, he and the guards disappear.

I groan and rest my head on Jameson, my nerves completely shot. I can't believe this happened. I don't know what to feel or how to think. All I want to do is to return to our suite and curl up in bed.

"Mr. Gallagher, due to these strange circumstances, it's in everyone's best interest that you also bear the outcast marks and join your brother," Zara says, flicking her attention to me.

"What?" My voice rises in volume.

Mr. Goldman nods his head. "I agree. I've had enough with these damn rebels, and the last thing we need is more rebel vampires coming in to try to steal what is rightfully ours."

"He's not a rebel!" I thrash in Jameson's arms, but he doesn't let me go. He links his fingers into my hair and presses my face into the crook of his neck.

I sink my teeth into his throat, my wild side breaking free, wanting nothing more than to show the board that they're messing with the wrong brother of mine. I can't just let Ashton face the same consequences as Silas. He'd been by my side. Ashton is one of the few here for me, and when the world feels against me and my guys, his loyalty and love is exactly what I need.

Freeport huffs a breath. "I'd like to request a coven union with Ashton Gallagher. With the banishing of Silas, and the recent deaths of several of my other coven members, I'd like to show him mercy to make up for my brother's mistake."

"Are you kidding me?" Mr. Woodsman says. "We will not take this kind of manipulation."

"I have to agree, Mr. Baron. If you wanted a coven union or a Blood Vow with any of the Gallaghers, you should have done so properly. Our decision to outcast Ashton stands." Viorica materializes in front of Ashton as Zara gets behind him.

He doesn't react.

He doesn't fight.

He accepts their conviction with his head held high.

"Wait." Bronx's deep voice echoes through the air. "I'm submitting my request to a coven union with Ashton Gallagher. I will take full responsibility of his actions from this moment on. You can trust me that he won't be an issue and if he is, you can outcast me yourselves."

My heart speeds in overdrive, a flicker of hope burning through me.

Viorica drops her hand to her side. I peek over Jameson's shoulder at her as he remains facing the wall to keep his body between mine and the others. It helps hide the fact that his blood drips down my chin.

"You do understand what such a request means, correct?" Viorica says, shifting her gaze to me.

Bronx swallows. "I do, but may I have a moment to tell my mate?"

Ice travels through my veins the second his eyes meet mine.

"Brother, we should discuss this," Mikkalo says, his voice lowering.

"Agree." Both Jameson and Everett say.

"Gwen will agree with me." Bronx closes the space to us and leans closer, bringing his lips to my ear.

I shiver at the sensation of his cool breath.

"Dandelion, if we agree to bring Ashton into our coven..." He swallows, his voice catching in his whisper. "If Ashton joins our coven, it would mean you can't. I'd forfeit our Blood Vow. Blood bonds aren't allowed within the same coven."

Tears swell in my eyes at the pain in his voice. I know it kills him to say the words as much as it kills me to hear them. But we all know that a Blood Vow for me is impossible. I can't transform. It was just a way to get the board to allow me to stay with Bronx.

"So after the baby..."

"You can proceed to Blood Match with one of the Royales as a personal donor," Viorica says, catching my quivering words. "Or perhaps you'd consider transferring your contract to another coven with the intent of a Blood Vow."

Freeport grins. "I'd like to propose one."

I glower. "No fucking way. I'd rather spend a short life with the Royales as a donor than ever spend eternity with you."

"As you wish, Ms. Royale," Viorica says. She looks at Freeport. "You are excused, Mr. Baron. Please be prepared for the challenge in three days. If you fail to show up or show up late, you will lose your one opportunity to oversee a region."

"I look forward to the rise of the Baron Region," he says with a bow.

Mr. Woodsman proffers his hand. "You are also welcome to join us at the Donor Life Corp Ball to meet with the city heads in all of the territory tomorrow night."

"It would be my pleasure." With one more bow, Freeport vanishes.

Mr. Goldman clears his throat. "Well, we don't have all night, Misters Royale. Let's proceed with the coven union."

Zara glances at me. "Such a shame. You'd have made a lovely Royale Heir, Gwen."

Ashton steps a foot closer. "You don't have to agree, Gweny. I'll accept the consequences for my transformation. I can't take this from you."

Viorica drops a stack of papers on the table. "I'm sorry, Mr. Gallagher. It's already done."

12

BROKEN VOW

"THIS WAY, MY DHAMPIR. WE have to hurry." Laredo drags me forward before scooping me off my feet at vampire speed. He buries his face in the crook of my neck, inhaling a long breath. Teasing me with his fangs, he grazes them along my collar to yank my shirt to the side to play-lick my skin.

"Laredo!" I screech. "Knock that shit off."

"You like it," he says, his deep laugh vibrating over my neck. "Just admit it."

Pulling away, I narrow my eyes at him. Both of us know I'd never. The second I do, it's over for me. He might always get his way. "You wish."

"More than wish. I dream and pray and beg the universe." He laughs as I crinkle my nose and bites his bottom lip, sending a trickle of blood down his chin.

The bastard. He knows exactly how to get to me. I also love messing with him. There's always been something exciting about sneaking around behind Grayson's back to suck on Laredo's neck. It helps that I have a good time with him. And he's hot. Charming. It could be worse.

"Be careful. You could lose that lip of yours." Drawing my tongue over his chin, I lick my way up to his mouth but don't meet my lips to his. "You know I bite."

"I look forward to every moment you sink your teeth into me, Gwen. You should know this by now. I'm your perfect blood source. Always ready to give you the world with nothing in return. Your presence is enough." He touches my cheek, drawing my attention from the blood still dribbling on his chin to his dark eyes. "I hope to continue to prove it to you. Perhaps you'll let me show you exactly what you're missing by playing the good little sister to your stubborn, over-protective brothers. They just can't accept our destiny just yet."

Warmth blossoms in my cheeks at his words. He sounds so serious. "Ha-ha. You're so full of shit. You only don't take anything in return because my brothers give you *what you need."*

He cocks an eyebrow. "I'd have to disagree. They don't...have what I'm looking for. Only you do."

The world suddenly slows, and I shiver in Laredo's arms, the wind lifting my hair from my warm neck. He sets me on my feet but keeps his hand locked to my waist. He'll touch me for as long as I allow him to, always pushing and testing, seeing how far I'll let him take things...and tonight, I'm in a great mood.

So I kiss him.

Standing on my tiptoes, I graze my lips to his, tasting the sweetness of his blood. His hand slides around my back, and he pulls my hips to his, letting me feel exactly how much I turn him on.

Sucking his bottom lip into my mouth, I nip him again, kissing and sucking to get a better taste. And he lets me. He hums under my fervent mouth, slowly drawing his hand lower to cup my ass. Tingles prickle over my body, and I imagine how it would feel if he continued his exploration. He'd be cautious and gentle, though I know he might like things rough. He gets off when I'm teetering on the edge of unleashing my wild side.

"You're so magnificent, Gwen," he murmurs. "I can't get enough of you."

I dig my fingers into his shoulder blades, locking him in place. "And I want more."

Laredo chuckles and tilts his neck, offering me a taste.

"There might be no turning back if you let me."

Reaching between us, I touch his bulge through his pants. "That's what you think."

"I know, my beautiful dhampir. You won't want to. You won't be able to help yourself once you claim me." He gives my ass a squeeze, the tips of his fingers testing how far I'll allow him to go.

My body turns wild, my heart pounding as slick warmth builds between my legs. Lately, I've been attracted to Laredo more and more. I don't know if it's all the time we've been spending together or his sheer persistence, but whatever it is...he's right. One of these days I'll allow him to go further. I can't stop thinking about what it would feel like if he touched me where I like. He'd be far better than the few times I've slept with a rebel before.

"I'm so fortunate Grayson found you. My life could've been much, much worse," I whisper, kissing him again to excite him even more with my affection.

He grins against my mouth, releasing a moan as I touch his boner through his pants again, wanting nothing more than to make him crazy. "You have no idea. Not everyone sees you as the powerful, marvelous woman you are...who I imagine to taste incredibly sweet."

"Wouldn't you love to find out?" I tease, stretching his lip with my teeth only to let it go with a laugh.

"You'll love every second of my mouth on you. I promise." He grazes his fangs across my lip. "You'll ask me to do *it again and again."*

Easing back, I meet his sparkling silver gaze. "Kind of like you with me. Always begging and pleading."

"Mmmhmm. I'll blow your mind."

I break away and kiss my way down his throat, tasting the sugariness of his skin. Using my teeth, I drag his T-shirt from his shoulder, stretching out the collar. He moans softly at the sensation of my mouth sucking his skin hard enough to leave a mark. Lifting me up again, he relocates us from in front of the house and into the shadows next to the shed. He presses my back to the wall and adjusts my legs around him so that only our clothes stay between us. But clothing doesn't stop us from enjoying each other.

Laredo slips his hand into my pants, popping open the button in the process. I moan so loud before he even touches me and sink my teeth into his shoulder. Electricity zings through my groin as his fingers rub my clit over my panties, just teasing and testing me.

I break my lips from my bite mark and meet his flashing eyes. "It's not enough. Harder, faster. More. It feels so good. I don't want you to stop."

"Anything for you." Laredo releases a deep rumble from his throat and watches my face as I gasp with his touch. Desire darkens his features. Our closeness shifts something inside me, this moment unexpected and exciting, my caution completely annihilated.

Bringing my lips back to his, I kiss him for real instead

of only tasting his blood. He opens his mouth wider, caressing his tongue against mine, continuing to work his finger over me until he manages to tug my panties out of the way and—

"Laredo. You're late. Hurry. The Gallaghers will be here any minute." A familiar voice sounds through the night.

I jerk from Laredo and peer in the direction of the voice but can't see anyone. It's weird, like I know who it is, but I just can't place the man's name. Or see him in my mind. It annoys the hell out of me.

Laredo groans and cups my face, our chests caressing with our panting. He ignores the man and picks up where he left off, sliding his finger into my pants. "You go. I want to stay and take care of my dhampir." He's not talking to me.

I pull away from Laredo again. He might be able to ignore the rude interrupter, but I can't.

A figure lurks around the corner, casting a shadow across the ground from the porch light. "You must go, Laredo. They might know otherwise. We can't risk it. You can catch her in a good mood another night."

Laredo glowers toward the shadow. "Do not even think about touching her. She's mine." Bringing his mouth to mine again, he kisses me softly and moves from the wall. "Hold on tight, Gwen. I need to relocate."

The world blurs, and Laredo spins me around, making

me screech. He lets me go, tossing me into the air to mess with me. I brace for the fall, expecting to hit the ground one of these days, but two strong arms catch me.

Laredo chuckles. "Sorry about that, my dhampir. I needed to take care of something for a second."

I frown and pat his chest. "Next time just set me on my feet. You have to stop pulling that shit. I hate it."

"Let me make it up to you," he murmurs with a soft smile.

"It sounded like you had somewhere to go. Who was that? I didn't know you knew people around here." I meet his eyes, a strange feeling cascading over me.

He combs my hair behind my ear. "It was just another blood source from the community covering for me. You know how your brothers hate the attention I show you."

I roll my eyes. "They can screw off. It's not like they allow me to hang out with anyone else."

"So does that mean I can finish what we started?" he asks, leaning closer.

I search his face, the nagging feeling refusing to go away. It kills the moment.

It's now that I realize the strange feeling arises because something is different about Laredo. I blink a few times in confusion, noticing the blood is gone from his mouth where he bit himself. I knew vampires regenerated fast but...

Caressing his lips to mine, he cuts off my thoughts without waiting for my answer.

I jerk back and slap him, my body screaming.

Touching his cheek, he cocks his head to the side and studies me. "What's wrong? You're frightened."

"I—" I shiver.

"It's okay, my dhampir. We can do whatever you want."

I swallow, suppressing my nerves. The blood source from the nearby rebel nest must've been lurking around, setting off my fear instincts like crazy. It's something I can't always control and drives me crazy. "I think I'm okay. Just...distract me for a moment—"

"Gwen, Laredo? Where are you?" Grayson calls. Footsteps sound near the gravel path in front. With his voice, my fear dissipates, replaced by disappointment.

Laredo groans and sets me on my feet. "I suppose we can finish this later."

I puff out my bottom lip, wondering if I can somehow revive the moment between us. "Or we can hide a little longer."

"Anything for you, Gwen. I'd hide with you forever."

"Forever is a long time."

"It's not. You'll see. Forever is never long enough."

Something cool touches my head, drawing me from my dream of Laredo. Laredo and his brother. I know that now. A dozen small instances flood back to me, making me feel so stupid for not questioning it sooner. Or maybe it was because I did and Laredo mind manipulated me to stop being suspicious.

With a groan, I shake my head and shift to my side to meet Bronx's intense gaze. Darkness shrouds the room, the only light illuminating from a com device on the wall near our bedside. Soft music trickles through the air, and I rub the sleep from my eyes, wondering what time it is.

"I'm sorry to wake you, dandelion," Bronx whispers, sliding his muscular arm under me to pull me closer. "But I think you need to drink some blood."

At the mention of blood, my stomach growls like crazy.

He chuckles and shifts, grabbing something from over my head. Stuffing falls from his fingers and tickles my cheek. "You really had it out for your pillow today. If I didn't think you'd drain me completely, I'd have moved you to ravage me instead."

I sit up and stare at the mess of stuffing lying around my head. "Shit. I did this?"

He holds up the sheet to show off a rip in the fabric. "This too. What were you dreaming about anyway? I was thinking I could pick up where it left off. Sounded good."

I grimace and flop back on the bed, covering my eyes with my hands. "It was what I think was a memory...with Laredo."

I brace to hear his growl, but instead he trails his fingers across my hands, getting me to drop them from my face. He remains expressionless as he processes my comment. I wish he wasn't so good at hiding his feelings, because I want to know how much it bothers him that Laredo now manages not only to invade my waking hours but also my sleep. It's like I can't escape the bastard.

Bronx blinks a few times and finally reacts by rolling on top of me. "I don't want to continue where you left off then."

I suck in my bottom lip. "I'm sorry."

He shakes his head, quirking the side of his mouth into a smile. "Don't be. I now want to make sure that your next dream is about us."

Puffing a small breath, I nod. "That's what I want too...but where are your brothers?"

"They're with Ashton." Bronx studies my face with his comment. "I asked if I could be alone with you. I just want to make sure you know that I will fix this."

I close my eyes, breaking our stare. "Bronx, nothing needs to be fixed. You saved my brother. I know it wasn't what you really wanted and you made the decision for my benefit. I can't even transform, remember?"

He groans and puts more of his weight on me. "It's more than that. Things might get tougher around other covens. They'll start to question why."

"Well, I don't care."

He bobs his head. "It doesn't change my vow to you, Gwen."

Stretching up, I brush my lips to his. "Good, because you're my forever. I don't need a damn ceremony or useless venom bite to tell me as much."

He touches my cheek. "I love you."

"And I love you."

Bronx kisses me deeper, slipping his tongue into my mouth while holding me close and resting his legs between mine. His stiff erection tests the resistance of my panties, and I reach between us to pull his cock free of his underwear. Moaning, Bronx flexes his muscles, his carnal desire igniting my own. I want him so badly that it's all I can think about. Him and me together, how good he feels inside me, how he makes my whole body sing and crave more over and over again.

Breaking from my mouth, Bronx kisses down my throat and to my chest. Locking his fingers to the bodice of my nightie, he shreds the fabric right down the middle and sucks my nipple into his mouth, grazing my sensitive flesh with his fang. And damn it does it make me yearn for his bite.

I moan softly, running my fingers through his hair and squirming under the sizzling sensations that blaze across my skin. He works his way lower, scratching my skin with his teeth just hard enough to get me to arch my back.

"You're driving me crazy," I whisper through a gasp. "This is torture."

He catches the sheer fabric of my panties on his fangs and drags them lower until he rips them away from me. Propping himself on his elbows, he trails his gaze over my naked body, the desire on his face as prominent as his hard erection keeping space between him and the bed.

Trailing one hand from my knee to my thigh, he gets me to spread my legs wider for him. He starts slow by teasing me, tracing his finger over my clit, stroking my body while watching my face. I can barely handle it, my desire overpowering all of my senses. So I grab his hand and guide his fingers to press harder, to move faster, to give me exactly what I want.

He hums, letting me take complete control to get myself off for a couple of minutes until he can't help himself from taking over. Lying down between my legs, he pulls my body to his face, slipping his finger inside me while licking and sucking my clit in a way that makes me scream in pleasure, the heat and intensity of our passion prodding me to give in to my deep-seated nature.

I lock my hands to his arms and manage to drag him back to me. He releases a playful growl because I don't let him finish me off, my desire to bite him far stronger than I realize. Aligning our bodies, I guide him into me at the same time I sink my teeth into his shoulder, getting exactly what my body wants.

He moans with his deep thrust, rocking his body so hard into mine that I hit my head on the headboard. Grunting, he slides his arm around my back and embraces me to him to keep me close until I finish sucking on my bite mark.

I break away with a gasp, loving every minute of Bronx's movements. He thrusts hard and fast, and the bed rocks and bangs the wall over and over again until my muscles spasm and tense with my orgasm. Only then does he decide to change positions, easing away for only a second before flipping me onto my stomach. He traps my legs between his, closing my body, but continues to thrust inside me deep enough that I bite the bed to try to quiet my sounds of pleasure.

Leaning down, he kisses my shoulder, hugging his arm across my waist so that I feel the daunting extent of him. His fangs tease me, setting me off, and my body builds to my point of release again.

"Bite me," I beg, gripping the pillow. "I want you to so badly. Just a prick."

He pants and licks my skin, breathing hard against my shoulder. "I want to so badly, but—"

"Bite me," I repeat. "Please. I can't stand it."

Bronx groans and sinks his teeth into the back of my shoulder, his body tensing with his climax. He licks the drops of my blood and presses his lips into the puncture wounds to staunch them with his kiss. My body hums and sings, so excited and satisfied by his giving into me that I can't stop myself from wanting to go at it again and again.

Bronx rolls off me onto his back, his chest rising and falling as he catches his breath. I shift to my side, and he pulls me the rest of the way on top of him, letting me straddle his waist while feeling the raw deliciousness of his body against mine.

I lick my lips and grin at him. "I'm ready for more."

He hums, gracing me with his sexy smile. "So insatiable. Hot. Sexy."

"Starved for you," I tease.

Shaking his head, he touches my cheek. "Not as starved as I am for you. Just that small taste...I know I can never live without you, dandelion. Ever."

"It's a damn shame that you ruined the chance to do so." Laredo's voice trickles through the room.

Scooping me up, Bronx wraps the blankets around us and launches from the bed. His fury about the intrusion only makes mine worse. When Bronx enters the living area, it's me who flies from his arms and tackles Laredo, shoving him into the floor.

Bronx doesn't allow me to stay on him long, releasing a deep, threatening growl, probably hating that Laredo prodded my nature enough to manipulate me into getting within a foot of him—while naked at that. The thought is the only thing that helps me keep my shit together. Also the fact that Bronx carries enough fury by the intrusion for both of us.

"Give me one good reason why I shouldn't punch your heart out," Bronx says, extending his fangs longer than I'm used to.

Laredo turns his head and looks at me. "Because Gwen needs me."

I glower. "You fucking wish."

"You don't believe me? Check the com device you've been ignoring." Laredo motions to the com device Bronx left sitting on the coffee table.

Punching Laredo in the stomach, Bronx sends him to his knees and zooms across the room to retrieve his com device. He taps the screen a few times and jerks his head up, glowering. It suddenly beeps in his hand, the screen glowing with an incoming call.

Bronx returns to my side and relocates me into the bathroom with him, leaving Laredo alone. I hop onto the counter and sit, searching Bronx's eyes as they flick across the screen. Accepting the call, Bronx touches the screen to project the video of his brothers on the blank wall. The three of them devour me with their gazes without looking at their brother. If I knew they were alone, I'd totally flash them my boobs.

"Gigi, lose the sheet. I need to look at your sexy body to cheer me up. Things fucking suck." Jameson pops out his bottom lip.

I tighten my mouth. "What do you mean?"

"We gotta steal Bronx. The board wants to meet with us all together." Mikkalo's eyes flash silver. "And because you're no longer considered...a soon-to-be true Royale, you can't join us. The board fears that someone could extract information from your mind."

"And they won't allow any of us to miss the meeting.

Viorica trusts her security too much." Everett remains expressionless. "I tried to get a hold of Rio, but he's unavailable."

"We even considered letting you hang out with Samantha and her match." Jameson squishes against Mikkalo to get a better view.

Bronx releases a low growl. "That son-of-a-bitch." His words aren't toward anything his brothers say but directed at Laredo. "He knew. How the hell did he know?"

I turn my attention to the bathroom door, imagining Laredo standing right outside to listen in on our conversation. I bet he's smug as hell.

"Laredo, we need to talk." Bronx hands me the com device and disappears. I'd follow behind him if it weren't for the scary-ass noises he releases. Also the sound of furniture getting thrown. It's not like I'd want to intervene anyway. Laredo deserves whatever Bronx does.

Jameson clicks his tongue, getting me to look at him. "So as I was saying, drop the sheet."

I laugh at his persistence, his teasing helping to suppress my worry from rising. Sliding off the counter, I peek into the bedroom and catch sight of Bronx and Laredo whispering in the corner of the room. I close the door, pouting my lip at Bronx and lean my back to it to make sure he doesn't open it while I give Jameson what he wants.

Setting the com device on the sink, I clutch the sheet around me. "You first, Jamie. Show me your goods."

He tips his head back and laughs in surprise. "Fuck, I love you."

Mikkalo twists his lips to the side. "Seriously, Gwen?"

"Would you prefer to show me instead?" I tease, biting my lip.

Everett smirks at me and the video feed blurs for a second. Filling the screen with his image, he whispers, "Ready?"

I laugh and nod. "Yeah."

I squeal with a high-pitched giggle as Everett props the com device on something and steps back. He quickly undresses, pulling his shirt off first, followed by dropping his pants. Excitement warms my thighs, and I devour his naked body, fully ready and willing to tease the hell out of me.

He strokes his cock a few times and grins. "Your turn."

I laugh again and drop the sheet. "You going to call your brothers?"

"In a sec. I want to have you all to myself for a moment longer." His eyes flash silver. "Turn around for me."

"Fuck. I miss her spankable ass already." Jameson's voice erupts through the room. "Hurry the fuck up, Bronx! The quicker you get here, the faster I can get back to our girl."

I peek at the projection over my shoulder, sweeping my hair from my back to give the three of them a better view.

Everett growls. "Bronx bit you?"

Ah, hell.

I stiffen and grab the sheet, covering myself up. Spinning on my feet, I meet Everett's narrowed eyes. He trails his gaze over my body in search of more bite marks. I pick up the com device and meet his smolder with my own.

"It was a bite and nothing more. He didn't drink and I asked for it. Don't you dare say anything. You know why. I'm in good health." I lock my gaze to Everett's on the screen, waiting for him to get himself under control. It's not like he didn't nip me before.

He sighs. "Okay, okay. I'm sorry. I just worry with everything."

"Well, don't. I'm fine."

"And you're about to be better." Laredo's voice trickles through the door before he gasps, probably getting hit again.

"Gwen, I brought you some clothes. Will you please get dressed? Laredo will be staying with you for a little bit. If he tries anything, punch his heart out." Bronx sounds like it pains him to even say the words.

Flinging the door open, I meet his broody gaze. "I'd rather be alone."

Bronx sighs. "Me too, dandelion, but I worry. I think Laredo has good enough sense not to try anything stupid."

I shift my gaze to his, and he smirks at me. I groan, hugging the sheet tighter. "I'm going to go back to bed." I point to Laredo. "You stay on the couch. I don't want to even have to look at you."

Bronx engulfs me in a hug and takes his com device from me, cutting off his brothers' connection. "I'm really sorry about all this."

"You don't have to apologize."

Squeezing me close, he kisses my forehead. "I'll be back. Call if you need me."

Bronx disappears like if he stays another moment, he might not leave me. Laredo clears his throat, staring at me from the doorway to the living area. I clutch the clothes Bronx brought me in my hands and step back into the bathroom.

"Gwen..." Laredo's soft voice stops me from slamming the door.

I look at him without a word.

"Can we talk? Please? I've been waiting so long for a moment alone with you." His smooth voice begs me, pleads with me, reminding me of a hundred conversations we've had before. All the nights we spent just hanging out while my brothers were out doing who knows what.

"I have nothing to say to you, Laredo," I say.

He frowns. "Will you just listen then?"

I sigh. "Will you leave me alone if I do?"

"Yes, I'll do anything you want. You're my dhampir."

Clenching my fingers into fists, I snap my gaze up to his. "I'm your no one, Laredo. Get it straight. You're nothing to me."

13

FACING THE PAST

THIS IS TORTURE. COMPLETE AND utter torture. I swear it feels like days have passed me by, but I know it's not even sunset yet. And I'm getting hungry. Bronx didn't think to leave me any of his blood, probably because he thought he'd be back by now.

My stomach growls for the millionth time, and I curl on my side and shove another cracker in my mouth. I don't want to eat them, but if I don't, I might go wild. The burning in my belly increases by the second so much so that even the fifth glass of water does nothing to help.

A small tap sounds on the door. "Gwen, are you okay?" Laredo asks without intruding on my privacy. I know he wanted to talk, but I just didn't have it in me right after Bronx left. So I hopped in the shower, got dressed, and did exactly what I told Bronx I'd do and went back to bed.

"Can I get you anything?" Laredo adds when I don't respond.

"You could bring me my com device," I say, propping myself up. "I think it's on the table by the door."

Soft footsteps pad away from the room, and I close my eyes and clutch my stomach, waiting for Laredo to come. Upon the quiet creak of the door, which he leaves open, I turn my attention away from the ache inside me and to Laredo, whose appearance causes a whole other pain in my very being.

Now that he crosses the room, his eyes flashing, his brows lowering on his forehead in concern, I can't help myself from remembering a few moments of our time together and how often he took care of me. I never admitted it before, but he was a lot more than just my blood source. He was my companion and the one always there after my dad died. But it doesn't excuse all the lies and secrets. Things I never thought I'd be able to understand because I thought he was dead—which is another thing I don't know how I'll get over.

"You don't look well," Laredo says, offering me my

com device.

I flop back with a groan. "You're right. I feel like shit."

Tapping my finger on the com device, which isn't technically mine but Jameson's, I stare at the screen with a picture of me in lingerie, smiling like crazy in one of our many blanket forts. A wave of warmth washes over me with the memory of that peaceful night a few weeks ago. I wish we could have more like it.

Everett's face flashes on the screen as the line connects. "Is everything okay?"

I purse my lips. "How much longer will you be?"

"A few more hours at least."

Tears uncontrollably burn my eyes, and I turn away. Why am I crying? This is so dumb. A few hours isn't even that long.

"Gwen?" Everett asks. "What's wrong?"

I swipe my hand across my cheeks, smearing the tears. I can feel Laredo's gaze boring into me, and it takes everything in me to ignore him and concentrate on Everett. "It's just...I'm so fucking hungry."

Everett groans. "Did you check the kitchen? Jameson always keeps a stash of things for you."

I stare at the empty thermos on the nightstand. It was the first thing I went after not long after Bronx left. "I need more."

"I'll see if I can break away for a few minutes to get you some—"

"Mr. Royale." A deep voice cuts him off. I glower at the screen at Mr. Goldman's interruption. "Ms. Royale can call the kitchen staff to bring her something. If she doesn't want to, then she can wait. You are not leaving until we're through. We all want to get out of here, you know."

That fucker.

Everett's eyes flash silver, and he looks ready to drop the line and come to me anyway. "Just hang tight, okay?"

A hand touches my knee, drawing my attention to Laredo. He slinks around the bed and steps into view behind me. He and Everett share a silent conversation with their eyes, and then Everett slowly nods his head.

"If you can't, it's okay. Take whatever you want and need." Everett doesn't have to say what he means out loud, because I already know what he's insinuating. And I hate it.

I sigh. "Just hurry."

The line clicks off, and I toss the com device on the end of the bed and pull the blankets over my head. I listen to Laredo's quiet movements as he exits the room, leaving me alone. My stomach roars again, causing me to curl in on myself. I thought I was bad before with how much blood I'd consume, but it has gotten worse and worse with my pregnancy. I'm almost afraid by how bad my blood consumption has gotten. If I drank this much before, I'd suffer blood bloat.

"Gwen, here. Sit up."

I smell Laredo's blood before I see it. It triggers the

memory of my dream last night, reminding me of a moment of teasing between me and Laredo...and his twin. Fuck. Just the thought pisses me off.

Throwing the blanket off my face, I meet him with narrowed eyes. He stops in his tracks, his eyes widening. He looks almost afraid. Extending his arm out, he holds a glass of blood as a peace offering. I'm so thankful he doesn't just hold out his bleeding arm. I don't think I could resist taking him up on his offer, especially finding myself already crawling to the edge of the bed to snatch it from his grip.

I gulp it in one swallow, the familiarity warming my insides. "Fuck."

"Is it okay?" he asks, risking to close the space to me. "I know how you hate using a glass. I just thought—"

"I hate that I still like it," I grumble. Staring at my bare feet, I hold the glass out to him. "Can I please have more?"

Laredo sits on the edge of the bed a few feet away from me. I can't take my eyes away from him as he bites his arm again and drips his blood into the glass, filling it all the way to the rim. Instead of handing it to me, he carefully tips it to my lips, not allowing me to chug it how I want until he's certain none will spill.

"I know you don't want to hear this from me, but you're as beautiful as ever, Gwen. I'd be lying if I said I didn't find comfort and relief being around you again. It killed me having to do what I did, especially because I've failed you. I accomplished nothing, and the Barons are still after you." Once again, Laredo fills the glass with blood. Shifting on the bed, he meets my eyes. "There isn't a day that passes that I don't regret my actions. I wish you and Livorno didn't have to pay such a steep price for my decision. Or your family. I am truly sorry. I hope you can forgive me and let me help you."

I bring the glass of his blood to my mouth because I need a minute to process his words. He sounds so sincere in his admission, but just because he's sincere and has regrets doesn't change the fact that I'm the one having to deal with the consequences. I'm the one who had suffered greatly. But then again, if he hadn't pulled this bullshit move, I'd have never met the Royales. I wouldn't be on the cusp of something scary-amazing with my unborn daughter. I would still live a nomadic life with my only purpose being preparing for my end at the fangs of a vampire.

"It going to take time," I finally say. "You hurt me. I grieved for you. I was so lost and alone, and I was so angry that you died. That you bit me with venom and changed everything." I lick my lips, my throat burning as I do my best to suppress my emotions. "But mostly, I don't even know what I should believe with you. I don't think I can ever trust you. You stole my memories. You hindered me by not allowing me to learn how to process my emotions. And you never let me know that it wasn't you alone taking care of me. I feel cheated that you and Livorno tricked me. You could've just come clean. Things would've been different."

"And risk you falling in love with him? Choosing him? You were mine, Gwen. Not his. It was bad enough that—"

I bring my finger to his lips and cut him off. "You're so fucked up."

"I suppose I am, and I guess I deserve my fate now, watching you with others, seeing how easily they share you. How you manage to love all of them equally. How you enjoy making love to them." Laredo slowly raises his gaze to me. "How happy you all are together, and now with the baby..."

"You should've told me that too." I whack him on the shoulder, ignoring his other comments. I don't even want to get into it about my relationships with the Royales. It's none of his business.

"You were so against sleeping with blood sources and managed to resist me for three years. I didn't think you'd give in so easily like you had, Gwen. I know it's in your nature to charm and seduce but..." His eyes flash silver. "But I guess there is more to it, and I don't know you as well as I thought I did. This you surprises me on so many levels."

"This me is who I always was, Laredo. The version you knew of me before was manipulated to be who you wanted me to be." I scoot back on the bed to lie on the pillows now that my stomach chills the fuck out. "And I'm still trying to manage. I'm so confused because of you."

"I can help you," he whispers like he's afraid of how I'll respond. "I can unlock your mind completely."

I clench the blankets in my hands. "Do you really think I'm going to trust you? And even if I did, I'm dangerous if I don't drink enough blood. I could hurt someone."

"You don't have to starve for me to do it. Do you not remember how close we used to be? I know you on a level unlike anyone. I think I can manage to do so in a few hours. Or maybe in your sleep. If you allow me in, I can connect with you. You have to be willing and open."

Except I can't.

I don't know if I want to.

I feel like I already know what I want to know. And being that close with Laredo again? No. It's not worth it. My guys wouldn't like it as much as I wouldn't. None of us trusts anyone apart from each other. Laredo still clings to this fake life we had together. He swears he was doing things to protect me, but he wasn't. He was doing things to protect himself and to possess me. I should've always known, considering he calls me *his* dhampir. It's never been something sweet or loving. He calls me what he thinks I am—a possession to him.

"I don't think so," I say, turning on my side to break his stare. "I don't care that much. It's merely an annoyance."

He sighs. "Gwen."

"No, Laredo. I still don't believe your intentions of being here. Now please, leave me alone. I've given you enough of my time. Thank you for your blood. I'll make sure to be more prepared, so I never have to ask you for such an offering again. If I wasn't worried about my unborn child, I might've just let myself turn wild on you. You did always used to say that the world would discover I can't be tamed."

Laredo isn't quick to leave. The weight of his stare burns over me, sending heat across my skin.

And then he growls.

I bolt upright to watch him disappear as the bedroom door swings open. One of the security personnel storms the room without saying anything. I scramble to grab the dagger on the nightstand and to get to my feet. The man sweeps his gaze over the room.

He closes the door and locks it. Pulling a small gun from his belt, he raises it and aims it at me. "Miss, I'm going to need you to drop the weapon and come to me."

I inhale a few short breaths, clutching the dagger tighter. He's crazy to think I'm going to do anything he says. "I think you're in the wrong room. Misters Royale will have your head for this mistake."

The vampire flashes his fangs, extending them enough that it'll surely be a kill bite if he manages to sink them into me. "You have five seconds. Don't fight. If you come quietly, we won't have a problem."

I open my mouth to scream only to have the vampire fly at me. He dodges around me and locks one arm to my waist and the other over my mouth. Panic rises in me at his cool breath blowing strands of hair from my shoulder.

"That's it. Easy now. It's a long run out of the building, and I don't want to hurt you, but I will if I have to," he murmurs.

I bite his finger, getting him to yank his hand. "Laredo!" I yell, knocking my head back into the vampire's chin.

He roars and spins me around, lifting me off my feet. The world blurs, and I screech. A threatening guttural rumble erupts through the air. Laredo appears a few feet in front of me, ready with a dagger.

Flashing his fangs, he says, "Let her go, brother."

Brother?

"What the hell, Laredo? I thought you were dead," the guy says.

"Let Gwen go. Now." Laredo steps closer. "She is not yours. She's chosen her beloveds and is bearing the future of her choice. I will not allow you to intervene."

"Fuck off. Thaxton—"

Laredo stabs the vampire from over my shoulder, sinking the blade into his neck. With his free hand, he grabs the front of my shirt and yanks me toward him. But the vampire doesn't let me go and stumbles with me, crashing into my back. Sharp fangs sink into the side of my neck, sending fire exploding through me. I screech at the sensation of his venom.

"Gwen, shit," Laredo calls.

The world blurs and shadows, and the ground falls out from under me. Cool arms wrap around me, and I blink through the haze as the strange vampire gets to his feet. Laredo drops me on the bed and zooms at him. The two of them break into a fight, punching and stabbing, biting and tearing at each other.

I tug myself toward the head of the bed to find my com device. I smack my hand on it, praying that it will automatically connect to one of my guys. A chair smashes on the wall over my head, startling me. I roll out of the way and fall to the floor, dragging myself under the bed. The pain grows more intense by the second.

A snarl prods at my human rationale, setting off my fear instincts like crazy. It suddenly cuts off before a thump sounds nearby. Blood splashes across my face as a head splats against the floor. I don't have a chance to move or scream or anything as fingers lock around my ankles and drag me out.

"Oh, my dhampir. Here, drink," Laredo says, biting his arm. "I'm so sorry I failed you and keep failing you. But don't worry. I'll do better."

I wiggle in Laredo's arms, thrashing against the pain. "Ev-Everett."

"You don't need your health keeper. I got you."

The world spins.

"Laredo, stop." More fear crashes through me as he carries me at vampire speed from the room. "Stop."

"We can't stay here. It's not safe."

I can't find the strength to fight.

I can barely keep my eyes open.

The last thing I see is a flash of light from the last rays of the setting sun.

"I should murder you for this." Jameson's angry voice drags me from the dark recesses of my mind.

Relief floods over me, and I pull myself together enough to get my body to cooperate to open my eyes. A cool hand touches my forehead. Everett's familiar scent engulfs me as he offers his arm to my lips.

My stomach twists, my body rejecting his blood offering. I cover my mouth with my hand, feeling strange wires stickered to my skin. Peering down, I glimpse the ultrasound belt around my waist, the soft light trickling from beneath the heavy blanket.

I swing my attention to the glowing projection on the wall, my heart fluttering like crazy. I don't think it'll ever not be mesmerizing to see the tiny fetus growing in my belly or knowing that in a few months, I'll get to hold her in my arms.

"I don't see anything concerning." Rio stands on the other side of the bed, peering over his tablet.

Bronx hovers beside him with his arms crossed. Looking to me, he offers me a pout. I don't think I've seen him this worried since the last time a fucking Baron bit me. "Are you sure? You ran every possible test? This is her second venom bite since we've found out."

"In normal circumstances, I'd be worried, but Gwen's unlike anyone I've ever encountered. Is there anything else you can tell me about the last time apart from her aversion to your blood?"

Everett touches my cheek once more, attempting to steal my attention away from Bronx and Rio's discussion about me. "Please try to drink. For me. The bite mark looks infected despite your blood work."

I purse my lips. "I feel worse too. Starving but...the venom. I'll throw up. I know it. I'd rather wait it out."

He sighs. "Laredo, you were right. Will you try to give her your blood? You're a Baron. She needs something. It's been far too long already. The bastard must've done more venom than a normal attack bite."

I shift on the bed and raise my hands, palms out. "No. Stay back."

Laredo freezes in his tracks, especially because Mikkalo releases a warning growl from his spot sitting in the chair not far from me. He's been so silent that I didn't realize he was here. He catches my gaze, and I reach for him. Jameson fills his place near the door, guarding it.

Mikkalo plops down on my other side and wraps his arm around my shoulders. I snuggle into him, burying my face in his chest. All I want to do is cuddle the hell out of all my guys, but fear still clings to me.

"You want to try me?" Mikkalo asks, biting his arm.

My stomach twists again, but I link my fingers around his wrist and bring his arm to my mouth anyway. I gently lick his skin, hating my reaction. I know it bothers him. Not because I'm averse to his blood, but because he can't take care of me in the way I need. I know how awful it feels. I hate that I can't feed him either.

Mikkalo groans and pulls me onto his lap to hug me. The ultrasound belt falls away, setting the room aglow. Rio quietly turns it off and disappears from the room. If he told Bronx anything I should know, Bronx will tell me.

"Thanks for trying, Gwen," Mikkalo murmurs, kissing me softly.

"I'm sorry. I just..." I let my voice trail off. I can tell by one look in his eyes that he doesn't want me apologizing for something out of my control.

"What about Bronx, Gigi? He's the only one you haven't tried yet." Jameson leaves his spot by the door, and I try not to react that he lets Laredo stand in front of it. Maybe it's because I'm in Mikkalo's arms, next to Everett, with Bronx hovering near. No matter, I still can't help my nerves.

I open my arms. "What about you, Jamie?"

He scoops me up. "I can't handle your rejection again. It makes me want to murder Laredo for failing to protect you. He should've never let anyone into our suite."

"The guy was dressed as security." Did I just say something that might sound like I'm defending Laredo?

By the look Jameson gives me...ah, hell.

"Still, Gwen. Jameson is right. I was just...there is no excuse." Laredo leans forward on the chair, resting his elbows on his knees. "It's quite clear that I'm incapable of giving you the life you desire and need. Not alone at least."

"Not with us either," I say, finally composing myself enough to glare at him.

"But maybe a few days longer," Everett says. He moves across the room and hands Laredo a cup. "Please fill it up and leave. It's better to give her some space right now, especially in this state. If she's emotional, she tends to be more reactive."

"I said I don't want his blood," I tell Everett. "I just want him to leave."

Jameson moves to the bed and sits down next to Mikkalo with me in his arms. Bronx joins us on his other side, and the three of them engulf me in a hug that steals my breath while also helping me breathe more easily. They take turns kissing me and smothering me with their affection until the door to the room clicks closed.

The bed shifts behind me, and Everett cages me between his chest and Jameson, not even caring that he has to sling his legs over his brother's to fit with us. My stomach roars, the potent scent of blood wafting through the air. I clench Jameson's shirt in my fingers and try my best not to react.

But I can't help it.

I'm starving.

Everett holds the glass of blood over my shoulder to Jameson. Before he can even reach it, I snatch it away and gulp it, running my finger along the inside in an attempt to get every last drop. The four of them stare at me in silence, but no one says anything right away. I can't tell what they're thinking, but I'm sure they feel badly that I must rely on someone else because the Barons are complete assholes.

I swipe my hand over my mouth and blush. "Disgusting."

Mikkalo tips his head back and laughs. "Especially because I can't wait to kiss you." Leaning in, he brushes his lips to mine, giving me the affection he knows I crave.

"You're setting the bar too high, Mik. Someone get our girl a towel to wipe off that bullshit." Jameson tugs his shirt off and tosses it to me. "So savage."

Bronx bumps him with his shoulder. "Then hand her over."

"Fuck no. I plan to bang the hell out of her right now. You guys can stay or go, but the cure for my need to destroy everyone who crosses my path is the kind of distraction only our girl can provide." Jameson says the words so seriously, I half expect for my panties to rip free before I can blink. He smirks at me. "What do you think? A little extra love?"

I laugh and pat his cheek. "Always, Jamie...but first. What's going on? What time is it? Where are we?"

Jameson groans. "Always with the questions."

Bronx slides his arms around me and pulls me into his

lap. I rest my head on his chest with my legs over Jameson and Mikkalo. Everett links his fingers through my hand, rubbing his thumb over mine.

"Gwen, we were preparing for war." Bronx rests his head to my temple. "Viorica and the board members don't want to even consider the Barons for the board seat. They think they're planning a hostile takeover of the territory and have the numbers and power to do it."

I groan. "They're going to ask you to give me them."

"That's what the meeting was initially about, but we made them see reason. Viorica is an intelligent woman. She didn't come into power by accident. She knows that once you give someone like the Barons something small, they'll try to take more and more."

"So what happens now? Will the board cancel the challenge?" A blip of hope rises within me.

Bronx sighs. "Unfortunately no. It's up to me to win and take Freeport's heart. If I can't, then a battle is imminent. But no matter what, my brothers will get you through this. We have a backup plan."

My chest clenches at his words. "A backup plan?"

"Laredo will teach them how to be unstoppable vampire rebels. He will take my place."

14

BLOOD OF THE PAST

"I BROUGHT YOU SOMETHING." EVERETT carries the biggest container I've ever seen of vampire blood. I gawk from the shower and wipe my hand over the glass to see if it's magnifying my vision or something. "I know you have to be starving."

Mikkalo slides his arm around my waist, slipping his fingers low enough to tease me while pressing his chest against my back. Bronx and Jameson were called away again, Bronx as our coven leader and Jameson as our head of communications, which mixes up our schedules a bit. But I don't mind. My guys have cared less and less about keeping our time together straight. If someone needs more of my attention, we compromise.

"Bring it here. We're not ready to get out." Mikkalo continues his exploration of my soapy body, running his fingers higher to my breasts.

"And don't forget the glass. I'm wild, but I'm not a total beast. Get naked while you're at it. I've missed you. I could use all the distraction right now, but especially to drink...that." I twirl my finger at the jug, knowing exactly where it came from. It looks like enough to weaken a vampire, so I can't help but wonder if Laredo is lying down somewhere or feasting on a bunch of donors. And fuck. I don't want to think about that. "If Bronx can pretend he's not drinking someone else by letting me have his attention, then I can do the same."

"Hell yeah," Mikkalo says. "Let's do this. I can't stand the sound of her hunger. Even the shower and music doesn't muffle the noise enough." My cheeks burn, and Mikkalo twists me around and squats down to kiss my belly. "You gotta go easy on your mama, baby girl. She doesn't like to be as wild as I love her to be."

My heart spills with love, the warmth cascading in good waves.

"Now go to sleep. I'm going to distract your mama," he adds.

I crack up and pat his shoulders only to have him get on his knees to lift my leg to his shoulder. Everett enters the shower and steals the moan from my lips, stretching over Mikkalo's hulking form to do so. My giddiness turns into blazing lust, and I clutch onto Everett because my legs weaken at the sensation Mikkalo creates with his mouth, flicking his tongue so fast that I reach my climax in a matter of minutes.

"Your turn, brother," Mikkalo says, smiling. "I want to feed our girl."

I can't even catch my breath as Everett scoops me up and presses my back into the cool shower wall. Mikkalo stands behind him with a glass of blood, carefully holding it to my lips while Everett slides his raging boner inside me. I accidentally slosh blood over him with my scream of pleasure, but he doesn't care, moaning as my lips find his shoulder to suck and lick it from his skin.

Mikkalo releases a hum of a breath, spilling some blood over his arm. He offers it to me, and I automatically sink my teeth into his skin, my senses fooled into acting on my carnal desire to get what I need from my guys. He purrs deep in his throat with his excitement and desire, his relief that I don't recoil as his blood mixes with Laredo's donation.

He pours a bit more, turning our hot shower session into something that could be found in one of Bronx's sexy movies. Everett moans and kisses my throat, working his mouth down to my shoulder. He guides my body to his over and over, sliding in and out of me harder, faster, deeper in a rapid pace to drive me wild.

Mikkalo plays with my breast with one hand while slipping his other hand lower to rub my clit to add more pleasure to this hot moment. He nips the back of my shoulder with his teeth, and I gasp and practically whimper for him to bite me.

It's Everett who does, sinking his fangs just deep enough into my skin to arouse another orgasm from my body. My muscles pulse and tense with hot intensity, and Mikkalo pours blood onto Everett, encouraging me to bite him too.

The second my teeth bite into Everett's skin, he cums, thrusting hard enough that I bang into Mikkalo. Mikkalo holds me in place until Everett slows and eases away. Kissing me softly, he smiles against my lips and whispers he'll get my things ready.

Disappearing, he leaves me with Mikkalo who takes over for him, bending me over in the shower to slide into me from behind. I brace against the wall through another round of pleasure, loving the sensation of Mikkalo's body bumping against mine, how his balls slap against me just right and how sexy he sounds with his release.

He doesn't let me stay bent over for long and scoops me up to kiss me the entire time we finish bathing and rinsing the spilled blood from our bodies.

"That was so hot, Gwen," Mikkalo murmurs, turning off the water.

"I feel so good. Perfect. You always know exactly what to do to help me." It's me who wraps a towel around him, yanking him close to kiss me again.

With the heat of our bodies pressing together, his soft tongue tasting mine, his strong arms creating what feels like the safest place in the universe, I easily push the rest of the world out so it's just me and Mikkalo and our love radiating from our souls.

If a soft knock didn't sound on the door, I'd consider seducing Mikkalo again for another round of pleasure.

"Hey, dandelion. We're back. I need to discuss a few things with you." Bronx sounds like he doesn't want to interrupt us, and it pains him to do so. "Whenever you're ready. I don't care if we're late."

Mikkalo grabs another towel and wraps it around me, guiding me to the door. Just because Bronx says he doesn't care if we're late doesn't mean we actually should be.

Opening the bathroom door, I find Bronx, Everett, and Jameson sitting on the bed in a quiet discussion, looking over Jameson's com device. I search to see if Ashton is around, but I don't hear any signs of him. Neither do I hear Laredo.

"Laredo's in Ashton's suite," Jameson says, turning his attention to me.

I shrug my shoulders. "Okay. Good."

Jameson's eyes suddenly light up, and he hops from his spot and materializes in front of me. Running the pad of his thumb over my bottom lip, he stretches my mouth for a second before leaning in to kiss me.

"You bit Mikkalo," he says, lowering his voice. "Are you feeling better?"

Heat bursts in my face at the memory. "I did. Everett too."

"Fuck yeah." Jameson unfastens the buttons on his shirt and thrusts it away from him before I can summon the nerve to tell him how they got my crazy ass to do so. "My turn. Come here."

Mikkalo roars a laugh and play-punches Jameson from over my shoulder. "It took a lot more than asking to get her to do it. We might've taken a blood bath—er, shower."

Jameson cocks his head and gives me a long once-over. "Gigi, you pulled a Caine? How...fucking hilarious." He chuckles and cups my cheeks, talking about the creepy vampire at Night Palms Castle that I caught nude in a blood bath. "We might have to wait a few more hours to take that kind of donation from Laredo."

I crinkle my nose. "I don't actually want to bathe in his blood, no matter how mad I am at him. The bastard hasn't even faced me after the bullshit..." I glance at Bronx and sigh. "We're still not done discussing things."

Because I'm not cool with his arrangement. What if this was Laredo's plan all along? It was convenient for him to suddenly arrive after the Barons announced they would challenge the Royales for their board seat.

Bronx clenches his teeth, flexing his muscles, knowing I might be on the verge of snapping at him. "I know, Gwen. And we will. Just not now. We have to get to the gathering. All of the city heads from every region are arriving now. We must make our appearance and gain support."

I grimace. "What? I thought I could just stay here. I'm no longer Blood Vowed to you. You said it yourself that it might cause problems for me since other covens will want to question why you no longer find me worthy."

Mikkalo releases a soft growl. "She's right. We're staying. You made that decision without us, so I'm making this one without you."

"Mik, you're our head of defense." Bronx straightens his shoulders.

"I was also supposed to be first in line before you handed the position over to the asshole who our girl hates." Mikkalo tightens his hold on me.

"You agreed with me," Bronx snaps.

Shit. Things are turning personal with their flaring anger.

Everett senses it and manages to intercept me from between his brothers. Jameson materializes in between them and places a palm on each of their chests. They step closer, testing Jameson's strength to keep them apart, and Jameson shoves them.

"Knock this shit off before you scare our girl." Jameson swings his fists and hits Bronx and Mikkalo in the guts one after the other too quickly for them to react as they refuse to take their glares off each other. It's enough to knock some sense into them. "We all agreed, but it is only a backup in case. It won't come to that. I believe in you, Bronxy. You have our girl to fight for, who I know you'll never fail."

I can't stop the smile from crossing my face at his comment. I love it when they say stuff to make the other feel better.

"He's right," I say from Everett's arms. "That isn't going to happen, especially because I didn't choose Laredo. I chose you. You can't honestly think he's capable of replacing you, Bronx. You have one hulking, muscular, tall, handsome, sexy-ass body to fill."

Bronx puffs a breath through his lips. "I just worry."

"Don't." Breaking away from Everett, I close the space to him. I motion for the rest of his brothers to come to me, so I'm caged in their delectable, muscular circle. "None of you should worry. For one, the board obviously supports our coven. And two, I support you. I won't let anything happen, even if I have to reveal who I am."

"Absolutely not, Gwen." Bronx purses his lips.

I cock an eyebrow. "It would ruin the Barons' plans."

"And destroy your future." Mikkalo squeezes my hand. "So no. It's not worth it. None of us could live with ourselves if something happened to you and our daughter."

"Yeah, Gigi. That isn't how we'll change the future for us. We don't need the world to know how truly wild you are." Jameson cups my ass, totally taking advantage that I'm in a towel. "Save that for us. In private. Bedroom or shower. Blood bath or not."

I sigh and rest my head to Bronx's shoulder. "I hate this."

"I know." Bronx kisses my forehead. "But it'll be over soon. I won't let you down."

I bob my head, a dozen thoughts whirling through my mind. I don't say it out loud, but I won't let Bronx down either. Nor will I let down Jameson, Everett, and Mikkalo. They're not the only ones who can come up with a backup plan.

Now, I just have to figure out mine.

15

VAMPIRE BALL

I THOUGHT THE GATHERING IN Crimson Vista was a huge event. It pales in comparison to the ballroom at the Blood Match Center in Midnight Valley. I stroll next to Bronx with my arm intertwined with his with Mikkalo at my other side. Jameson leads the way with Everett protecting our backs.

From my spot tucked safely between them, I can't see much of anything apart from the dazzling rainbow lights that dance across the walls and reflect over the glass ceiling like stars come to earth in a brilliant lightshow. Music pulsates through the air, the sound vibrating over my skin. My white gown turns red with the shift in lighting, and I spin on my heels, trying my best to distract my guys to get them to loosen up enough to let me have a look around the grand room.

Jameson snatches me by the waist, spinning me out only to reel me into his arms again. He slides his fingers through mine while placing his other hand on the small of my back, swaying our bodies to the upbeat tempo of the music.

Mikkalo cuts in, sweeping me into a dip that sends my leg into the air. I laugh and hold onto him, nearly forgetting what a great dancer he is. We haven't had much time to just do something fun the last few weeks that this feels so good. I don't even care if I might not have as good of rhythm or that I sense vampires watching. All I care about is that all four of my guys smile at me and take turns to show me the affection I crave.

Bronx tugs me to him and kisses me so passionately that I can't stop from gripping his lapels. His hand slides down to the small of my back. He pulls me to him, setting me off with his scent.

"Can I show you off, dandelion?" he whispers in my ear. "I want to prove to these bastards that you're still my girl."

I ease away from his broad chest and peek around him

at the sea of people—a blend of vampires and donors—chatting and dancing, some feeding, but all looking to be having a good time. And I want to so badly, but a part of me freaks out a bit.

"Or maybe we can sit, and you can let me hand-feed you?" he adds, sounding a bit nervous now that I haven't immediately responded.

I bob my head. "That sounds nice. I could use something more to eat. Maybe some water."

Jameson steps up beside us. "I'll handle that. Bronx, you find Gigi a table to sit at. Possibly away from...everyone."

"Or I could pick." I grab Bronx by the tie, making him laugh.

Everett and Mikkalo excuse themselves to greet some of the other covens and to scope the room for possible threats. I search around for Ashton but don't see him. I'm too nervous to ask Bronx where he is because I'm not so sure I can keep my voice down.

"Gwen!" a deep voice calls, drawing my attention to Declan. I haven't seen him since Silas had bitten Ashton, and a part of me feels awful that I haven't asked to see him. "Over here."

I shift to look at Bronx. "Can I sit with my brother? Looks like they're all donors."

"Anything you want." Bronx's words surprise me.

I half expected him to tell me that we could invite Declan to join us instead, so he could keep me far away from everyone. I'm thankful he doesn't. I just want to pretend this is all normal and not some gathering before the possible start of a territory war.

Declan rushes from his seat and engulfs me in a hug, spinning me around. "Fuck, Gweny. I've been worried. No one will tell me shit. I tried to visit with you, but your suite was empty. I thought you left without a goodbye because of Ashton."

I tip my head back and force myself to smile, hoping I look as okay as I can be. "I'd never abandon you intentionally like that. I was...sick." I touch my stomach. "My prenatal health keeper wanted to monitor me for a while because I couldn't bring myself to eat."

Declan lifts an eyebrow. "Are you up to eating now?"

"Jamie's bringing me something. Can I join you?" Shifting my gaze, I assess the table he pushed from, wondering if they're donors from Macon's coven. My jaw nearly drops at the sight of two girls each holding children in their arms—one an infant and the other a toddler. And now I can't stop looking.

"Yeah, of course. I was just talking to a few donors from Ombre Noire. They live with the city head coven...and are related to one of the coven members. Can you believe it? Macon said she—"

"Mr. Royale, it's a pleasure to see you again." A man materializes next to Bronx and extends his hand.

Declan's eyes widen for a split second before he composes himself. Without a word, he links his fingers through mine and tugs me the few feet to his table and away from Bronx and the vampire. Bronx doesn't follow me, though I can tell he wants to. Instead, he watches me along with the handsome vampire with darker hair and eyes than Bronx. The guy remains expressionless, studying me and Declan as we both sit down.

A tiny hand locks into my hair and yanks, surprising the hell out of me. I yelp and freeze, unsure of what to do with the tiny human now intent on stealing a chunk of my hair. The baby giggles the sweetest laugh, and I turn my head and smile at her.

"OhmyGod, I'm so sorry," the girl holding the infant says. "Jade, let go of her hair. That's not nice."

I laugh and swivel in my seat completely. "It's fine. I should get used to it. I'm expecting a baby in thirty-twoish weeks according to my health keeper."

Her eyes widen and she drops her gaze to my stomach and back up again. "But you're a Blood Match."

Touching my stomach, I say, "Technically yes, but currently no. I have to wait until after my pregnancy."

"How?" she asks before realizing the obvious answer to her question. I don't think I've ever seen someone blush so hard. "I mean, I've never heard of a pregnant Blood Match."

"Things just happen," I say, trying not to give extra information. "It was a bit of surprise. Unexpected." I cringe. It was supposed to be planned according to the story Viorica told the board.

"It was shocking as hell," Declan says, bumping his shoulder to mine. "I never imagined Gwen would get pregnant."

"Why? Are you the dad? Do you not know how babies are made?" This comes from the other girl. She looks nearly identical to the girl next to me, who is surely her twin. "Austin says that the cities purposefully don't teach sex education, so it's okay if you didn't know." I don't even know how to respond. She looks on the verge of informing me with whatever information she knows about sex. Turning to her sister, she adds, "I bet she is strictly a blood source to her mister. Not everyone gets lucky like Jewel had."

"What about you?" I ask, now suddenly desperate to change the conversation. "Is that how it happened?" I motion toward Jade. "I mean, was it a surprise. She's adorable by the way."

Both of the girls widen their eyes. The one closest to me tips her head back and laughs. "Oh, no. Jade is our cousin and Dougie is...the brother of our other cousin's coven mate."

Sounds complicated. "That's interesting."

"Want to hold her? Jade seems to really like you. I could use a break for a bit to eat before my food gets cold." The girl automatically hands Jade over, not giving me a chance to think about it.

I sit frozen with the baby in my arms, her chubby fingers tangling in my hair as she leans in and gives my chin the wettest kiss in existence.

"Dana, Fallon. What did I tell you two? If you need help, just ask. You can't hand Jade to a stranger." A brunette with big blue eyes materializes with a guy as big as Bronx by her side. "I'm sorry...Ms. Royale. It's not often the girls leave our city."

The tall vampire releases a low growl, startling me, and I jerk my arms out to hand the baby back to who I think might be Dana before the guy attacks me. Except Dana isn't prepared, and the baby slips from my hands. I screech out, fear colliding through me. Three intense growls vibrate across my skin. Then four more.

"Fuck. It bit me." Jameson rests on his elbows, holding the baby against his shoulder.

The brunette snatches Jade from his arms.

I hop to my feet and grab her hand. "I'm so sorry."

Her eyes flash silver at me, and I realize what a huge mistake I've made putting my hand on a vampire. A woman I had no idea was one...actually, she's the warmest vampire I've ever felt in my life. The only times my guys feel warm are after the shower or a round of hot sex because I heat them up. But she looks like she hasn't participated in either.

"Jewel, come on. Let's finish our rounds so we can go back to our suite. It's getting late for the kids." A blond vampire guy with green eyes takes the baby from her. He cradles Jade on his shoulder and bounces on his feet.

I can't stop myself from inching a bit closer. He looks like a natural. I wonder if he's also a health keeper. "Jewel?" The name sounds familiar. I sort through my thoughts for a moment, finally recognizing where I heard it from. "Sammy Vaduva spoke of you."

My comment stops the vampires from disappearing.

"Fucking Samantha and her big mouth," a black-haired vampire says. His eyes flash silver, and he runs his hand through his tousled strands. Turning to me, he asks, "What nonsense did she say?"

Bronx's muscular chest presses into my back as he towers behind me. Jameson and Everett take places at my sides, and Mikkalo steps right in front of me, blocking my view. I nearly smack Mikkalo on the ass for interrupting and putting an end to my conversation, but then I remember where I am and what I'm supposed to be. Vampire customs mean I shouldn't speak to anyone, but damn it, does it annoy me that they pull this card now.

"Mr. Divine, you may ask Ms. Vaduva yourself. Now, if you'll please excuse us, Gwen must eat. I'm sure you've already heard of the news." Mikkalo shifts his arm and reaches his hand back to grab mine. "Her and the baby's health is important to our coven."

A small intake of breath comes from Jewel. Using the tall guy's shoulder, she stands on her tiptoes in an attempt to look at me. "You're the pregnant Blood Match whose blood brother's unauthorized transformation ruined your Blood Vow."

"Babe, not a good time." The dark-haired guy swivels and looks at Jewel. "None of our business, either."

She narrows her eyes and ignores him. "I'm so sorry that happened to you. I couldn't even imagine. I'd be devastated if my Blood Vow to the Divines had been canceled. Are you okay?"

Did she imply she made a Blood Vow to all the Divines? Sammy had mentioned that we had a lot in common. Now it makes me study the Divine Coven and Jewel more.

"If you ever want to talk..." Jewel's voice trails off as she stares at my guys. Turning to the black-haired Divine, she pulls him close to whisper in his ear. "Dude, see if you can arrange something. I want to talk to her more."

"Beautiful, I don't think that's a good idea right now, and I'm sure Kingston and Austin would agree. I'm sure the Royales won't agree anyway. It's better to stick to ourselves and our current alliances in these uncertain times." This comes from the tall guy. "The defense heads have been discussing prep for war. It involves them."

"War? Then I definitely want you to arrange a meeting. Diego, she looks so sad," Jewel says. She glances at the blond vampire. "Austin, do you really agree with them?"

I try to remain expressionless as they blatantly whisper in front of me, using a tone humans aren't supposed to hear. I shift on my feet and glance to Everett. He shrugs his shoulders, and I realize he doesn't hear them. I don't think any of my guys do. They're waiting for them to return to our conversation. It's a vampire thing. No one considers it rude to suddenly exclude other covens from their conversations. And fuck...I think the Baron venom made my dhampir side worse.

"Actually, I'd love to talk sometime." I brace myself for their sudden scrutiny at my late response and interruption of their conversation. But I can't help it. My curiosity gets the best of me, especially with the baby. I've never been around children much. The most experience I have is holding a kid for a few minutes during one of the shit show situations the Barons created. "Jade is so adorable. Maybe you could give me some tips. None of us has experience with infants."

Jewel tilts her head. "What of the father? Most humans don't allow their young near vampires, and it sounds like you include the Royales in your desire to learn more."

Fuck. I don't even know how to respond. I hate the idea of anyone believing that I'd ever sleep with someone else outside of my guys, but it's the only believable explanation since vampires can't procreate with humans, which I'm supposed to be.

"Seriously, babe," the vampire, Kingston, whispers. "You're going to get us in trouble. These guys have a blood feud with a back-world coven."

"But if we can help—"

Jewel and Kingston vanish at vampire speed. Austin and Diego glance at each other and then motion to the girls at the table, getting them to leave their seats. If my guys weren't caging me in, I might try to go after them. There is something strange about the Divine Coven, and my curiosity won't allow me to let it go.

"Well, that was weird." Declan draws my attention to him sitting at the table. "Macon did say they were a bit unconventional but that the board lets them get away with it because they ended the last territory war against their own coven leader and Blood Rebels."

I've heard my guys talk about this. I know several regions fell a few months ago, but hearing my brother mention Blood Rebels...it scares me a bit. The ties the Barons have to Blood Rebels are strong. They had an entire community at their disposal. It's how Laredo knew so much about the elders and the rebel life enough to trick my brothers.

Bronx releases a small grumble. "Careful, Declan. People are listening."

"Yeah, brother. I could hear you across the room." Ashton startles Declan by placing his hands on his shoulders. "I hadn't realized how obnoxious your voice really was."

Declan shoves his chair back in an attempt to collide into Ashton, but Ashton is too quick to move. I dodge between Mikkalo and Everett to get a better view, taking care to keep the table between my brothers and me. It hurts that

I hesitate.

The same hurt I feel crosses Ashton's face. "Hey, Gweny. You look beautiful. How are you feeling?" I know he knows about the venom bite.

"I'm better. Still have a little aversion. Is it okay to get closer or...or are you still suffering from blood hunger?" I twine my fingers together. I want so badly to hug him.

Bronx nudges me. "I think he can manage."

Ashton smiles, flashing his fangs. He catches himself and covers his mouth like he doesn't want me to see them. "Bronx is right. The first day was rough, but I have much better restraint."

No one has a chance to stop me before I dash forward and crash into him, nearly tackling Ashton to the floor. He laughs, bracing on the table, his strength crazy now that he transitioned. He lifts me up and spins me around, making my heart incredibly happy in this moment. I'm so relieved that he's okay.

I bury my face in the crook of his neck, catching the strange new fragrance of his skin. My stomach screams, erupting with a fiery pain. I dig my fingers into his shoulders, attaching myself to him, so he can't push me away.

And then I bite him.

The world blurs as Ashton relocates me. His blood fills my mouth, quenching the blood hunger igniting inside me. My dhampir side doesn't care that he's my brother. All I want is to drink his blood to get my body to chill out.

Two hands lock onto my waist, and I release an unexpected guttural growl from my throat. "Damn. What do we do?" Mikkalo's voice sounds from behind me.

"Just let her. It's okay." Ashton gently touches my back. "I don't think she'll kill me."

Everett shifts my hair to look at my face. "I don't know about you, but I kind of prefer this over Laredo. I know it bothers Gwen to rely on him...and technically, Ash is of the Baron bloodline. Obviously our blending of blood didn't affect things too much."

"Fuck, you're right." Jameson gets super close, meeting my eyes. "Though I don't care where the blood comes from as long as you don't starve. I know you'll attack me with that sexy, pouty mouth soon enough...even if it's not to bite me."

"Man, she's my sister," Ashton says, growling.

"Get used to it, brother. You're a Royale now." Mikkalo slaps Ashton on the back. "When we get all this shit settled, you can have our suite in Crimson Vista. We plan to return to Night Palms Castle anyway. Will be nice to always have someone in the city we can trust."

"I look forward to it," Ashton says.

I finally manage to ease my mouth away from Ashton's neck. Embarrassment floods through me. I can't believe I just drank his blood. Or bit him. Talk about something I never thought I'd do. But hey, it's one way to assure I don't get blood lust.

"An-n-n-n-d you survived." Jameson chuckles, quickly snatching me away from Ashton. He twists me in his arms and frowns at the sight of my face. "Damn, Gigi. What a beast." Lifting me above his head, he kisses my belly. "You know I'm going to remind you of this for eternity, mini-beast."

I laugh and wiggle in his arms until he brings me back down. "Don't you dare. She can't help it."

"Obviously neither can you," Mikkalo says. "Makes me curious, though. Think if Ashton bit one of us with his venom it'd encourage you to get over your aversion sooner? I mean, the blood shower worked."

I twist my lips to the side, my mind automatically wandering to that sexy, crazy, and a little bit freaky lovemaking session with Mikkalo and Everett. "I'm willing to try. I'd prefer to drink from you."

Jameson groans and bonks his head to my shoulder. He grazes his fangs along the collar of my dress, nipping the fabric. "Of course you are willing, Gigi. You're not the one getting bitten by your brother. Venom hurts."

I snap my teeth at him, getting an inch within his ear. "I understand, Jamie. I wouldn't want to either...but I guess I won't be biting you next. Sucks because I wanted to so badly."

He narrows his eyes. "How badly?"

I laugh and pat his cheek. "There's only one way to find out."

"Which you'll never know, and I will," Everett says.

He materializes behind Jameson and hooks his arm around his neck. Jameson growls, flashing his fangs, dipping his head down in an attempt to bite Everett. Mikkalo chuckles and tugs Jameson's arm free from me, restraining him. Bronx howls a laugh. I expect Bronx to grab Jameson's other arm to leave me clinging to him, but instead he pulls me away.

"I don't think so, Ev. I got our girl this time." He extends his own arm to Ashton. "All right, Ash. Time to test your venom, brother. As coven leader, it should be me. Consider this a lesson."

I can't stop the laugh from bubbling from my throat. Their playfulness eases my nerves. This all feels so normal despite the circumstances. I might not get a Blood Vow with my guys but having Ashton here, knowing he'll always be, brings me joy and love. It feels right.

I snuggle against Bronx. "You're so sweet, Bronx. I'll make sure to give you all the extra attention. Anything you want."

Everett groans and drinks me in as Bronx holds me. "Damn. So sexy."

"Damn is right." Mikkalo drops Jameson's arm and steps closer. He touches my back between my shoulder blades. "I want to be back up. I'll experience a hundred venom bites if that's what it takes to take care of you."

Jameson growls and punches Mikkalo in the gut, sending him jumping back. "No fucking way. It's going to be me."

I wag my finger at him. "I'll consider it, Jamie. I think Bronx is enough for now. I don't want you all to suffer on my behalf."

"I'll suffer if I don't," he murmurs.

Mikkalo smacks him on the back of the head. "I'll guarantee it."

The two of them break out into a play fight, and Everett steps closer, keeping them away as they wrestle. "Probably should hurry, Bronx. Now's good when they're distracted."

Bronx waves his arm, drawing Ashton's attention away from the fight. He stands in silence, probably wondering how the hell to handle this entire situation. Bronx adjusts me to cling to his side. Draping his arm over Ashton's shoulders, he gives him a little shake.

"Come on now, Ashton." Bronx guides him away a foot to face the wall. "I want you to extend your fangs all the way. You'll know you're releasing venom when you feel the heat."

I can't stop from gawking at Ashton extending his fangs completely. His eyes flash crazy silver. Without waiting, he locks his hands to Bronx's arm and sinks his fangs in. I gasp at the sight, a wave of anger rushing through me. It's the strangest thing. I know Bronx asked Ashton to do it but just seeing him comply sets me off.

Bronx stiffens at my reaction.

I try to smack Ashton, wanting him to get away. Then I release a low noise from my throat as I stare at Ashton's mark on Bronx.

"Whoa, shit. Get her out of here Bronxy," Jameson says, dragging Ashton back. He shields him, raises his palms out. "She's turning into a wild beast."

"Looks like our girl doesn't like anyone else biting us," Everett says. "Interesting how possessive she is with us, even against Ashton."

"Damn. Now I don't want to be your backup, Bronx," Mikkalo says. "You might want to listen to Jameson."

"Hey, Gigi. Chill the hell out, okay?" Jameson says, snapping his fingers in my face.

I growl, the deep, unsettling sound echoing through the air. Gasping, I cover my mouth. Embarrassment washes through me. "Shit. What's wrong with me?"

"Nothing, dandelion. You're perfect...but we'll be back," Bronx says to his brothers. "I'll call if I need you."

And like that, the world blurs.

Bronx presses my face into his broad chest, silencing any and all noises that escape my mouth. My mind has trouble catching up with my body. I jerk away from Bronx's chest to peer around the dimly lit room. A soft moan trickles through the air from behind one of the privacy curtains.

I freeze at the strange new scent. It's not human blood. I know it. My sense of smell goes off like crazy.

Bronx doesn't have the chance to stop me before I thrash away from him and run at dhampir speed to the small room. Latching my fingers to the curtain, I yank it open. A deep snarl reverberates through the air at my intrusion. Bronx yanks me away, flipping me over his shoulder. We both stand in shock at Kingston and Jewel stepping from the room, armed and ready to fight.

"Whoa, shit," I whisper, gawking at the ruby blood dripping down Jewel's chin. My eyes dart to Kingston's unbuttoned shirt where a definitely not vampire bite ravages his pec. I know a dhampir bite when I see one. It's too deep from super strength to be human.

Bronx steps back, his muscles tensing and flexing against me. "Fuck."

Kingston slides his com device from his pocket and taps the screen. "Hey, bro. Get Austin. We have a problem. The Royales saw Jewel."

I raise my hands, fear crashing over me. "Wait. Wait. Please. I'm sorry. I smelled your blood. I couldn't stop myself from intruding."

Kingston snarls again, standing protectively in front of Jewel.

Jewel grabs Kingston's arm and drags him back. She locks her arms around his broad chest to hold him in place. "Let her talk, dude. Look at her face. Blood."

I swallow my nerves and turn from Bronx to Jewel. "You're a dhampir."

Jewel loses color. "You know because you were a Blood Rebel."

Shaking my head, I risk stepping closer. I take a breath. "I was, yeah, but not by choice. I know because I'm a dhampir too."

16

THE DIVINES

OKAY, SO TALK ABOUT A room full of broody, buff, and extremely hot vampires. Apparently dhampirs have a type. It blows my mind, seeing Jewel with her coven. She's been playing the role of a vampire for who knows how long. A part of me feels a bit jealous that she pulls it off. Another part of me worries that she'll get caught. If she gets caught, it could be me next.

Shifting in my seat, I sit across from Jewel in the sitting area of our suite. She perches on Austin's lap while I rest against Bronx's chest, concentrating on the thrumming of his heartbeat on my back. I want to make a joke about our similarities with our guys, but each of our covens are so on edge with each other, this whole meeting turns more awkward by the second.

I clear my throat for the third time, trying to decide what to say first. I have so many questions and don't even know where to begin or if she'll even answer them. "So..."

"You know what? I have an ice breaker, because this shit is tense as fuck. I'm dying to know...is your girl wild as fuck or is it just ours?" Jameson leans over Bronx's shoulder and kisses my neck. "Not that there is anything wrong with her beastliness. We just—fuck, we can't take her anywhere without her getting into trouble. Like a few days ago, she launched herself at Macon and bit him. It's getting worse." He grins at me. "And better, at least for me. Shit, I love you, Gigi."

Diego tips his head back and roars a laugh. Reaching to Jewel, he slides his fingers under her chin so that she looks up at him. Blush stains her cheeks, and her eyes flash silver, an indecipherable expression crossing both of their faces.

"Fucking A. Jewel is a sexy-ass savage." Kingston bounces her on his knees, holding her in place with one arm. With his other hand, he tugs down his shirt to show off the mark she left on him. "I mean, look at this. This is her love bite, and because of it, we rarely go anywhere anymore...but that was my vow to her. Bed for life."

"Dude!" Jewel snaps, growing redder by the second. I thought her cousin won the award for deepest blush, but I'm pretty sure it belongs to Jewel. "You can't put that all on me when you beg. Now enough."

Mikkalo chuckles. "Can't blame you, Kingston, though I love when Gwen surprises me. You never know what to expect."

I swivel and point at him. "Don't instigate. This is not that kind of meeting. If you want to trade stories, you better arrange your own time."

"Yeah, guys." Jewel looks at Kingston and Diego. "Keep it up and you're out. Austin will be the only one allowed to stay."

Smirking, I narrow my eyes at my guys, glancing to Mikkalo, Jameson, and even Bronx. "And Everett will be the one to stay with me."

"Damn health keepers," Kingston and Jameson say at the same time.

Clearing my throat, I draw Jewel's attention to me. "Actually, maybe we can send everyone out. If you're okay with it, I think it might be easier to talk. I can already tell Jamie's on the verge of playing a game of twenty questions with your coven."

"A hundred questions," he murmurs.

I fake-glare at him. "I don't think I could survive the embarrassment of anything they'd want to discuss."

Play-growling, Jameson flicks my shoulder. "And leave

you two alone to plot? Hell no."

Bronx shifts me off his lap and takes my hand. "If this is what you want, and it's okay with the Divines, then we'll give you as much time as you need. It'll give me a chance to bring up some region-related things. I have a few things of my own I want to discuss with Jewel's mates."

Jewel shifts to the Divines, and the four of them have a silent conversation with their eyes. The three coven brothers then turn to each other, their eyes flashing silver. I can't read any of their expressions as they decide what to do. It's Jewel who gets to her feet and struts around the coffee table to sit beside me.

She smirks. "You know they're all going to eavesdrop, right? This isn't going to be real privacy."

"I'm used to it. My guys can't help it either, but at least this way we might avoid their unnecessary commentary. It's just—I can't believe you're a...you're like me. I've wondered my whole life if I was destined to be alone to figure this shit out and now I have someone who I can compare things with." I ease from the arm Bronx rests on my shoulders and motion for him to get up. He kisses the top of my head and goes to his brothers. They join the Divines and head into the hallway, but I know they won't go far.

Jewel combs her fingers through her hair and ruffles the dark, shiny strands. "Your life seems as complicated as mine was. This Baron Coven—were you with them before? Did they mind manipulate you?"

I don't know how much I should really say, but Jewel seems honest enough, and we both carry huge secrets about who we are that I let myself open up a bit. "Not romantically. I'm a descendant of a woman who their prior coven leader bit a long-ass time ago. They tried to stake a claim on me, but neither my dad nor I ever signed any contracts. They're a bunch of assholes waging a war for not getting their way."

She sighs. "Seems like that's always the case."

"Your coven's why the Royales ascended into the region head position?" I already know the answer, but I want to hear it from her.

"Loyalty is a tricky thing among vampires if you haven't realized it. I just happened to be in the middle of something that was bound to happen. Vampires can't stay ghosts to the system forever if they want power within the territories." She shifts her gaze to the door. "Which is why the Baron Coven registered, right?"

"Only some. I don't even know how many. All I know is they've ruined my family. Broken bonds I had with my brothers. And now they want me and my child. They want future heirs because they think dhampirs are the key to shifting power in the world."

Jewel frowns at my words, her blue eyes blinking a few times as she tries to remain expressionless. "Friggin' shit balls. My niece..." She lets her voice trail off. Without her having to say the words, I think Jade might be a symptomatic carrier of the dhampir gene too. I don't think she's worried about herself at all and only that cute little baby's future.

"Jewel," the soft voice sounds from the doorway. Austin runs his fingers through his blond tresses. "I'm sorry to interrupt, but we have to go."

Her eyebrows shoot up on her forehead. "What? Why?"

"We can't get involved in this impending war. It's not safe for you or Jade. We need to find..." He closes his eyes for a split second before rushing closer. Lifting Jewel in his arms before she has a chance to protest, Austin brings his lips to her ear and whispers, "We need to find Orl—our brother. Brayla's waiting with the girls."

Neither of them realizes I hear the words, and I decide against asking why Austin's other brother isn't here or who Brayla is. Instead, I hop to my feet and cut the two of them off. There are still so many questions I want to know if Jewel has the answers to.

I raise my palms to them. "Wait. Wait, please. Just a few more minutes. There is so much we still haven't talked about."

Jewel puckers her lips, her forehead crinkling. "I'm sorry, Gwen. We make decisions together in my coven regarding the safety of our family. If my guys think it's unsafe, then I agree with them." It looks as if it pains her to say the words.

"Beautiful. Austin. We gotta go." Diego looms in the doorway with Bronx behind him. I don't see Kingston or the rest of my guys.

Jewel reaches out her hand to me. "Stay safe, Gwen. As soon as we get our city prepared, I'll reach out to you. This won't be the last time you see me...just, for now. Until things become more certain."

Bronx and Diego shake hands, and Bronx says, "Thank you for the offer. You can contact us through Rio Mercy. He is our most trusted ally and Gwen's obstetrician."

"Hell, okay." Diego turns to me. "We wish you well with your pregnancy, Gwen. It can't be easy having this thrown at you like this."

Austin makes a strange noise in his throat. "The likelihood of your future heir being symptomatic is rare, so don't worry about it. It'll most likely take after its father."

Shit. They don't know.

Bronx clears his throat and shakes his head at me, knowing I'm a second away from spilling our secret about vampire and dhampir procreation. A huge part of me wants to argue with him and do it anyway, to warn Jewel of the possibility, but then my stomach twists, stealing my breath. We can't let anyone else know. Not yet. Not until the Barons are dead and out of our lives forever.

Jewel disappears with Diego and Austin, leaving me with Bronx. He closes the door behind him and scoops me up, engulfing me in a hug that ensures I won't fall apart at any second.

"Gwen, I'm sorry you didn't get more time," he murmurs, combing his fingers through my hair to pull it from my face. He caresses his lips to mine, savoring the taste of my mouth for a moment. "But I understand where they're coming from. Their city is just as new as our region, and they're thriving. They have children to look after."

I bob my head and sigh, resting it against his. "I know. And I know we'd do the same. It just sucks."

"We only have to get through the next few days. Once I win the challenge tomorrow, things will get easier. Laredo—"

I cut off his words with a kiss. "I don't want to even think about him right now. Only you. I know you'll kick Freeport's ass. You'll prove just how powerful you are, and then we can focus on taking out the rest of the damn Barons. One by one and together."

His lips stretch at my comment, and he grins against my mouth. "Always together."

Strolling toward the bedroom, Bronx kisses me tenderly, exploring my mouth with the softness of his. He slips his tongue over mine, caressing it with deep, even strokes that burst tingles through me the longer we kiss.

I unfasten the buttons on his dress shirt and glide my fingers over his taut chest, mapping out every inch of his skin. Shrugging from his shirt, he continues on to unbuckle his belt, kicking off his pants as we reach the bed. Lust darkens his beautiful brown eyes, and he sets me on my feet and spins me around to unzip the back of my gown.

I shiver at his fingers trailing down my spine while he bends into me, kissing my shoulder. He grazes his fangs over my bra strap, tugging it down with his teeth. With a flick of his hand, he sends it dropping to the floor to join my gown. I spin in his arms and meet his lips for another kiss.

Setting me on the bed, Bronx hooks his fingers to my panties and pulls them off. His eyes roam over my body, his gaze tracing all of my curves, his hot desire prominent as his erection presses against the fabric of his boxer-briefs. My eyes dart to the circular fang punctures on his arm left by my brother, and my stomach growls embarrassingly loud in a moment where all I want to think about is Bronx inside me, how good he makes me feel, the heat of our passion, and how just the thought of touching me makes him hard with lust and feral need.

"Want to try?" Bronx asks, knowing that I didn't get much earlier because of our confrontation with the Divines. "The venom hasn't worn off just yet."

I bite my lip and shake my head. "No, not yet. I have another idea."

Arching up, I lock my fingers to his hips and tug down his underwear to expose his erection to me. His body flexes as I link my fingers around the base of his shaft and bring his tip to my mouth and glide my tongue around. There's something about taking care of him this way that satiates a part of my need to feed him. Just taking control and giving him my attention, tasting the sweetness of his skin, knowing how much he enjoys the feeling of my tongue and mouth licking and sucking him turns me on. He claims that masturbation is a stress-relief for him, but I'm pretty sure this is better.

His whisper of my name, so soft and like a breath of pure desire and love, fills me up with heat and warmth, pushing away all the bad feelings that lingered with me from earlier.

I roll my tongue on the bottom of his shaft as I suck him as far as I can into my mouth. Bronx moans and stands between my legs, digging his fingers into my shoulders. I rub and lick him, cupping his balls in my palm to run my thumb over the smooth skin. I want so badly to give him everything he wants. To hear him moan. To make him cum for me. I want nothing more than for him to feel every ounce of pleasure I have to offer.

"It feels so good. You're incredible, dandelion," he murmurs, playing with my hair.

I peek up at him watching me and smile, warmth blooming across my cheeks. "And you're delicious. Just what I need."

He chuckles and moans as I work over him with my mouth, sucking a bit harder and bobbing my head to pull his hard cock in and out of my mouth until he clutches onto my head and whispers he's about to cum. I don't pull away, tasting his sweetness flood my mouth, a flavor not unlike his blood. I slowly ease away and pinch his ass with a smile, loving how his face lights for me with the love we share.

Dropping to his knees, he decides to return the gesture, pulling my legs onto his shoulders to kiss the sensitive skin between my thighs. I moan under the zinging sensations he creates with his mouth, his tongue flicking my clit just right until I orgasm for him.

Using his broad shoulders, he nudges me higher up on the bed and adjusts himself between my legs. He leans forward and steals my breath as he thrusts into me so deeply that only the pillows protect my head from hitting the headboard. His raw desire lights silver in his eyes, his face turning serious as he meets my gaze.

I link my fingers to his neck and pull him closer, kissing him deeply with each of his desperate thrusts. The passion we share burns through both of us, warming his cool skin. I nip his shoulder and work my mouth up to his neck to leave a hickey on his skin. Sliding his hand under my ass, he pulls me impossibly closer and rocks over and over into me that I burst with small, loud moans that match his rhythm. Pleasure cascades over me in wave after wave, my body wanting to ignite all over again.

The sensation of our bodies meeting again and again turns my mouth desperate to take more, to experience everything I can from Bronx. He nips his lip with his fangs, testing to see how I react. My body trembles with anticipation. The droplets taste slightly different but good, the Baron venom still in his system enough to turn my body wild.

I use my dhampir strength and roll him off me so I can climb on top. I rock my body to his, twisting my hands into my hair to keep it out of the way to give him the best view of my body. I moan with my nearly-frantic movements, the sound of my voice increasing in volume as he rubs his hands over my nipples while I ride him hard and fast, experiencing the intense pleasure he elicits inside me.

His hands travel down my stomach and to my ass, and he guides me faster on him, my body bouncing up and down with his movements. I don't even care how loud I am. I let go of all my nerves and just enjoy this moment driven by our carnal need to be together.

Bronx's fingers tighten on my ass cheeks, his nails biting into my soft flesh. It sets my body off, and I lean down and sink my teeth into his shoulder. He grunts with his climax, banging my body against his a few more times as I drink.

"You make it impossible to ever want to leave this room," he whispers, stroking his hand up and down my back. "I can barely think of anything other than you."

Easing my mouth away from my mark on him, I say, "Good. That's what I wanted. Just me on your mind."

"And how beautiful you are," he whispers, rubbing his thumbs to the curves of my breasts. "How smart and strategic you are. The way the scent of your skin sends my body wild. The taste of your lips. Your throat. Your breasts." He kisses his way down with his words. "Your stomach and hips. That perfect love button of yours."

I giggle and shake my head. "Keep going and you'll get exactly what you want. I'll make sure of it." Linking my fingers through his, I stretch his arms over his head and lock him in place.

"Is that so?" he teases.

"You're mine, Bronx. All mine."

He pulls the blankets around us, not giving a damn that the party goes on without us. All he cares about in this moment is me and him and our closeness.

We're so wrapped up in each other that neither of us hears the door open. Nor do we hear the soft footsteps until it's too late.

"Mr. Royale," Freeport says, extending his fangs with his glower. "I thought by now you'd come to your senses."

Bronx releases an intense growl and grabs a dagger from the nightstand.

Freeport raises his arms in surrender. "There is no need for that. You'll have plenty of time to fight me tomorrow...unless you hear me out. I'd like to make a deal."

"A deal?" I cringe at the sound of my voice echoing through the room.

Freeport risks stepping a foot closer to stand tall in the doorway to our sleeping quarters. He meets my eyes. "Yes, my infuriating intended. A deal. I'm sure neither of you wants to continue with this challenge that you'll surely lose, but I cannot back down and show weakness."

"Fuck that. Get out! We don't make deals with assholes." Anger rushes through me, and I shift off Bronx, taking the sheet with me. "Now get out!"

Freeport doesn't budge, crossing his arms over his chest. If Bronx didn't grip my arm, I'd fly out of bed to attack the intruding douche. Why Bronx doesn't? I wish I knew. I flick my gaze to Bronx with a silent question furrowing my brows. Bronx doesn't react, keeping his eyes locked on Freeport while Freeport trains his creepy stare on me.

Inching closer, Freeport narrows his eyes. "It seems Mr. Royale wants to hear what I have to say, my beloved. If you want me to leave, you'll have to make me. But I must warn you, if you fail, I'll take you away this instant. It is your choice, Gwen. But so you know, this bargain is with the Royales. Not you."

This asshole.

Bronx envelops his arms completely around me, pinning me to him to stop me from launching off the bed to tackle Freeport. Freeport is so confident and full of himself that he will underestimate my capabilities. I could end this right now.

But Bronx refuses, still not looking at me. He keeps the blankets securely around us while remaining armed and ready to fight if he has to. "Go on, Mr. Baron. What is your deal?"

"Bronx," I whisper-hiss, wiggling in his embrace. I'm about to lose my shit. "Don't give him even a second of consideration for anything he has to offer. He will say anything to get you to comply. The only reason he barged in here is because he's getting scared. He knows you'll kick his ass."

"Dandelion, please." Bronx squeezes my hand. His gaze finally turns to mine, his eyes seemingly searching the depths of my soul. Yet, his expression remains nearly unreadable.

I sigh and turn to Freeport. "Give me one good reason not to yank your heart out right this second and be done with this bullshit."

Freeport takes my comment as an invitation to enter our sleeping quarters.

It's me who growls to get the asshole to keep his distance.

I flick my gaze past him and wonder where the hell Laredo is. Or my guys. I expected them to hang out nearby.

Freeport straightens his shoulders. "I'll be honest. I never imagined that you'd have the gall to go through with the challenge for the board seat, Mr. Royale. I'm rather impressed that you think your power matches mine."

"It does," I snap. "You're so full of yourself to think you're even an ounce as good as Bronx."

Freeport tightens his jaw and ignores me. "With the new predicament of canceling your Blood Vow with Gwen, if you win the board seat, you'll endanger her life. As you've probably figured out by now, Gwen carries the regenerative trait that all vampires do. She cannot die naturally or age past maturity. Do you really want to jeopardize her? Others will notice, and she will only grow stronger." He almost sounds concerned but not for me. There's no way.

I sit up, keeping the blanket in place to stay covered. "Then maybe you should've thought about that before having Silas bite Ashton." I glower, daring him to argue.

Freeport snarls, flashing his fangs. "That was not on me. Your brother...is as reckless and uncooperative as you. He deserved the fate of an outcast."

"But it *is* your fault! You transformed him." Fury replaces my anger, and I clutch the sheets hard enough that I start to lose feeling in my fingers. It takes everything in me not to launch at him. I know I could break Bronx's hold in this moment. Freeport stabbed at my dhampir nature so much that I have an all-consuming need to destroy him. "You made him a deal he was incapable of following through with. My brother is stupid. You set us all up for this bullshit."

Freeport takes a step back, his eyes blinking with flashes of silver. He's nervous, and he should be. "Perhaps you're right, but that is beside the point." I knew it. He only agrees with me because of it.

"Then get to the point, Mr. Baron," Bronx snaps, speaking up. His muscles ripple around me. "You've been here long enough."

"The point is that I don't want the knowledge of the dhampir mutation to get out as much as you don't. I'm sure Gwen will do something that she can't take back if we proceed. So, I'd like to make a deal with you in regards to Gwen to prevent that from happening. I'll call off the challenge if you agree to entrust her in the Baron care until your heir comes of age. At that point, you'll have enough power to take over the board and can manipulate the law in your favor."

Bronx tenses, his chest rumbling with an inaudible threatening growl. I don't think I've ever felt him tremble with his anger, and it prods at my fear instincts a little bit. "You want me to take over the board? Bullshit. I'm not stupid."

Freeport puffs out his chest and cracks his knuckles at his sides. "Under my authority. You will work on my behalf, not unlike how Donor Life Corp was before the recent downfall of Mitchell Divine. But we won't fail. We'll grow stronger as a territory. Agree to my terms, and you can keep your dhampir and heir thereafter, but there is one more thing to make this work."

I study Freeport in silence, waiting for him to continue. My mind is already set against his deal.

He's crazy if he thinks my guys are going to entrust me in their care or that I'll go through with that willingly. I'd rather risk exposure.

"You're wasting time, Mr. Baron," Bronx mutters. "Just say what you want."

His eyes turn to me, his jaw twitching as he prepares his words carefully. "I want Gwen to bear another heir but with me. I want to continue the Baron dhampir mutation."

Oh, no he fucking just didn't say that.

"Are you kidding m—"

Bronx covers my mouth with his hand, trapping me in my place. He risks me biting him to get me not to respond. "And you'll drop out of the challenge? Leave us alone for good?"

Freeport nods his head, a small smug smile tightening his mouth.

He looks ready to point and laugh at me because Bronx doesn't respond with an automatic no. It drives me crazy. The edges of my vision shadow the longer he fights to keep me in control.

"Upon my heir's eighteenth birthday, you will hand her over and you can have Gwen and yours," Freeport responds, extending his fangs a bit at his condition. "She will be betrothed to my next in line."

I thrash so hard that I finally break away from Bronx's hand to yell, "No fucking way!"

Freeport ignores me. "I will permit visitations for your coven to our rebel nests at any time. You will not be kept from Gwen or your heir. Consider this to be a formal permanent alliance with the benefit of our protection. You will not regret it."

"And if it's a boy?" Bronx asks to my utter dismay. I can't believe he continues to humor such a horrible deal.

"It won't be. I assure you." Freeport tilts his head and proffers his hand. "Do we have a deal, Mr. Royale? I need an immediate answer. The rest of your coven thinks more with their hearts and will fight you. You must stand strong and flex your power as their leader. Let this be your first lesson to a fruitful, powerful future."

Bronx shocks the hell out of me by abandoning the bed to extend his hand out to Freeport. "You must bow down to me at the challenge. The board cannot know that we've made prior arrangements."

I nearly lose my shit.

"Deal."

Freeport disappears as I scramble to my feet. Bronx intercepts me and hugs me to him, kissing me to stop any sort of reaction. I jerk away from him and swing my hand, slapping him across the face.

He drops me to the bed and puts space between us. "Gwen, calm down."

"How can I calm down?" My voice rises with shock and anger. I clench my fingers into fists so hard that I break the skin on my palms, sending rivulets of blood streaming between my fingers. "You just arranged a deal to hand me to the Barons for eighteen years. Eighteen years! You agreed to let him force a child on me. How could you do this? How could you even consider this?" I point to the door, flinging my blood at him. "Get out. I want you out."

"Gwen, please. Take a breath. I don't want you to attack me before I can explain." Bronx shuffles a foot forward, his arms open with his need to embrace me. He braves my wrath with a tight jaw. "I love you. I love you with everything in my entire being. You have to believe me that I'd never go through with this."

I blink my eyes, trying to get my oncoming tears under control. My heart aches at just the thought of his agreement with Freeport flitting through my head over and over. "Then why agree to such a thing at all? How could you even without intent?"

"Because I didn't trust that he wouldn't attack if I denied him. We can use this to our advantage." He locks me in his stare. "Trust me. This is a good thing."

I clutch my twisting stomach. "Fuck. I'm going to be sick."

I slump on the edge of the bed and cover my face with my hands. It takes everything in me to calm down. My mind and heart battle over this whole fucked up situation. I know

Bronx is doing what he thinks is best, but making even a fake deal with the Barons will have consequences. He might have just doomed me.

"Dandelion," Bronx says softly, touching my back. "Look at me."

I shake my head, my chest clenching, my heart so heavy it feels as if I'll lose it and die. "Get your brothers. I need them."

"Gwen."

"Get your brothers!" I scream.

Bronx disappears.

17

THE DEAL

I DON'T KNOW HOW TO feel or think or even what to say. I'm trying so hard not to be pissed off at Bronx. I know he had his reasons, and he was trying to stop from fighting and possibly losing his life against Freeport, but damn it. This is all so fucked up.

Mikkalo, Bronx, Everett, Ashton, and Laredo speak in low, rumbly voices in the corner of the room. I thought I was angry, but I'm nearly certain Mikkalo and Bronx would have tried to murder each other if Everett didn't get in the middle. Ashton remains stone-faced and Laredo steals glances in my direction.

Jameson slides me onto his lap and spins the two of us to face the wall. He couldn't speak without yelling, so I invited him to sit with me. Because I feel sick as fuck. My stomach clenches in persistent knots. I hate being angry at Bronx. I hate it.

"Gigi, can you kiss me, bite me, fuck me, do something to distract me," Jameson whispers. "I've never wanted to murder my brother like I do right now. I don't know what the hell he was thinking to engage at all with the Baron asshole. He should've called us for backup. And the deal? I know he doesn't plan to hold up his end, but shit. He's now jeopardizing more than himself."

I hang my head and lean more into him. "I'm scared." It's all I can manage to say.

"I won't let anything happen to you or our daughter or any of our future children. Do you understand? I will steal you away and go into hiding if I have to. I have connections in other territories. We could just—"

"I can't leave your brothers. It has to be all of us," I whisper. "I can't imagine having a life apart from any of you."

"I'm just not sure I can agree to this. Bronx crossed a line." He swivels and glowers at Bronx.

"Whenever you're ready and will let me speak to you, I will explain why I disagree. I made a decision that would benefit us the most, Jameson. What you're thinking about—it's dangerous. It'll jeopardize our coven even more."

Jameson snarls. "Bullshit! This isn't about our coven. It's about our family."

Before I can react, Jameson sets me on the bed and launches at his brother. My dhampir nature kicks on, and I catch the back of Jameson's shirt just as fast and swing him toward the wall. I link my fingers to the front of his shirt and rip it open, bringing my mouth to his bare chest.

I bite him.

Jameson groans and slides his hand under my ass to get me to wrap my legs around him. "You're playing dirty, Gi-gi."

I lick the blood drizzling from my bite. "You wanted a distraction, and my aversion is pretty faded with the venom bite Ashton gave you."

"It was Laredo, but whatever. I need more from you." Jameson pulls my body harder into his.

The world blurs around us, and I gasp as my back hits the cool bathroom wall. I didn't even realize Jameson ripped off my panties on the way in here, and his cock throbs against my slick wetness, ready to push inside me.

"Fuck, Jamie," I whisper, resting my elbows on his shoulders, clutching his face in my hands. "What are you waiting for?"

Jameson growls under his breath and cocks his head to

the side. "That."

Bronx stands in the doorway to the bathroom with his arms across his chest. His eyes soften when they meet mine, and he opens and closes his mouth like he has something he wants to say to me but doesn't know what or how or if it's even worth his breath.

My chest clenches in agony, the pain of our confrontation with Freeport still tender and raw, cutting through me at the memory.

Raising my hand, I motion for Bronx to come in and close the door. I don't mean to cut Everett and Mikkalo off, but they're in far better control of their behavior, and Jameson is a bomb ready to explode. And Bronx? This is between us.

"Gwen, Jameson," Bronx starts, stepping closer. "I'm sorry how I handled the situation."

"You should've let our girl handle it and just backed her up. I bet she wanted to, and you were too damn stubborn to trust that she can devour the whole fucking vampire population if she wanted to, but especially that dickhead Baron. Now would've been the perfect time with her out for their blood." Jameson's fangs click near my ear, the sound of him extending them unintentionally turning me on. "But fucking no." Jameson twists so he's the one with his back to the wall, using me as a shield or a buffer between him and his brother.

I hug Jameson tighter. "Thanks, Jamie. I wanted to

murder Freeport."

"Which would have made things worse!" Bronx's voice echoes through the small room. "You two act too much on your emotions that you fail to see what I'm strategizing to do. I would never put Gwen in danger. You have to trust me, damn it. Mikkalo and Everett do. Ashton and Laredo. They get it."

"That's not the point," Jameson and I say in unison.

Jameson huffs a breath. "Just the fact that you thought it was even an ounce okay—even if you didn't mean it—to offer our girl up for eighteen years to build a family with assholes that have tormented her all her life—fuck, Bronx! Even if Gwen decided she wanted to take the Barons up on their offer, you can't make deals regarding her future heirs, even if they aren't yours too. It makes me worry about what will happen to this beautiful, precious baby girl if she doesn't share your blood."

Agony crosses Bronx's face a second before his expression turns into rage. He flies at the two of us and yanks me away from Jameson. Strong arms engulf me from behind, and Mikkalo shields me against the wall as Bronx and Jameson blur in a fight. Glass shatters as Jameson hits the mirror before the tiled wall cracks under Bronx's hulking body slamming into it.

Everett, Ashton, and Laredo enter the tiny bathroom and manage to pull the two of them apart. I've seen Bronx lose control, Mikkalo too, but I haven't seen this side of

Jameson, and it guts me catching his eyes solid silver. He's always been passionate, but that passion turns him deadly.

"Jamie, please," I whisper. "You're scaring me. I know you're angry—"

"I feel like he betrayed us, Gigi. He's my brother, and I know you're in love with him—"

Bronx growls from Laredo's hold, cutting Jameson off. "If you'd listen, you'd know that I am using Freeport's fake defeat to my advantage. The challenge will happen tomorrow, brother. I will fight Freeport. He will die."

"So all of this bullshit to buy you a few seconds?" Jameson asks, clenching his fists. "And what happens if you fail?"

"You will ensure our girl and our baby girl have the life they deserve," Bronx says softly.

Panic and heartache crash over me in a waterfall of fear that leaves me breathless. Sobs escape my mouth, my eyes burning with tears. It was one thing to have Bronx strategize using me to his advantage. It's another thing that he thinks about the possibility that his strategy won't work. And then what? I can't lose him. I don't care that we don't always see eye-to-eye. I don't care that we both piss each other off sometimes. We get through it. We work it out. But this? No. I can't allow it.

Shaking my head, I break from Mikkalo's loving arms, now feeling cold without the quiet comfort he brings me. "You are not putting that shit on any of us, Bronx. We're in this together. I will not let you take on this bullshit on my behalf. If I have to reveal what I am to protect you, then I will. I don't care anymore. This isn't all about me no matter what you think. I know you're afraid of what the world would think of me or how it'll try to use me. But the world—no, the fucking universe—should tremble in fear." I bring my hands to my stomach. "I bear unimaginable power, remember? Born from the Royale line and me. It makes me stronger than ever."

Laredo lets Bronx go, drawing my attention to him. "Gwen, no. I didn't go through all of this to have you act so carelessly."

"Fuck off, Laredo! This isn't your choice. Stay out of it," I snap.

No one has a chance to react or fight or move.

Laredo rushes me, scooping me into his arms. Sinking his fangs into my shoulder, he injects me with his venom, sending my head spinning.

The last thing I hear is Bronx yelling my name.

Laredo kidnaps me.

The world turns dark.

"She's growing stronger and more anxious by the day. Her blood consumption is twice as much. I think it's time to separate her from the Gallaghers." The soft voice trickles through the air.

I remain still in bed with my back facing the door.

"She will put up a fight. I don't think she's ready." Laredo's light footsteps cross the room. He rests his hand on my shoulder, brushing my hair from my neck. "Not to mention the fact that they won't let her go either. They don't understand the lifestyle she needs. Grayson threatens to murder me if she drinks even a drop more than what he thinks she needs. He'll hinder her."

I try not to shiver under Laredo's fingertip trailing up and down my arm. I count my breaths, hoping he doesn't realize I'm awake. If he does, he and whoever he talks to will disappear.

"That's what I'm afraid of, brother. The more time you allow me to spend with Gwen, the more I realize how marvelous she really is." The other voice sounds so familiar, but I can't pinpoint who it belongs to.

"Make no mistake. She is mine. Do you understand?" Laredo releases a low growl. "I did not risk everything to have you try to take her from me."

Another far deeper growl rumbles through the air. "Perhaps we should give her the choice."

"Never."

The world shakes, dragging me from my memories. I jerk upright and flail my arms, trying to hit anyone within arm's reach. Strong fingers grip my wrist and yank me forward, and I crash into a solid, muscular body.

Laredo restrains me to him, holding an arm across my stomach and another one an inch away from my mouth.

Blood drips from two puncture wounds in his flesh, setting off my belly to scream like a beast.

"Take a breath and drink, my dhampir. You'll feel better when you do." His cool breath tickles my ear.

I buck harder and attempt to head-butt him, but he leans out of my reach. "Laredo, I'm going to kill you for this!"

Laredo silences my yell with his arm, forcing his blood into my mouth. My stupid body automatically latches onto him, my hunger forcing me to drink what I need. Laredo moans from behind me, his body awakening to my closeness. It's enough to get me to pull back and sink my teeth deep into his arm. He doesn't loosen his grip like I expect but only tightens it.

"Don't tease me, Gwen. It's taking all my restraint not to remind you of all the good times we've had." He shifts my body on his lap to move me between his legs so that I can't feel his excitement. "I want to remind you that there is life outside of the Royales."

I dig my nails into his skin, pulling back. "I don't care if there is life outside of them. Any life without them is a life I don't want. Now, let me go, asshole."

"I'll let you go once you calm the hell down." Laredo offers me his other arm, acting quick to adjust his hold on me. "You're out of control."

"Because you kidnapped me!" I screech.

Flipping me off him, Laredo pins me in place and covers my mouth with his hand. He bows forward to close the space between our faces and meets my eyes. Silver light reflects in his gaze, lit by my feral nature on the verge of consuming me completely.

"I'm sorry I had to, but you left me no choice. I can't allow you to make such rash, dire decisions based on what you think your heart wants." Laredo releases a low growl, pushing his weight more into me. "I will not allow you to reveal what you are to save the man who put himself in such a position. It is not your job to clean up and handle Bronx's mess."

"But it is," I say, my voice mumbling against his hand. "And you have no right to try to stop me."

"The hell I don't, Gwen. I've devoted my life to you. I'm not letting you go so easily. It was one thing to come to terms with the fact that your heart opened for others—that I can accept. I can also accept that you've chosen to take on their coven name and bear one of their children. All of those things are decisions you can make. But choosing to reveal you're a dhampir? Purposefully wanting to risk your entire eternity and that of your child? You're not thinking clearly. It's more than your life you risk. You risk many others. You'll break the hearts of those who live to care for you. You'll be the reason for the end of the Royale line." Laredo flashes his fangs at me. "You don't actually want that, and neither do your mates, but you all will end up destroying each other with your love-clouded decisions."

"So what now? Do you really think you can imprison me forever?" I struggle beneath him, waiting for him to lose focus long enough for me to strike him in the balls. From my position, I know we're in some sort of room—maybe a basement—and I can see the top of one door.

"Just until the challenge ends." Laredo searches my face. "When the fate of the Royale Region is revealed is when I'll figure out what to do next."

Anger and fear radiate from my heart, cracking me open piece by piece. "You can't do this Laredo. If something happens to Bronx—I'll destroy you. I'll kill every damn Baron, the board, the whole damn territory. No one, and I mean no one, will stop me."

Laredo's eyes flash silver, his stern face softening. "I'm sorry, my dhampir. You can threaten all you want but some things are just out of your control. Once you realize it, you'll learn how to better plan for your eternity."

I close my eyes, thinking of a dozen ways I can murder Laredo from my position, but all of them involve overpowering him. In this moment, I'm not so sure that I can. I've never felt him this strong in my life. I don't know if it's because of his sheer will to keep me away or that I'm currently an emotional mess, but either way, my dhampir abilities are refusing to manifest.

Laredo takes my reaction to him as defeat and eases his weight off of me a bit. "I hope you know that I hate that it came to this. I really thought I could work something out with the Royales. I thought if I worked on you enough, you'd remember what a good life we had together before my damn brother failed to get you away from Crimson Vista safely."

I tense at his words. "Laredo, this life you keep mentioning was a fucking lie. It was far from good. You manipulated me into thinking that you were good for me, but all you did was steal pieces of me away until I was left with only the things you liked."

"My dhampir, that's not true. I only took away the things most dangerous to your survival and things you begged me to make you forget." Laredo frowns with his words. "I hardly think making you forget about the Barons or my brother or the pain caused by your family is something you should hold against me. You asked me to do it."

Fury ignites inside me, burning through my heart. "That's bullshit!"

He growls softly. "I'll prove it. Let me into your mind. I know you have it in you. Our connection runs soul deep."

I heave a few breaths. "Are you crazy? You expect me to open my mind for you? You'll manipulate me into compliance."

"I won't, Gwen." He props himself over me, supporting himself on his elbows. "I've never done that before. I wouldn't."

"You did! I know it. I felt it. I remember it." Tears burn my eyes as a dozen thoughts swirl through my mind of

Laredo's silver gaze capturing mine and how he'd manipulate me. "You even murdered Jonathon because I chose to sleep with him. How can I believe you now? You betrayed me, Laredo. You claim that you're okay with the Royales, but you're not. You think I belong to you like some sort of possession. I remember the argument you had with your brother."

"My brother? My brother is why you're in this mess. He hated having to be me. He's the real reason your brothers were separated. He didn't go through with the plan. He called the authorities to ensure they'd get picked up instead of just separating you from them for me." Laredo's breath mingles with mine, his chest pressing against me with his heavy breathing. "And I never—and I mean, never—would have killed someone you chose to give affection to. That wasn't me. Livorno was responsible for that, Gwen."

"Liar!" With my fury, I manage to break my arm free and punch Laredo in the side of the head. I shove him off me and kick him right in the balls, sending him rolling into the wall.

I spin on my feet and dash toward the door, locking my fingers around the handle. It doesn't budge under my strength, remaining stuck. Bringing my fists up, I pound against the wood, cracking it under my sudden strength. I'll tear the door down if I have to. There is no way I'm staying here with Laredo. I have to get to my guys. I have to help Bronx. I have no idea how much time has passed, but I fear

I might be too late.

"Gwen, stop," Laredo says, digging his fingers into my shoulders. He drags me away from the door and presses my back into the wall, cupping my chin with his fingers.

His eyes flash silver, blinking so quickly that they glow, stealing away the dark depths of his gaze. He locks his stare with mine, flaring his nostrils. I wiggle and thrash, trying my best to swing my legs to kick him, but he sandwiches my knees between his, restraining me with his whole body, trapping my arms between our chests.

"Gwen, don't look away," Laredo says, his voice deepening.

Panic crashes through me at the sensation of an invisible heavy weight cloaking my body. This is impossible. He shouldn't be able to open my mind. I consumed vampire blood—his blood. This can't be happening.

"I want you to relax and stop fighting. I'm not going to hurt you." Laredo leans closer, his breath mingling with mine and caressing my lips. My heart picks up pace, though the rest of me turns placid in his arms.

"Laredo, stop." It takes all my free will to spit the words out. "Don't do this."

He clenches his jaw. "I have to. It's the only way you will see things clearly. Right now you only have broken memories to piece together without a guide. You're not going to ever be whole and aware without my help."

He's lying. He's done this too many times before.

The hope I carried to overpower him dies with my body's compliance.

I can't get my arms or legs to move, my gaze to break away, or my mind to keep him out. This is it. He's going to steal the best parts of me away. He'll take the love I have for the Royales and ruin it. He'll destroy me like everyone else wants to do outside my little family I just got.

"Gwen, open your mind to me. Let me in," Laredo whispers. "I'll be gentle."

Fuck. Fuck. Fuck.

My head spins, my vision going dark. A strange emotion flows through my mind, foreign and indescribable. I've never felt anything like this before. It's like Laredo fills me up in an intimate way that no one else can do. I realize what I feel is him—possibly his soul, and everything he carries within him. His devotion. His needs. His desires. His hope for me. It's the strangest thing.

His eyes remain glowing, though I watch as a tear drips from his bottom lashes and onto his cheek. My heart clenches at the sight and my inability to reach up and wipe it away. There is something scary and fascinating about the sight. Vampires don't show weakness. It's not in their nature. But here Laredo is, linking with my mind, letting me feel and experience everything that he is and how much turmoil swells inside him.

"Please forgive me, my dhampir. Please," he whispers, running his thumb under my eye. He doesn't manipulate me with his words. He begs me instead, rubbing away my tears. I'm crying too. I had no idea. Every sensation that crosses my skin and every emotion that prods my soul no longer belong to me. It's all Laredo. He consumes my very being. "I never wanted our lives to be this way. I want you to know that."

The invisible weight pinning me eases just a bit. "But it is what it is. Laredo, please. Just let me go. You can't make these decisions for me. No one can. Not the board. Not the Barons. Not my brothers or even the Royales. This is my life. Mine. No one else's."

"I'm sorry," he repeats, leaning so close that his lips brush mine as he says, "Remember. Remember everything. You will now have complete clarity. Everything stolen from you will return to how it should be."

Pain pounds in my head, my brain feeling as if it expands against my skull. A whimper escapes my mouth, the noise soft yet so full of agony that it makes my chest clench. Laredo continues to rub his thumbs across my cheeks, swiping away the spilling tears as the broken pieces of my life come together. It feels as if every ounce of heartache and grief he eased from me now slams into me harder and hotter than ever.

"Laredo," I whisper. "Let me go."

"You need to rest. Let your mind heal. Everything will be over soon." He loosens his arms around me. "You need time to process."

Process? I don't know if I even want to. It's the strangest thing finally seeing my life as I lived it and not as I was forced to think it went. And I now see the complete truth. I can pick apart the moments where I spent time with Laredo and the moments I spent time with Livorno. I finally realize the truth. Laredo isn't entirely to blame. His brother was responsible for a lot of the bullshit in my life. But even so, Laredo was there every step of the way. He didn't do a damn thing to put a stop to it.

The only thing he's doing now is trying to stop me from fighting for the future I want and deserve—one free of manipulation. One I can love and live freely. A future where I can raise my daughter to embrace who she is—not a gift to humanity or a vessel of power. I can raise her to know that she has complete control over her life and no one can change that. She will know the power she bears is hers and hers alone.

"Laredo, let me go," I repeat, pushing through the swirling emotions of our mental link.

"Gwen—"

"Let me go!"

Laredo's hands drop from mine, and he falls back, hitting his ass to the floor. Frozen in shock, he remains in his spot with wide eyes. "Gwen, wait. Don't leave."

I fly at him and grab him by the collar. Hoisting him from the floor, I use my dhampir strength to pin him to the wall this time.

He slackens in my embrace, his fangs protruding from beneath his lips. I catch my silver gaze reflecting back to me. Once again, Laredo's emotions crash through me as I lock him in a stare.

"Gwen—"

"Shut up," I command.

He snaps his mouth shut, his eyes growing impossibly wider and full of fear. It's now that I realize something is different. Off. He doesn't shut up because I asked him to. He can't open his mouth because I commanded him not to talk.

Ohmyfuck.

My heart nearly leaps from my chest as it catapults itself at my ribcage. This isn't supposed to be possible. I shouldn't be able to manipulate a vampire's mind. I mean, I've tried it a dozen times before. It's taken everything in me to try to break free from mind manipulation and it never worked. But now?

I let go of Laredo with one hand and touch it to my belly. My pregnancy is the only thing different—and the venom bites. Laredo bit me. A Baron bit me too. I thought my dhampir abilities were getting more powerful after I could hear a conversation no one else could hear between the Divines. And now this?

"Tell me where we are," I say, keeping my eyes trained on Laredo.

"Midnight Valley." Laredo's face reddens with his

words.

I release a breath. Thank the universe he didn't take me from the city.

"You will take me back to the Royales." I dig my fingers into his cheeks. "You will help me stop this bullshit with the Barons."

Laredo releases a low growl. "Okay."

Leaning closer, I lock my gaze hard to his, feeling everything wild inside him. "You will never manipulate my mind again. Do you understand?"

"Yes."

"You will let me live my life as I want. You'll let me be free."

18

MIND CONTROL

DARKNESS SHROUDS THE CITY AS Laredo carries me through the dirty streets of Midnight Valley. This part of the city belongs to the donors, nestled far from the crumbling tower of the Blood Match Center.

Laredo hasn't said a single word since strolling with me through the lobby of one of the human towers. The single security guard nearly shot the both of us, and it took Laredo disarming him and manipulating his mind to get us out.

"We still have quite the bit of distance to walk," Laredo

says, hugging me tighter.

Neither of us mentions what happened in the basement of the tower, but I know it's on both our minds. I just—I want to suppress it. I have too much to worry about to deal with the fact that I mind manipulated a vampire.

"Then pick up your speed," I snap, giving Laredo a shake. "I will eat your heart in front of everyone if we're too late."

He groans. "I can't. It's too risky to be seen running with a donor. The authorities will think I'm kidnapping you."

"You did kidnap me, asshole." I pinch my fingers into his shoulders again. I wish he'd let me ride on his back, but he refused to leave me exposed to an attack from behind. My fear was the only reason I agreed.

Laredo growls, getting his fangs awfully close to my ear. "I did not. I was saving your life, which you're about to ruin. If I knew how to break the damn mind-fuck you did to me, I would, my dhampir. You're making a huge mistake."

"You made the mistake, Laredo. Not me."

"There's still time. Look at me and fix this. We'll figure out another way that'll make us both happy." He tips his head back, trying to get me to look into his dark eyes instead of the empty street behind us.

"No fucking way. I'm never looking at you again." I feel awkward as hell with my body wrapping around his, but I don't know what else to do. He's obviously literally taking me back because I commanded him to. It's just...

My. Damn. Stomach.

His scent does nothing to help the burning in my belly. And of course he would smell so good, considering he bit me with his venom. I want to bite the hell out of him, but I know how he enjoys it, and it's the last thing I want to do.

But again...my stupid, roaring stomach. I'm sure vampires might hear us from miles away.

"Gwen, don't bite me, please," Laredo whispers, stretching his neck to the side. This jerk. He's playing his usual game, trying to get me to do the opposite of what he asks, knowing how stubborn I am.

"I won't," I mutter, pressing my nose to his skin. Damn it. He smells so good.

"I need to be in optimal condition for what's to come. If you drink too much you'll weaken me," he adds.

"Wait. What? You're serious?" I ask, arching back to look at him and then I immediately regret it and bonk my head back to his shoulder.

"I'm utterly serious, my dhampir." He runs his fingers through my hair, playing with the strands cascading down my back. "I know not to test you now."

I squeeze my eyes shut. If I ignore him, we'll get there faster. I can intervene and get the Barons to stop this bullshit. I can—

Laredo moans and slides his hand down to the small of my back. Blood floods my mouth, sending sweet tingles across my tongue. I flare my nostrils, the scent of his blood overpowering everything. And ohmyfuck. So good.

"I suppose a little won't hurt me," he murmurs, his voice turning husky.

I can't believe I bit him. What is wrong with me? I know I had issues with self-control before, but it seems even worse.

With all my willpower, I try to get myself to pull away from his shoulder. I need to stop. He's right about my blood consumption weakening him. He might piss me the hell off. Laredo might have betrayed me to the stars and back. But in this moment, I kind of need him. My guys need him. He knows our enemies better than we do.

"Gwen," he whispers, turning into an alleyway. My back hits the brick wall of the towering building as he presses his body hard into mine. "You're so incredible. Enchanting. It's like you cast a spell on me, and I want to bow before you. I want to lift you up so you can rise."

Ugh. His words snap me from my blood hunger enough to get my shit together.

"Please, my dhampir. I need to kiss you." Laredo combs his fingers through my hair, moving it from my face, now sticky with his blood. "I feel as if I'll die otherwise."

What. The. Fuck.

I raise my hand and cover his mouth before he starts puckering his lips or some shit. The tips of his extended fangs prick my palm. I flinch at the sensation of my blood dripping from the punctures. Laredo glides his tongue over my skin, and I shiver and drop my hand away.

His eyes flash silver. "Please, Gwen. I've been a patient man. I know your heart and body belong to others, but I must admit that I'm so madly, deeply, and truly in love with you. I'm begging you to break this mind manipulation you have on me. Please. It burns me from inside out like the sun against my skin. I'll do anything. If you want me to reveal myself to the board and Barons, I will. I'll stand beside your mates and fight. But you can't. You need to remain the pretty little secret we share."

Whoa. How the hell am I supposed to respond to his admission?

Swallowing my nerves, I meet his gaze. "Laredo, stop. Just stop."

I don't want to hear any more.

This is too much.

"Just release me, my dhampir. I swear to you that I'll still take you to the Royales. I swear. I just—I can't stand this." His voice whispers against my lips as he leans closer to me. His dark eyes flash silver in his desperation.

Why do I feel so badly?

Inhaling a long breath, I cup his cheeks in my hands. "I—I don't know how."

A tear trickles from the corner of his eye to drip across my finger. "I'm so, so sorry for ever doing this to you. I just wanted so badly to protect you."

Fuck. He's getting to me. It's hard to continue to look at him. He sounds so sincere.

But still.

"Laredo, I don't know how," I repeat. "I don't know much of anything about myself anymore. I didn't even know this was possible."

He presses his lips together in a tight line, sharpening his features. "There's so much to learn. We can learn together. I can show you. Once we get through this, I'll tell you everything I know. We'll figure this all out."

"With my mates," I say, locking my eyes with his.

He nods. "Yes. Just open your mind to me again. Open your mind and release me from your hold. I will not betray you."

Do I believe him? Should I believe him? I have no idea. A part of me screams not to be an idiot. Laredo could be tricking me in an attempt to get me away. If he manages to get into my mind, he could reverse our roles and control me. And then what?

If only a huge, irresistible part of me—the part that can now distinguish memories from my past that separate Laredo from his twin—moments clear and pure, unsullied by the mind manipulation wants me to give in. That part of me trusts Laredo. He was there for me after my dad's death. He fought for me. He went against the Barons for me.

A wave of warmth washes over me as our minds open to each other and link together. The new emotions coursing through my being no longer belong to me. And they're so pure and intense, hot and desperate. Intoxicating. Intimate.

"Laredo," I whisper, swallowing the burning in my throat. "This is insane."

"You're confused about me. I feel it. You hate that a part of you craves me. Wants me." His eyes flicker with pops of silver. "There is no need to be ashamed."

"You have no idea what I'm feeling." Anger snaps the strange feelings out of me, drawing my focus from everything Laredo is to everything he's ever done to me.

"But it's not enough." He touches my cheek, tilting his head without breaking our eye contact. "The damage is done, isn't it? The only way to salvage it is to doom any sort of future I could have with you. The Royales will never allow it. Not now. They'd never understand my reasoning."

Fuck. Laredo's emotions capture mine again and steal control. I expected this. I knew better. But here we are with him latching himself to my mind to mess with a piece of me. I can feel the ache growing and growing, consuming me as I lose the power I have over him.

"Gwen, release me," he says, his voice deepening. "Let go of my mind."

"You're free," my mouth says without my permission.

"Very good, my dhampir." Laredo rolls his shoulders and adjusts me in his arms, easing me from the wall. "Now listen to me. Don't look—"

A guttural growl vibrates through my core, the deep

harsh noise snapping the lock Laredo tries to put on my mind. For a split second, my heart leaps into my throat, a sense of relief flooding through me. But it doesn't last long. My hope explodes to burn away with the faint hint of a strange scent. What I thought could have been one of my guys finding me turns out to be one of the many I want dead.

"Little brother, you bastard. I knew you were too smart to fall by the hands of the godforsaken authority. And look who you have. Beautiful Gwyneth. Freeport will be so pleased. I'm sure to replace Thaxton as first in line now." The sultry voice digs under my skin, making my flesh crawl. The last time I heard the voice was when we stumbled upon the Baron Estate within the rebel nest.

"Stay back, Duncan," Laredo says, twisting to set me on my feet behind him. "Gwen is mine."

The Baron douche, Duncan, extends his fangs. "You can't claim what doesn't belong to you. You are last in line and should've never been graced with an ounce of my future intended's presence."

Ugh. Every single one of the Barons thinks they're going to get to claim me. It pisses me off. Fucking entitled bastards. They swear to know everything about dhampirs but they know nothing. It's something I can use to my advantage.

Inching a step away, I try to focus on my surroundings. With Laredo's attention on Duncan, he stops concentrating on me. All I need is a few feet of distance. If I can get that, I can summon my dhampir speed. I can get out of here. I can—

Laredo unsheathes a dagger. "Gwen, run."

Spinning on my feet, I don't hesitate and bolt away and toward the main street. The city remains eerily quiet for being after dark, and it sets off my human fear instincts, pushing me to move faster. Snarls and growls echo through the air from behind me as Laredo and Duncan break out into a fight. It takes everything in me not to glance over my shoulder and instead watch the world in front of me.

A shadow catches my attention at the mouth of the alley, and I slow down, wishing I had a weapon on me. I expect another Baron to materialize in my path to snatch me away, but Corona steps into view.

That fucking dick.

Rage kicks my body into action, and I rush forward, my dhampir side grabbing a hold of me. I've been waiting what feels like forever for the moment to kill this monster. To taste his bitter blood. To put him through the pain he caused me.

He straightens his shoulders without flinching and reaches into his jacket.

My heart threatens to escape me at the sight of the gun. Extending his arms, he aims his weapon at me, his fangs peeking from beneath his lips. I skid to a stop and spin around, searching for somewhere to duck for cover. I might be able to handle a lot, but I'm not bulletproof. I'm more vulnerable than ever.

A loud pop blasts through the air.

I flinch and brace for the pain. For the agony.

Corona growls, dragging my attention back to him. A human man stands behind him with a gun while Corona bleeds from the neck. He releases a strangled roar, his voice wet and guttural. Blurring with his spin, he flies at the man.

The man yells as Corona grabs him and lifts him off his feet. Corona extends his fangs for a kill bite, and a dozen moments of him killing humans flash through my mind. I launch at him and hop on his back. He roars again and drops the man. I lace my hands around his neck to hold on. He spins me around, and I dig my fingers deeper into his throat, jabbing him in the bullet hole with my index finger. I don't think I'll ever get over how gross and slimy insides feel, but I suppress my need to shudder and rip my fingers harder into his skin.

"Gwen, stop. Please." The feminine voice pulls my attention from my feral desire to tear Corona's head from his neck. Brooklyn stands a few feet away with a dagger in her hand. "I don't want to hurt you, but I will."

A hoarse, scary-ass noise escapes my lips at her threat. It's enough to get her to take a step back. Corona thrashes in my arms, spinning as fast as he can in an attempt to knock me away. My back collides into the brick wall, and I gasp in pain, nearly losing my hold on him. But I refuse to let him get away this time. This is the moment I've been waiting for. No one can stop me. We don't need this fucker anymore. And now that I'm in this horrible position, stressing over the fates of the ones I love, I don't care if I'd face consequences as a donor.

"Gwen," Brooklyn warns again.

"Get out of here or you'll be next!" I scream, clawing my hands deeper until the tips of my fingers scratch at something hard and unfamiliar. Bone.

Brooklyn flies toward us at the same time I screech and sever Corona's head from his body with my bare hands.

Fuck.

Shit.

Ah, hell.

Brooklyn screams, her voice wailing through the air. She catches Corona's body as I let it go and land hard on my ass. I scramble to my feet, pushing through the pain. I don't trust that Brooklyn will mourn long before she comes after me. She's always blamed me for all the bullshit.

Shoving Corona's body away just like I expect, Brooklyn hisses and tries to grab for me. I kick her in the chest, knocking her back, and stumble a few feet until I find my footing. I glance behind me into the alley to look for Laredo and Duncan. All I see is darkness.

Brooklyn vanishes, leaving Corona's body discarded on the ground. Fear trickles through me, and I slow down at the end of the building. The man who shot Corona pushes from the ground and peers around. Our eyes meet, and he raises his gun at me, set off by my dhampir nature. I don't have to see myself to know I'm a mess. Blood covers my entire front, and I bet my eyes flash like a vampire's. The only thing I'm missing is a pair of fangs.

A figure materializes behind the man, and I point my finger. Laredo grabs the man before he can pull the trigger and disarms him. I stare in shock as he bites into the man's neck, drinking his blood. Instead of trying to help, I do the most selfish thing and flee. If Laredo catches me, he'll take me away. I won't have a choice. My body aches with the exhaustion of fighting with Corona. But I keep moving.

If I didn't think some shadow dweller would come after me, I'd yell for help. I know my guys have to be looking for me. They wouldn't just let Laredo disappear. Mikkalo's probably scouring the feeds now.

Unless he can't.

The challenge might have already started. Fuck. It could be over.

No.

I suppress the wave of hopelessness trying to consume me and jog to the end of the block.

The hairs on my arms rise as Laredo stalks me, keeping his distance but still following me. I think the only reason he hasn't tried to grab me is because he knows I'm on the verge of losing myself to my nature. I might rip his head off the same way I did Corona's. Except with Laredo, I'll eat his heart too.

"Gwen, stop. Please. We have to go." Laredo's voice sounds through the air. "You're a mess. Anyone who sees you—"

Laredo releases a growl and disappears. Two figures blur through the street as Laredo thrusts a shadow dweller into the wall.

And what the fuck.

It's like this whole damn city is determined to stop me from reaching the Blood Match Center.

"Run!" Laredo shouts. "Run and don't stop. If the Barons catch you, they will take you and Freeport will end Bronx. Go, Gwen!"

I should've known that an ordinary shadow dweller wouldn't attack out of nowhere. The Baron Coven probably lies in wait.

I know that Freeport and Thaxton would not expect their brothers all to register. They wouldn't come here to challenge my guys without a backup plan.

Ignoring the sound of the vicious fight, I push my legs to run despite my body only wanting to drop to the ground to curl in on myself. I wish Laredo didn't steal my shoes. It's bad enough that I'm wearing a dress.

"There's no point in running, Gwen. It's over. If you don't submit to me, one of my brothers will catch you." Thaxton materializes in the middle of the street ahead of me. I nearly eat shit on the ground trying to stop myself. He smiles, showing off his long fangs. "We have a deal with the Royales. That won't change. This is for the best for everyone."

My heart clenches at his words.

"Isn't that right, Mr. Royale?" Thaxton waves his hand.

Ice washes over me at Thaxton's words. Two strong hands capture me from behind, Mikkalo's scent engulfing me in both relief and confusion.

"Gwen, please don't fight," Mikkalo says, his soft voice digging into my soul to rip me open. "We discussed this. Remember?"

I gasp in a few small breaths, trying to get myself in control.

"It's only eighteen years. You'll learn how little time that really is in our eternity." Mikkalo eases his arms from around my stomach to spin me around. His eyes lock onto mine, a dozen emotions crossing through his gaze, though his jaw remains tight. "Please don't fight us on this. Thaxton is right. This is the best solution for everyone."

My heart throbs. I know he's only saying the words, but a huge part of me is fucking scared as hell that my life might turn into that. There are so many Barons and the rest of the world seems against us too.

"It's the only way to ensure your safety. With the turn of events with Ashton, anything else would be too risky. You'll learn to love our life. We will treat you well." Thaxton's voice purrs through the night. "I promise."

Tears burn my vision. "I will never." I can't say anything else. I can't even pretend.

Thaxton glowers. "I'll prove you wrong. Mikkalo, grab her. It's time to finish this bullshit."

19

THE CHALLENGE

"JUST LET ME GO. I'LL take care of him," I whisper, hugging Mikkalo as tightly as I can. I'm afraid if I let him go, someone will try to swoop in and steal me away. I've been kidnapped enough for one day.

"I can't, Gwen. Others are watching. Just try to stay calm and trust me, okay?" Mikkalo strokes his big hand in circles on the small of my back.

"I do trust you. It's just—fuck. Where have you guys been? I thought you'd come searching for me." I rest my chin on the crook of his shoulder.

"I didn't have to search for you. I knew where you were the entire time." His voice remains low and even. "I was afraid this would happen, so I attached a tracking device to your bra."

I jerk my head back to meet his eyes. "My bra? Seriously?"

"I knew Laredo would steal your jewelry, but I knew he wouldn't risk taking anything else off you. I figured it'd give me a few hours before you changed." His eyes search my face. "Did he hurt you at all?"

I shake my head. "Only my heart. I was freaking out that I was too late."

"You almost were. Bronx and Freeport are joining the board now." Mikkalo's soft voice sends panic through me.

"Fuck," I whisper.

"Take a breath, Gwen. We have this handled." Leaning in, Mikkalo uses his nose to move my hair from my neck. He brushes his lips to my skin, getting me to tilt my head up. I practically crash my mouth to his, my need to drown in his quiet affection the only thing stopping me from launching toward Thaxton to collide into his back. I want to so badly. About the same as I wanted to murder Corona.

I'm powerful enough. I know I could take on all the Barons.

I might have to.

"Enough, Mr. Royale. I will not stand her and watch

you sully my brother's intended. She's all yours to do what you please with after our coven gets what we want, but until then, hands off," Thaxton grumbles in warning, pissing me off.

Mikkalo grips me in his arms, nearly squeezing the breath from me. "Watch it, asshole. She's on the verge of attacking."

"Then the two of you can stay out here." Thaxton strolls ahead toward the towering Blood Match Center. "I'll see you after the challenge. My coven is watching. If you try anything stupid or let Gwen go, then they've been instructed to take your head and heart."

My body quakes with furious tremors, and if Mikkalo didn't plead with me to calm down, I'd lose complete control. Someone besides the Barons would see what I'm truly capable of. My dhampir secret will get out.

"I know you're upset, Gwen, but just another minute, okay?" Mikkalo whispers. "I swear to you we won't miss anything. We have a plan."

"Which is?" I whisper-hiss.

"Proceeding how we planned, but I need you to be in complete control. I know how you react when you're scared and stressed. I can't take you up there until I know it's safe for us. What you said earlier—what made Laredo kidnap you—it got to all of us. We were split on what to do and if we should leave you in Laredo's care until it was over..." He stops talking at the tensing of my muscles.

"Are you fucking kidding me?" I can barely control my voice. "Was it—"

Mikkalo cuts me off with a kiss. "I will not tell you who wanted to do what, Gwen. I'm sorry. It's not important now. Just know that we all agreed that if we expect you to trust us then we sure as fuck must return the same respect. You're our girl. We want to be together, stand together, fight together—we're more than a coven. We're mates, Gwen. So please, take a breath, get your sexy little feisty ass in control, and let's support Bronx."

I bob my head, inhaling a few deep breaths through my nose. "And if all else fails, I'll just ma—"

"We're not going to fail. Now get ready. I gotta move fast. We need the element of surprise."

The world blurs before I have the chance to tell Mikkalo about my new, strange, and crazy-intense ability. I snuggle my face into his shoulder, blocking the cool air. Dozens of soft voices trickle around us. We move too fast to see any of the other vampires, but I know they've gathered to bear witness the rise or fall of the Royale Region.

"Fuck, give her here." Jameson's arms engulf the two of us, squishing me between him and Mikkalo. "Please, brother. I need to make sure she's okay."

"No. I'm the one who needs to make sure," Everett says. "You two need to go join Ashton. You're late."

"What?" I ask, my voice rising.

Jameson covers my mouth with his hand. "Late as in

we don't have much time to prepare, not late as in Bronx is facing the shit show alone." He brushes his lips to my temple. "Now behave. We'll see you in a couple minutes."

"Love you, Gwen" Mikkalo says, kissing my forehead. "Keep it together."

The world blurs again, and I don't have a chance to say anything or argue before Jameson and Mikkalo leave and Everett relocates me into a quiet, empty office. Setting me on my feet, he kneels in front of me, hiking up my dress faster than I can react. Usually he'd ask me if I was hurting anywhere, but now he doesn't waste any time trailing his gaze and fingers gently over my skin.

I flinch at the sting of his fingers touching Laredo's bite. "Shit."

"It looks bad, Gwen," he says, biting his arm. Holding it out, he waits for me to drink from him. "Please try."

I do as he asks and suck his arm, ignoring the knots twisting my stomach. I don't know if it's because I'm on the verge of a meltdown or because my body knows I need his blood, but either way, I manage to gulp a few mouthfuls.

"You have a couple scrapes and bruises on your back." Everett slowly grazes his fingers down my sides and glides his fingers along the waistband of my panties. "Here too. Did you fall on your stomach at all?"

I try to think back, but everything is a blur. "I don't think so."

He puffs a breath of air through his lips. "I think you'll

be okay."

Spinning around, I cup his cheeks in my hands. "Everett..." I let my voice trail off, so it doesn't hitch.

"Hey, hey. It's okay. We're all okay." Everett stands up and pulls me into his embrace.

A dozen thoughts swirl through my mind. "But for how long?"

Everett holds me by my waist, searching my eyes. "I—I don't know. I want to tell you forever, Gwen, but I know you do better when you know what to expect. My brother wants to protect you, but I know it's because he feels it's the only thing he can do now."

I don't think I've ever seen Everett so nervous. When Bronx announced he was going to challenge Freeport, his brothers' first reactions were for him not to do it. They didn't think the region was worth it. And now? I know Everett's mind hasn't changed.

"We have to do something, Everett. I know that your brothers strategized the hell out of tonight, but I'm afraid. What if something goes wrong?" I groan and rest my head on his chest. "We need a backup plan. I want it to be me."

He sighs. "Gwen, no. Not you. That's the one thing I completely agree with my brothers over. I will not put you in harm's way. Not before and especially not now." He slides his hands to my stomach.

"But Everett—"

He growls softly under his breath and meets my gaze.

"Gwen, no."

"Stop arguing for a second and think about it." Something indescribable crashes into me, stealing my breath away. It's now that I realize my eyes blink silver, reflecting in the glassiness of Everett's blue gaze.

His mouth parts in surprise, his fangs peeking from beneath his lips. "Whoa."

Whoa is right.

I snap my gaze from Everett and turn my back, a hurricane of emotions ravaging my very soul. I can't believe I just linked my mind with his. I didn't mean to manipulate him. But damn. It felt incredible—not manipulating him but feeling him on another level.

Sliding his arm around me, Everett gets me to turn around to face him. "Gwen...that was...the most amazing thing I've ever experienced. You connected your mind to mine. Did you feel it?"

I slowly nod my head. "It's how I got away from Laredo. His venom did something to me. My dhampir nature is stronger."

"This changes everything," he whispers.

"I can use it against the Barons."

Everett's eyes widen. "No. This changes everything because we can't stay. We have to get my brothers and get out of here. The board would kill you if they ever found out. It's one thing to be a dhampir—we might be able to brush that revelation off. But this? Being able to control vampires?

Fuck."

I furrow my brows. "It might only be temporary. This baby girl has my body all out of whack."

He tightens his jaw. "Even so, if that's the case, what about her? We have to protect her too."

"And we will. But right now? We need to protect Bronx."

"Gwen."

"Everett, no. I can't lose him. I can't risk it. You guys are important to me." I touch my belly. "And to her."

Pulling away, I turn my back on Everett and cross the room. I'm afraid he'll do something rash to protect me. If I go, he'll follow me. If someone else sees us, he won't try to run. I know he and his brothers put me before them, but that's not how it should be. We are all equally important.

"Gwen, please. Let me call my brothers. We might have time to withdraw." Everett blocks my way and pulls his com device from his pocket.

"Hurry," I say, preparing to rush past him.

Everett's com device lights up as Jameson's projection illuminates the wall. His gaze finds mine, and he blows out a breath of air. Neither of us says anything, just staring at each other in silence.

"Jameson, get Bronx and Mikkalo," Everett says, speaking first.

Jameson's eyes flash silver. "Viorica's preparing the contracts right now. Where are you?"

Everett tenses. "Just tell Bronx to cancel the challenge and meet us downstairs."

Confusion crosses Jameson's face, and he turns his attention away from Everett and to me. He doesn't ask, but I can see question after question flickering through his eyes. "Ev, please just bring Gwen. Bronx can't withdraw. It's too late. Viorica wouldn't let him even if he wanted to. You know why."

I gasp a few breaths, my nerves getting the best of me. Of course the board won't let Bronx back down. They want him to try to defeat Freeport before going to war.

"Please, Ev. Don't do anything stupid. Please just bring Gwen. Bronx wants to say...Bronx needs Gwen." Jameson scrubs his hand over his face, wiping away his frown to turn his expression hard.

The line clicks off, and Everett shifts on his feet and squeezes his eyes shut. "They'd want me to take you away if they knew." He says the words more to himself than me. "They'd do the same."

I grab the front of Everett's shirt and shake him. "Take me to Bronx, now. You will not rob him of what he needs from me. I have to be there. I have to."

He combs his fingers through his light hair with a sigh. "You're right. I can't do that to either of you. But Gwen, please. Don't try to intervene."

My words stay lodged in my throat. That's a promise I can't make. My body, mind, and soul won't allow it. So instead of saying anything, I force my head to nod and slide my arms around Everett's neck. He adjusts my dress and lifts me into his arms, cradling me against him. I listen to his soft breathing as he exits the small office and into the hallway. He speeds down the hallway and surprises me by exiting the building into a courtyard.

The collection of voices grows louder, the group of a few dozen vampires sitting in clothed chairs, facing an open grassy area. I half expect a cage or some shit, but only neatly trimmed hedges surround the small garden.

Everett doesn't give anyone the chance to spot us and races along the wall and into an alcove that leads into a small concrete corridor. I don't have a chance to prepare myself before Everett's arms fall away from me only to have Bronx catch me.

He showers me with a dozen kisses, ensuring his lips caress every inch of my face. "I'm so sorry, dandelion. I know I shouldn't have let Laredo take you like he did, but I—I failed you. I don't know if I can ever be the man you deserve."

I jerk my head back to meet his gaze. "Stop that. You're going to hurt my feelings."

Mikkalo slaps his back. "She's right, brother. Our girl needs you to give her that stubborn fucking attitude that drives her wild and not words that almost sound like defeat. The fight hasn't even started yet."

"Yeah, Bronxy. You can't choose now to start this bullshit." Jameson hugs his arms around the two of us. "Now hurry up and snuggle our girl, so I can have my turn to keep her ready for you when this is over. You know how hot she gets seeing you in action."

I can't stop the laugh bubbling from my throat. Jameson makes it easy to forget that we're on the brink of a war. "Jamie, I'm not sure I can wait. Can you stall?"

Jameson throws his arms up. "Fuck, I can try."

Bronx grabs the back of Jameson's jacket, stopping him from disappearing. "I need something to look forward to after."

I can't stop the pout puckering my lips at his words. "Bronx..."

"Dandelion, listen to me. I need you to try your best to stay in control. This will all be over soon. No matter what happens, you and our baby girl will be fine. That I promise you." He hugs me tighter and kisses my lips long enough to steal my breath, leaving me suffocating for more when he pulls away. "I love you."

I tighten my mouth to stop my damn lips from quivering. As much as the idea of Bronx fighting Freeport freaks me out, I have to remind myself that Freeport doesn't stand a chance.

Not with me.

I'm not some Baron descendant to be bred to bear power. I am my father's daughter, and family was always most important to him. And the Royales are my family.

They worry about letting me down, but I won't allow such a thing to happen. I made them a promise of forever, and I intend to keep it even if I have to destroy the world in the process—starting with the Barons.

"You better kick some ass, Bronx," I say, kissing him again. "We have a few debts we still have to pay to each other, remember?"

His eyes flash silver with desire. "I'd never forget."

I hug him. "I love you."

A strange whistle sounds through the air, drawing my attention away from Bronx. He sets me on my feet and hugs me one last time before hugging each of his brothers. Mikkalo and Jameson disappear with him, leaving me with Everett in the small concrete hallway.

I realize that Everett is keeping me out of view for a reason.

I try to drag him toward the courtyard. "We need to be closer."

"Not happening," Everett says, hugging me from behind. "We can see everything from here."

"But—"

"It is with great honor for us to gather here today to bear witness to the testing of strength and power of the leaders of two great covens." Viorica's words cut off my argument. "Due to the unfortunate loss of our board member, Zaire Royale, we now open a seat to the winner of the regional challenge, which will prove who is better fitted for such a prestigious position."

The crowd offers a small applause, but no one outright cheers. Every coven is as on edge as us. No one wants to see this challenge happen. No one wants a war either.

"Mr. Royale, please choose your weapon," Zara says.

I inch forward, tugging Everett with me. My heart sinks into my stomach as I watch Bronx stroll to a table of weapons and choose a dagger not unlike the ones I know he carries.

"Mr. Baron, please choose your weapon," Mr. Goldman says, motioning to Freeport.

Freeport tilts his head up and searches around. I automatically step back and hide the best I can. I don't want him to see me here. I don't want to see the satisfaction crossing his face because he believes he's going to get what he wants.

"Mr. Baron," Viorica says. "We don't have all day. Pick your weapon."

Freeport releases a growl and snatches a sword from the table.

Without hesitating, he spins and rushes Bronx. Everett holds me close, squeezing me so tightly that I'd have to fight him to get him to let me go. Bronx and Freeport spar, each getting in a few jabs as they blur across the grass.

But then Freeport freezes.

Bronx shoves his blade into Freeport's chest.

Raising his hands, Freeport stiffens and looks at the

board. "I'd like to surrender. I'm withdrawing from the challenge. If you do not agree, then you will face a war."

Silence falls through the air as the crowd looks to the board for their response. This is supposed to be a fight to the death, but Freeport still believes he and Bronx have a deal. He was to admit defeat in front of the board to make it look real.

I cover my mouth with my hand, suppressing any possible noise I can make.

Because this is it.

"I'm sorry, Mr. Baron. You agreed—"

Mr. Woodsman's head severs from his body and lands on the ground.

The rest of him falls over, sending blood splattering across the stone path. I stand frozen in shock at the sight of Silas standing with a sword in his hand. A cold smile crosses his face, and he bares his fangs.

"Mr. Baron!" Viorica yells. "This is an act of treason."

Freeport punches Bronx in the gut, knocking him away. Jumping to his feet, he rushes toward Silas. The two of them growl at each other. Freeport swings his weapon in an attempt to decapitate Silas.

Bronx takes advantage of the distraction and collides into Freeport. I dig my fingers into Everett's arms, my heart pounding in overdrive. Freeport roars, caught off guard by Bronx. He spins around to attack, giving Silas the chance to disappear.

"Come on, Bronx," I whisper, tensing.

My focus is too consumed by the fight that I see the shadow too late.

Everett roars and falls away from me.

Twisting around, I stare in horror as Laredo rams a dagger into Everett's chest.

I scream.

20

DESPERATE MEASURES

"STAY BACK, GWEN. I'LL CUT his heart out if you move. I just want you to come with me." Laredo twists the dagger a bit.

Everett clenches his jaw to stop from yelling. "I'm on your side, you asshole. I want to take Gwen away too. Far away."

Bronx's voice cuts through the air. As much as I don't want to turn away from Laredo, I can't stop myself from looking at the fight between Freeport and Bronx. I gasp at the sight of Bronx's swollen face and a gash across his fore-head. It doesn't slow him down though. He charges Free-port again with his blade, stabbing him in the shoulder.

A hand locks around the back of my dress and hauls me back. "Come on, my dhampir. It's time to go."

I swing my arm back and elbow Laredo. "You bastard!"

Everett shifts in front of me and cups my cheeks. "It's okay. I'm coming with you. We'll call my brothers when we're out of the city walls."

My eyes widen. "Everett, no. Bronx—"

"Go, dandelion!" Bronx yells, drawing my attention to him. He remains completely focused on Freeport, keeping his ground.

My chest tightens at his command. If only it didn't feel as if I'd die if I move even another inch.

Jameson appears in the doorway to the corridor. "Gigi, let Everett get you out of here. It's not safe. Mik caught sight of the Barons closing in on us."

"I can help," I say, pleading with my eyes. "If we leave, what if they catch us?"

Jameson growls. "They won't."

"But Jamie." I break away from Laredo and slide past Everett. He lets me. I don't know if it's the desperation in my voice or the look in my eyes, but he doesn't risk getting in my way.

Jameson steps closer and holds his arms open for me. "Everett, I'll take her. Go help Mik."

A whimper escapes my lips. "Jameson, no. I don't want to separate. You promised we'd do things together."

"Not this, Gwen." Jameson locks his fingers to my wrist to restrain me before I can make a run for it.

I snap my teeth at him, my dhampir nature awakening and unleashing my most dangerous side. Jameson spins me away and locks his hands around me from behind. I face the courtyard, catching sight of Bronx and Freeport again. The two of them blur in a fight. Thaxton stands in wait. Everett joins Mikkalo, now waiting for a command.

As for the board, they stand there uselessly. Viorica and Zara remain within the safety of their covens. Mr. Goldman hides behind a wall of snarling vampires. And Mr. Woodsman? Shit. I can't stop from staring at his decapitated body. I don't know if the Barons had planned for Silas to do that bullshit, but either way, he started a war. He messed everything up. He—

My heart nearly spills from my chest as Silas materializes behind Bronx. He shoves a dagger into Bronx's back and then jams one into his neck. I screech and try to run from Jameson. He tosses me to Laredo and disappears to help his brothers.

Chaos blurs the lines between who is an ally or enemy, and every coven turns to fight for themselves.

"Laredo, you have to let me go," I say, digging my fingers into his arm. He purposefully keeps me facing outward. Nothing I do, not kicking or stepping on his feet does anything to get him to release me. "They'll murder everyone. The Barons are psychos."

He tenses as I scratch his skin, squeezing my fingers tighter and tighter in an attempt to break his arm. "Then it'll be fewer people to worry about, Gwen."

"Damn it, Laredo. Let me go!" I jerk my head back and bash it into his nose.

He snarls at me and drags me back, moving at vampire speed. The entrance to the courtyard disappears as he runs with me down the hallway to who knows where. Panic gushes through me, the sounds of the fight growing more intense even with the distance between us.

The world suddenly spins, and I crash into the wall and slide to the floor. I sit on the cold concrete ground, stunned silent. Silas rams his shoulder into Laredo's chest, smashing him into the wall. I blink through my shadowy vision and try to regain control over my senses. It takes everything in me to push from the ground and even more to get my legs to work.

"Gwen, keep going. Grayson's at the end of the hall. The rebels are waiting to help." Silas flashes his fangs and chomps down on Laredo's neck, tearing a hunk of flesh free. "We're done with this bullshit. These assholes will never give us the power we deserve."

Rebels? What the hell? I haven't dealt with rebels since...those fuckers deemed me a traitor to humanity.

Ignoring Silas, I dash away and back toward the courtyard. At least half of the vampires fighting don't want me dead like the rebels. What will they think or do if they discover the truth about my pregnancy? I doubt they'll consider it anything other than an abomination.

"Gwen!" Silas yells.

Laredo manages to shove him away, but I pick up my speed and don't wait to find out what happens. They can both murder each other for all I care. The only thing important right now is getting to my guys and getting out of here. Everything else can be thought about later.

Soft light illuminates from the mouth of the corridor, and I slow down at the pungent scent of a mixture of vampire blood. My stomach twists and turns at the sight of the first body—a guy in a suit with a gaping hole through the back, his spine hanging out and his chest cavity clearly empty of his heart.

"Shit." My voice comes out a whisper, and I squat down and feel the guy for weapons. I find a blade tucked away on a leg holster and pull it free.

"This all could've been so easy, Mr. Royale," Freeport says, drawing my attention to him as he corners Bronx against the wall of the building.

Mikkalo and Everett stand on guard, surrounded by three other Barons.

"All I asked was for one thing, and you were too stupid to accept it. Now look what you've done." Freeport waves his dagger at the courtyard, pointing out the gore. "Do you really think the board will want you to claim a seat now?"

Bronx extends his fangs and charges forward, taking a split second opportunity to attack Freeport again. I inch my way from the corridor, sliding along the wall of the building and behind the tall trees. If I can find a moment of surprise, I can take the fucker down. Or at least help Bronx to do so.

Freeport drops to the ground and kicks his leg out, knocking Bronx's feet out from under him. Bronx hits the concrete and catapults back up, but he's too slow. Ramming his blade into Bronx's shin, Freeport sends him sprawling to the ground.

Bronx roars and rolls, trying to get back to his feet before Freeport restrains him. Silence draws through the air, the rest of the onlookers no longer fighting and now entranced by the challenge.

Freeport clicks his tongue. "You'll never overpower me. You should've taken the deal. Now I'll get what is rightfully mine and the board seat."

"Come on, brother," Mikkalo calls. "Take his heart."

Freeport jerks his attention to Mikkalo. "Or how about if my brother takes yours?"

Thaxton fakes Mikkalo out, allowing his other brother, whom I can't remember his name, to close in and stab Mikkalo. The gesture sets me off, and I can't stop from screaming out at the sight of Mikkalo's blood dripping from a stab wound to his chest.

The shrillness of my voice is enough to distract Freeport.

Bronx takes advantage and hops to his feet, flying at Freeport too fast for him to react. My presence pushes Bronx to fight harder, faster, showing the world exactly the power he carries. A figure rushes in my direction, and I drop down to my knees and slice my dagger in front of me. Thaxton trips, not expecting my sudden movements, and he crashes into the wall.

Launching to my feet, I bolt away from the wall and toward where Mikkalo, Everett, and Jameson prepare an attack on the Barons. They're outnumbered, but it doesn't stop them. The three of them blur in a fight, getting the Barons to back up.

"Dandelion, stay back," Bronx yells, drawing my attention to him.

I inhale a sharp breath of relief, staring in awe as Bronx overpowers Freeport. He shoves his dagger into Freeport's chest, slamming it all the way to the concrete beneath him. The scent of Freeport's blood trickles through the air, setting off my senses.

A look of horror crosses Bronx's face when our eyes meet. I don't have to see myself to know that my dhampir nature reveals itself in the form of my eyes flashing. My whole body tingles as I lose control over myself. I need to end this right now, no matter the consequences. The board is utterly useless. The Barons won't stop unless they're all dead. The only way I can envision a future is if I steal the power and take it for myself.

Bowing my head, I concentrate on moving at a human pace toward Freeport. He snarls and snaps his fangs at Bronx, managing to lace his hand around Bronx's wrist to stop his blade from cutting out his heart completely.

"Stay back, dandelion," Bronx warns again. "I will handle this."

Freeport releases the creepiest laugh in existence. "Is that so? I'm nearly certain you don't have the power within you. Gwen is mine."

Everything happens so fast that I don't have the chance to react. Freeport breaks his other arm free and thrusts Bronx over his shoulder and onto his back. Freeport somersaults with him and straddles his waist. Punching down his fist, he shatters Bronx's sternum and sinks his hand into Bronx's chest.

"Brothers, grab Gwen," he says, grinning at Bronx's holler. "Ms. Vaduva, announce my ascension to the board. As I'm not a completely heartless bastard, I'll give Gwen twenty seconds to say goodbye to Mr. Royale."

Bronx's jaw tightens under the pressure of Freeport's hand. "Brothers, don't let them have her. She's ours."

Freeport starts to slide his arm from Bronx's chest, causing him to shout again. The sound of his pain steals my breath. I charge closer, but Freeport holds his free hand out, stopping me. He meets me with a serious expression, his nostrils flaring.

"It's over, Gwen. Say your goodbye," Freeport says.

"Gwen, I love you." Bronx's voice turns into a whisper with his words. His body slumps back, his eyes rolling.

"No!" I scream. "Freeport stop! Stop! I'll go with you. I'll do whatever you want. Just don't kill him."

Freeport's eyes flash silver. "You're lying, Gwen. This must be done."

I thrash my head back and forth. "No, please. I'll let you into my mind. You can erase everything. You can have me to do as you want. Just don't kill him. Let them all go. If you don't, I'll shout to the world what I am." I keep my voice low. "I mean it."

"Prove it. Right now. I'll take just enough to make your mind malleable." Freeport extends his fangs.

I automatically touch my stomach. "What?"

"You heard me."

"Gwen, no. It's too risky. Don't agree. We'll get through this," Everett says from his spot. "Please. Bronx wouldn't want this."

I straighten my shoulders. "I'm sorry, Everett. It's what I want. We'll be okay. I'm strong enough." I rub my fingers over my belly. "We both are."

"Gwen—"

Freeport releases Bronx and slides his hand free. I gasp a small breath, knowing that his heart remains intact. Closing the space to me, Freeport stops in front of me. His eyes rove over my face. He grasps my chin, tilting my head to the side to reveal my neck to him. My guys yell and snarl, but the Barons manage to keep them back. The board continues to stare in silence.

"I'll be gentle," Freeport murmurs. "Relax."

That's easy for him to say.

Closing my eyes, I imagine what life would be like if everyone would leave my guys and me alone. I imagine a brilliant future at Night Palms Castle with our daughter. My heart swells at the thought. I can envision it all now. Nothing has been more perfectly clear. My guys wouldn't stand a chance against the sweet cuteness of our daughter. She would have the world at her fingertips. A life pure and untainted by the horrors the life of a dhampir seems to attract. She'll be the most magical and powerful being in all of existence.

Freeport's sharp fangs pierce my skin, stealing the daydream of my perfect future away.

Gasping, I clutch onto his shoulders, using his sturdy frame to support me. My mind swims with a dozen thoughts. It's the only thing I can do to suppress the pain and heartache shouting from my guys.

"My dearest Gwyneth, open your eyes for me," Freeport says, hugging me to him by my waist. "Let me get a look at you."

Fluttering my eyes open, I meet Freeport's solid silver gaze. My eyes blur, my body slackening in his embrace. Ice travels through my body with each painful breath.

"Don't look away." Freeport leans in so close that our breaths mingle, and his eyes are the only things I can see as darkness consumes the edges of my vision. "Open your mind to me. Let me in."

My ears pop at his words, my body screaming, my mind entangling with his unfamiliar emotions. I've never felt anything like it. The darkness he carries smothers all the light my mind managed to summon with thoughts of my future. Pain swells in my mind the longer I'm trapped in his stare. I can't move my limbs. I can't speak. All I can do is wait for this to end.

"You are a Baron, Gwen. Everything you experienced in your life was a lie. You were kidnapped by rebels and kept away from the coven you love." Freeport's words sink deeply into me, entangling with my will to fight his mind manipulation.

"I was kidnapped," my mouth says without my permission.

"You are so happy that we found you," he adds, a smirk playing on his lips.

A weird-ass wave of warmth courses through me. My insides clench as he manipulates more than my mind, rewiring my emotions into something I'd never carry for him or the Barons.

"You want me to take you home. You're so happy to be carrying my child." His words strike a nerve inside me.

Agony explodes through my being, but my body

doesn't react.

"Tell me you're happy to bear my child."

My throat burns. I can't stop my mouth from opening. "I'm so happy to bear your child."

The second the words escape my lips, my mind snaps its connection to Freeport. He startles and tightens his grip on me. It takes everything in me not to fight him. He'll do something crazy.

So I fake-faint, slumping into him like his gesture was the thing to break me.

Mikkalo growls and snarls. Jameson yells my name. Everett shouts for Bronx to get up and stop Freeport. None of them get the chance to intervene. The ground shakes and a loud explosion rings through the air.

The familiar sound of guns firing pops through the silent night.

The world blurs.

"Fucking rebels," Freeport mutters under his breath.

I groan and try to raise my head. Freeport cradles me in his arms, pressing his hand to the back of my head to stop me from looking around. Several other voices trickle through the air, and the temperature changes from cool to warm and back to cool again.

"You should've ended him when you had the chance," Thaxton says with a growl. "You knew better than to show mercy on a Gallagher."

He's talking about Silas. I know it.

"We'll deal with him later. Right now, we must leave the city. The Royales will come after her." Freeport rubs his hand on my back.

"And we're losing numbers. Gwen managed to kill Duncan. Morgan is also missing." Thaxton huffs a breath.

"Shit," Freeport says. "That leaves us with—"

Freeport roars and spins. The world falls away, and I brace for impact. I roll across the hard asphalt, unable to stop. Fire bursts across my back as I skid into a curb. I heave, my stomach twisting. Two strong arms lock around me and lift me from the ground.

"Gigi, take a breath," Jameson says.

I don't get the chance.

Jameson sinks his fangs into my shoulder, piercing me. He releases his venom in a hot wave, stealing my breath.

"Fuck, he bit her with venom," Thaxton says.

Freeport roars. "Just grab them both!"

The last thing I see is the city lights of Midnight Valley dim into darkness.

21

REBEL HEIR

"THERE'S SOMETHING YOU SHOULD KNOW, my dhampir." Laredo rests his palms on the counter on either side of my legs. Leaning in, he brings his lips to my ear. "One day, you're going to remember this moment as you lived it, and you'll forgive me for stealing it away."

My brows pucker with my frown. "You don't know me well, now do you?"

He nips my ear. "Infuriatingly stubborn. Sexy and seductive. Madly in love with me."

Tipping my head back, I laugh. "Yeah fucking right, Laredo. You seriously think I could ever love you? You know the only reason I keep you around is because you taste delicious."

"I love when you compliment me, Gwen." He hums in my ear. "I love how you must keep lying to yourself because you know I'm your weakness. With me, you know you're safe. You can let your guard down...you're free to be the woman you want to be. No asshole brothers. No rebels."

"No more sneaking around," I tease. "No hiding my hunger."

Laredo slides his hands from the counter and to my knees, easing my legs open to stand between them. "No hiding your desire...or curiosity to find out exactly what you do to me."

My smile fades at his words. "Careful, Laredo. You've caught me in a good mood."

He tilts his head and smiles. "You know, I can make it better."

I swallow and lick my lips. "Yeah?"

Brushing his lips to my cheek, he says, "Mmmhmm. Which is why you'll forgive me later."

"Laredo."

He twists his lips in a smile and kisses the side of my mouth. "Gwen."

"Do it and I'll never love you."

Easing away from me, he meets my eyes. "It's too late

for that."

I roll my eyes.

"You'll see."

A terrible taste floods my mouth, twisting my stomach. I gag and spit. Jerking upright, I flail my arms, my mind struggling to catch up with me. Shit. I'm so confused.

"Here, my beloved. Try again."

I shiver at the sensation of Freeport's breath tickling my shoulder. His heavy arm hangs over my side as he lies with me from behind. I nearly react by jerking my arm back to punch his dick, but the last moments before I lost consciousness flood back to me.

Cringing, I do as Freeport asks and link my fingers to his wrist. I can't even get his bleeding arm within an inch of my lips before my belly heaves again. I groan and flip over to my stomach. Freeport's arm moves with me and he taps his fingers to my side.

"We'll try again later. Would you like some solid food? I can have one of the staff cook you something." He continues to touch my side, playing with the fabric of my dress. "Or perhaps I can run you a bath? I'm sure you're still reeling from the challenge. I just wish I had rescued you sooner. It must've been terrifying being with that lowly coven after you escaped the rebels."

I squeeze my eyes shut, hoping my fake groan convinces him that the reason I react as I do is because I'm sick. "I need blood," I whisper. "Why is my body acting like this?"

Freeport sighs. "You were bitten with venom by someone beneath you. It'll pass."

"But I'm starving." My stomach rumbles, proving me right. "My—our baby can't wait that long. Where is the asshole who did this to me?"

I hold my breath, listening for Freeport's reaction. He doesn't respond right away, and fear swells through me. I can't help but think the worst. If something happened to Jameson, I won't be able to play along. I'll murder Freeport right here, and then I don't know what will happen. I have no idea where I am or anything.

"I can bring you some of his blood," Freeport says, sitting up.

I reach out and lock my hand to his arm. "I want to see him myself. You know I don't like cups."

Freeport jerks his attention to me, studying my face. I count silently in my mind to distract myself from reacting. It takes me counting to twenty-five for Freeport to finally break his gaze away from me.

"I suppose that will be okay. It'll be quite the punishment to be the thing he truly is to you—a lowly blood source." Freeport scoots from the bed and holds his arms out to me.

I stand up and slide my arms around his neck, letting him lift me into his arms. My body screams to punch him. To inflict the same pain he did to me. But my mind begs for me to chill the hell out. I need to get to Jameson first. If

I do something rash before I do, the Barons might ensure I never see him again.

"Please, go slow," I say, resting my head to his chest. I'm afraid if I look at him again, he'll expect something more from me. He thinks he mind manipulated me into believing my guys' baby is his. The fuckhead. It pisses me off just thinking about it.

"Anything for you, my Gwen." Freeport opens the bedroom door leading into a large sitting area. The place looks like he collected back-world furniture just like the rebels used to do after scavenging a ruined city. "I need to make sure my brothers know the rules anyway."

"The rules?" I peer around to search for every possible exit. Two dark-tinted windows, a balcony door, and the double doors leading to a grand hallway. I don't recall seeing anything in the sleeping quarters, though I didn't get a good look around. The last thing I want to think about is that I woke up in bed next to Freeport. At least I'm still in my same dirty dress.

"You are mine and mine alone," he says. "Just the way you like."

The Baron Coven is nothing like the Royales. For one, it's obvious none of them trusts each other. It's like they've come together as a necessity and not because they remotely care for one another. And two, they all seem to think that I'm a possession they'll eventually get. I wouldn't put it past them to turn on each other. I need to figure out how to use what I know against them. I need to learn as much as I can. They can't get away with this. They can't.

A door at the end of the hallway creaks open, and Thaxton struts from a room. He crosses his arms over his chest, standing tall. His eyes flash silver as they examine me in Freeport's arms. I can't read Thaxton's expression, but I know he's fascinated—this is another thing I can use.

"Sleeping beauty, it's lovely to see you awake. How are you feeling? I did the best I could for your injuries, but my brother would barely allow me to put a finger on you while you were unconscious." Thaxton flicks his intense eyes toward Freeport. "Perhaps now that you're awake, I can give you a proper exam. I'd like to check on the Baron's heir. You lost a lot of blood, no thanks to my brother."

Freeport growls. "I did what was necessary, and she is fine. Only hungry."

"You're a health keeper?" I ask, ignoring Freeport's assessment of me. I recall him mentioning something like that before. Trying to use his position to claim it's fine to feed on pregnant women.

"Something like that." Thaxton risks stepping closer. "Now if you don't mind, brother—"

"I mind," Freeport snaps. "My greatest concern is getting my beloved the sustenance she needs. She couldn't drink from me yet."

"Couldn't or wouldn't?" Thaxton flashes his fangs with a smile. "I can't blame you for either, Gwen. Maybe you'll let me try."

Swinging his fist, Freeport punches Thaxton in the jaw, sending him reeling back. I tense, bracing myself to be in between two angry vampires.

But Thaxton only laughs. "You're quite touchy, brother. Is it possible you carry doubt that Gwen might not be the one for you? I mean, the extent you went through to get to this point—"

Freeport extends his fangs in warning. "Shut up. Gwen's my intended. I am leader of our coven after all."

"Until she devours you in your sleep. You know the possibility. Dhampirs will kill those unworthy." Thaxton smiles, seeming to love messing with Freeport.

And I hate how much I enjoy it.

The fucker.

"She'd never. Now move along, Thaxton, or I'll see to it she drains you dry." Freeport points down the hallway. "And why don't you do something useful and have Gwen's ladies unpack her belongings. I'm sure she wants to get out of this dress as much as I want to see her out of it."

This. Guy.

Thaxton whacks Freeport on the back. "Good luck, brother." He smiles at me again. "Gwen. I'll see you soon, I'm sure."

He disappears, his laughter fading after him. Freeport mutters something I don't understand under his breath and continues on down the hallway. Two other vampires materialize from doorways, but neither of them says anything, just watching us quietly as we stroll past. I do my best to look around and map the house, trying to memorize every little detail of this huge estate. I don't know what I was expecting, but it wasn't this.

Freeport carries me down a flight of stairs and through a luxurious living room with the technology I'm used to seeing. Several screens light up the wall, and a man sits in front of them, scouring over the video feeds.

I gasp at the sight of Bronx and Mikkalo standing in the shade of a building without sun blankets. Fear trickles through me. The Barons are monitoring them. They're probably watching the board too. And hell.

"That's them," I say, realizing Freeport slows and penetrates me with his gaze. "My captors."

His tense shoulders relax. "We're just making sure they never steal you from us again."

I bob my head.

"Are you certain you want me to take you to feed on the one we caught? It might be best to just wait it out, beloved." Freeport strokes his fingers over my arm. "I worry about the stress it'll bring you."

Is he for real? It's twisted as hell that he continues this game of his, pretending like I actually belong here. He's a psycho. They all are. But I'm not afraid for myself. This is better than I expected. If Freeport believed he was unable to manipulate my mind, he'd cage me. Now this way I can manipulate them. It's the only way.

"You don't need to worry about me, Freeport." I hate even saying his name. "I'm plenty capable of taking care of myself. I have been for a while."

He puffs air through his lips. "I suppose you're right. Forgive me if I'm a little over-protective. I just love you so much."

I force myself to smile. "I know."

Freeport carries me at a quicker pace to a steel door. He presses his hand to the metal, and it swings inward, revealing a steep set of concrete stairs. Tapping something on the wall, he turns on the lights. Electricity hums through the air, and I try to peer down the long hallway but the overhead lighting's glow only goes so far.

I silently send a prayer to the universe. This could've been so much worse. I know rebels punish vampires with sun cages. The Barons could've trapped Jameson outside to suffer. A vampire can withstand the sun, but most wouldn't want to. The agony is too much.

"Now, I must prepare you. Your blood source has been drained enough to keep him weak. If you try to drink too much, you won't get more later." Freeport sets me on my feet and presses his hand to another steel door. It beeps under his touch, and he hits a button to send light through the room.

I nearly lose my shit.

Jameson hangs helplessly from chains with his eyes

closed. I've never seen him like this, and it hurts my heart. Tears burn my eyes, and I blink them away as fast as I can.

"He won't bother you any. Make it quick. I have a full night planned for us." Freeport waves his hand to motion me in the room. "Don't be gentle."

Something dark snaps inside me, and I link my fingers to Freeport's shirt and swing him into the wall. He freezes, his eyes locking onto mine. I release a low growl from my throat. My dhampir nature grabs hold of me, fueled by this torturous situation. I can't pretend any longer, but Freeport doesn't have to know that.

"Don't move or speak," I say, pinching his chin in my fingers. Goosebumps prickle on my skin as his surprise and annoyance wash through me as we link our minds together. Feeling him on this level unnerves me. He truly is psychotic. The darkness seeping into me sets me off even more. "You will obey my every command starting now. Jameson is not your prisoner. He is an ally, and you want him to join your coven because of his power."

"G-Gwen." Jameson's soft voice trickles through the air.

As much as I want to throw myself away from Freeport and into Jameson's arms, I remain trapping Freeport in my gaze.

"You will stop monitoring the Royales and declare they are no longer a threat. Do you understand?" I ask.

Freeport's eyes flash silver, his body rigid under my

grip. "Yes."

"You will respect my privacy and not expect anything from me," I continue. "I will get my own room. You will allow Jameson to stay with me as he will be the only one I will drink from. Got it?"

Freeport's nostrils flare. "Yes."

"You will not speak of this to anyone. You will forget my power. You will obey me because you had a change of heart. You will tell your brothers to back off." I pinch my fingers deeper into his chin. "Understand?"

"Yes."

"Now forget this moment. You will leave me with Jameson and wait for my call. When I do, you will have my private quarters ready and blood waiting for Jameson. You will never put a claim on me again." I shove my hand against his chest. "Now leave. Turn off the surveillance. It is no longer needed."

Freeport shakes his head and blinks his eyes the second I break my stare. He studies me for a moment, and I hold my breath, waiting to see what happens. Bringing his hand up, he offers me a smile and brushes my hair from my shoulder. His hard features soften, turning him a teensy bit cuter in the process. He obviously doesn't wear brooding well.

"Take all the time you need, Gwen," he says. Reaching into his pocket, he pulls out his com device. "Use this to call me when you're ready. I'll prepare a room. I understand that your privacy is important."

I tighten my mouth. "Thank you."

He nods. "I just want you to be happy."

Freeport spins on his feet and disappears up the long hallway and to the concrete stairs. I release a small breath, thinking about how the only way I will truly be happy is to end this bullshit once and for all.

"Gigi," Jameson whispers, drawing my attention from the stairs. "You're o-okay."

Rushing to Jameson, I touch my fingers to his wrists and yank at the chains. They snap under my desperate strength, sending him falling forward. He lands on top of me and groans, burying his face into the crook of my neck.

"Push me away," he whispers. "I'm too hungry."

I do as he asks and shove him off but only to climb on top of him. I sweep my hair from my shoulder and bow down, brushing my lips to his. "Bite me. It's okay. I need you to be strong enough to get up."

"But—"

I purposefully snag my bottom lip on his fangs, sending blood trickling into his mouth. He inhales a sharp breath, the click of his fangs extending even longer sounding in my ear. Sucking my lip into his mouth, he kisses me again, more fervently, like my kiss is the one thing that gets him to pull himself together. And maybe it is.

He breaks away from my mouth and softly kisses the skin of my throat before sinking his fangs into my flesh. My body turns wild under the sensation of his lips latching on as he gets what he needs. He doesn't drink for long, just enough to make me moan.

"Fuck, Gigi. Am I dreaming?" Jameson sits up with me and hugs me close. "Did you just—"

I cut off his words with a kiss. "Your dreams are probably far hotter and dirtier than this."

"I can't believe..." His voice trails off. "Shit. This is why Everett wanted to run. He knew. When? How?" It's like he's afraid to speak the words out loud, and I can't blame him.

"After Laredo's venom. I let him into my mind in a moment of weakness and he tried to take advantage of me. I just reacted. I think it's the baby or the venom or a combination." I keep my voice incredibly low.

"I need to get you out of here." He stumbles to his feet with me in his arms, using the cold wall to support us.

I shake my head. "Jamie, you need to rest for a bit so we can figure out how to get word to your brothers."

He sighs. "No. I'm good. We can't stay here. It's too dangerous."

"It's far more dangerous to leave and have the Barons hunting me again. We can use this to our advantage. Take them out." I clutch his cheeks in my hands. "You have to trust me."

Closing his eyes for a second, he rests his forehead to mine and shares my breath for a moment. "Bronx is going to kick my ass."

"He's going to thank you. Your quick thinking helped to save me. You ensured I wouldn't be here alone." I meet him with a smile. "Now can you walk? I'd like to thank you as well."

He moans and slides his hands to my ass. "Gwen...we shouldn't risk it. The Barons will question Freeport's change of heart."

I lift an eyebrow. "Let them. It'll cause a rift in their coven. They don't share the same bonds that ours does. They think they're powerful, but they haven't seen anything. We'll prove how weak they truly are."

Jameson lifts me higher to press his lips to my stomach. "Do you hear your mama, mini-beast? She's going to change the world for you."

"For us," I say, running my fingers through his hair.

"For us," he repeats. "Starting with ending these bastards."

"I will take all of their hearts."

Epilogue

TIME FOR CHANGE

"I WON'T TELL YOUR BROTHER if you won't," I say, licking my lips.

Thaxton quietly closes the door to my suite behind him, a smile playing on his lips. "You know I won't. He's an utter disgrace, thinking he'll bear future power with you. We all know when a dhampir wants something, she'll take it immediately. And you, my Gwen, have chosen me. Haven't you?"

I clench my jaw, forcing my lips to smile. "I have.

You're far cuter and taste better."

Thaxton unbuttons his shirt and eases it from his shoulder. "Would you like your bite now or after our fun?"

"After."

Thaxton nudges me toward the bed, and I grin, turning my gaze to look over his shoulder. Jameson cocks an eyebrow at me, waiting for my command. The second my legs hit the side of the mattress, I clutch Thaxton's cheeks in my hands.

He sucks in his lip between his teeth. "May I kiss you?"

I smile and crinkle my nose. "Not yet. I want to do something else first."

"Is that so?"

Leaning in, I stare into his eyes. "So don't look away. Don't speak."

Thaxton freezes in his spot as Jameson restrains him from behind, stopping him from slumping into me. His eyes widen, his mind realizing what's going on. I can't stop the smile from crossing my lips. This was far easier than the last time. I realize it's best this way—getting them to lower their guards before I go in for the mind fuck.

"I need you to do something for me, Thaxton. Can you handle that?" I ask.

His fangs peek out from beneath his lips. "Yes."

"I need you to give me a com device of my own. I'm tired of having to steal your brother's. Give me access to your spy cams as well." I pause for a second, letting my command sink in. "I also want you to arrange a daylight outing. There are some people I need to meet. Can you manage to do all this without telling your brothers?"

"Yes," he says, automatically.

"Tell no one."

"Okay."

I lean in a bit closer. "Oh, and Thaxton?"

"Yes, Gwen?" He remains frozen in Jameson's hold.

"Forget this is why I brought you here. You will remember that we had a good time, and you feel so powerful, knowing that I picked you as my blood source. But don't tell your brothers. They get jealous."

He grins. "I'd never."

"Now say goodbye and leave." I break my eye contact and grin at Thaxton, rubbing the back of my hand over my mouth. Jameson disappears before Thaxton gathers his bearings.

"Was it okay?" he asks, blinking a few times. "Did you get enough?"

I steady him on his feet. "I did. Thank you."

"So...see you later?" He caresses his fingers over my cheek, pushing my hair behind my ear.

"Yeah, sure."

Thaxton leans in to kiss me, and I turn my head, so he plants his lips to my cheek. "Goodbye, Gwen."

Thaxton disappears, closing the door behind him. I don't make it two feet toward the bed before Jameson scoops me up and tosses me on my back. I laugh and grab the pillow, pulling it over my head to muffle the noise.

Jameson drags it away and kisses me. "I need my mouth all over you. Your little seductress act gives me a raging boner. I want you to command me sometime."

I link my fingers to the front of his shirt and tug it up and over his head. "I command you to lose the pants."

Jameson chuckles, sliding between my legs. He unfastens my jeans too quickly for me to react and tosses them on the floor. I grin, devouring his body as he undresses completely. He wasn't kidding about his raging boner.

"Come here. I want my mouth all over you too." I wiggle my fingers, getting Jameson to return to me.

He tears off my panties and drags my shirt off to expose my breasts. "No bra," he murmurs.

"Nope. You tore the last one, and I'm only down to two," I say. "If you continue to rip off my undies, I won't have any of those left either."

He purrs deep in his throat and glides his fingers down my stomach. I moan at the gentleness of his touch as he slips his hand across my clit and continues on to dip his finger inside me, feeling the warmth and wetness of my desire.

"Who needs those anyway?" he murmurs, fingering me slowly at first while brushing his lips to my jaw. "Not us. We never leave this room."

I gasp and clutch his shoulders, arching my back as he continues to work me over, adding pressure to my clit with his thumb. He's right about never leaving the room. We've turned into each other's sole entertainment the last week, waiting on word from Bronx. I feared that the Barons would realize I got a message to him with Freeport's phone, but Mikkalo managed to intervene. And now we're supposed to wait.

But I'm getting antsy.

Jameson meets me for another kiss, stroking his soft tongue against mine. I reach between us and join my hand with his for a moment before lacing my fingers around his boner, lubricating it with my own excitement. He moans at the sensation, kissing me harder, deeper, more furiously. I inhale a breath and slide my hand up and down the length of his erection until he can't handle the teasing any longer.

Adjusting his body to mine, Jameson opens my legs to wrap around his waist. Pushing inside me, he takes his time to tease me a couple of times before thrusting until our bodies meet completely. He steals my gasping moans with an intense kiss, making sure little noise escapes my mouth. My body screams in pleasure, every cell buzzing under Jameson. I don't know if it's the situation or what but sex has been completely mind-blowing over and over again.

"It feels so good," I whisper against his mouth. "Just like that. Don't stop."

"Mmm. I love you. You're amazing," he responds, grazing his fingers between us to caress my nipples. "I'd say this was perfect if—"

I cut him off with a kiss. "Soon. No more thinking about them."

"Is that a command?"

He tests me by tilting his head to meet my eyes. His flash silver with his desire, and I can't stop from losing myself in their emerald depths. A second later, a wave of indescribable emotions cascade through me, Jameson's love and desire swallowing me whole as our minds link. He moans, keeping his gaze locked on mine, experiencing me on a level unlike anything we've experienced before. He always claimed not to be good at linking minds, but I open myself up to him as he opens himself to me.

"Oh, Gwen," he murmurs, my name a caress of breath against my mouth. "Gwen."

I smile. "Good, huh?"

He draws his hand lower to rub circles over my clit like he wants nothing more than to drown in the pleasure he feels from me and our mind link. My breathing quickens as tingles bloom from between my legs and to the rest of me. He moans and thrusts harder, faster, stealing my breath.

"Gwen, fuck. Whoa," he murmurs.

I can only moan my response, feeling my body clench and tense with my oncoming orgasm. Sinking my teeth in his shoulder the way he likes, I bite him at the same time that we both cum. I don't know if it was him feeling my pleasure or me feeling his, but my body hums unlike anything I've ever felt. I've never been so close—body and soul aligned—and it makes me both incredibly happy and sad. Happy because of how in love I am with Jameson, but sad because it feels like a huge part of me is missing with his brothers' absences.

Jameson wraps his arms around me and holds me close. "I miss them too, Gwen. We've never been apart for long."

"If you two miss us so badly, then why are you ignoring our knock?" Bronx's voice trickles from the balcony door. "Hurry up, dandelion. You don't want us getting caught, do you?"

I abandon Jameson on the bed and fly across the room at dhampir speed. Thrusting the door open, I drag Everett and Bronx into the room by their sun blankets with Mikkalo rushing in behind them.

"What the hell are you doing here?" I ask, sudden panic clenching my chest.

Everett closes the space to me first and kisses me, scooping me off my feet, loving the fact that I hug my naked body around him. "Do you really think we'd stay away from you?"

"We had to check to make sure this lucky bastard was taking care of you properly," Mikkalo adds.

Bronx hugs me from behind, sandwiching me to Everett. "You're our girl. Whatever crazy-ass plan you have. We're in."

I blink tears from my eyes. "You're not here to steal me away? Lock me in the safety of your room? Hide me from the world forever?"

Mikkalo joins our hug. "What kind of life would that be? We want to give you and our daughter the world."

Sliding from the bed, Jameson whacks Mikkalo on the back. "I don't know, brother. Having Gwen to myself for an entire week...heaven."

"I want more than a week," Everett says. "I want forever."

Bronx kisses the crook of my neck. "And we'll destroy anyone who tries to stop us. This is more than about the Barons. It's about the world."

"And we're going to change it," I say.

Jameson grins. "Damn straight. Just like you changed us."

To be continued...

OTHER REVERSE HAREM NOVELS BY GINNA MORAN

THE VAMPIRE HEIRS WORLD

La Vega Vampire Showstoppers:
Vampire Nights
Bloody Nights

The Divine Vampire Heirs
Blood Match
Blood Rebel
Blood Debt
Blood Feud
Blood Loss
Blood Vows

The Royale Vampire Heirs Series:
Rebel Vampires
Rebel Dhampir
Rebel Match
Rebel Heir
Rebel Fight

Academy of Vampire Heirs Series:
Dhampirs 101
Blood Sources 102
Coven Bonds 103
Personal Donors 104
Blood Wars 105

THE MATES OF MAGAELORUM WORLD

The Pack Mates of Lunar Crest:
The She-Wolf Games
The Wolf-Mate Trials
The Omega Hunt
The Witch Chase

Fated Mates of the Dragon Clans:
Caged by Her Dragons
Freed by Her Dragons
Saved by Her Dragons

SEVEN SINNERS WORLD

Her Personal Demons
Her Deadly Angels
Her Darkest Devils
Her Sinful Saints
Her Twisted Sinners

About Ginna Moran

GINNA MORAN IS THE AUTHOR of over forty novels including the popular Academy of Vampire Heirs, The Divine Vampire Heirs, and The Royale Vampire Heirs Why-Choose novels.

She always carried a fascination for all things paranormal and wrote her first unpublished manuscript at age eighteen. Her love of the supernatural grew stronger through her adult life, and she now spends her days with different creatures of the night. Whether it's vampires, werewolves, angel, demons, or mermaids, Ginna loves creating and living in worlds from her dreams.

Aside from Ginna's professional life, she enjoys binge watching TV, crafting and design, playing pretend with her daughter, and cuddling with her dogs. Some of her favorite things include chocolate, mermaids, anything that glitters, learning new things, cheesy jokes, and organizing her bookshelf.

Ginna Moran loves to hear from her readers so visit her online at www.GinnaMoran.com. You can also find her on Facebook, Twitter, and Instagram. To stay up-to-date on new releases, sign up to her newsletter. To interact with Ginna, join her Facebook Group Paranormal Center for Matches and Mates. You'll not only get exclusive access to extra stories, but you'll be able to participate in games and fun giveaways!